SCARLETT, PRINCESS OF THIEVES

HANNAH HITCHCOCK

"The idea is not to live forever, but to create something that will." Andy Warhol

To those who believe in doing what's right, not what's easy. This story is for you, the unsung hero.

CONTENTS

PLAYLIST

Me And The Devil - Soap&Skin

Into Your Arms (No Rap) ft. Ava Max - Witt Lowry

Dandelions - Ruth B.

Falling Like The Stars - James Arthur

(Everything I Do) I Do It For You - Bryan Adams

PROLOGUE

Many have heard of the legend of Robin Hood, the heroic outlaw, the rebel against tyranny, and the lover of Maid Marian. Who robbed from the rich and gave to the poor. Few have heard the whole truth, the story of Robin Hood and his band of merry men, *and women*. No songs in history were written about women. Not even of the bravest. One woman in particular was central to the legend of Robin Hood, but I bet you've never heard of her. She was his counsel, his conscience, and a fierce warrior. She was his beloved sister. This story is the tale of that woman.

"It's not fair!" She cried, throwing her embroidery to the ground with as much force as an eight-year-old could muster.

Grabbing her arm and shaking the young girl, nursemaid Edith shouted, "Now listen here young Lady. You will do as you're told or I will scold you for your insolence."

Robin made himself known by coughing loudly, asserting his authority. Even at eighteen, he had a commanding presence about him. He was his father's heir after all and even though Edith had been his nursemaid as a child, she wouldn't dare speak to him now like she did back then.

"That will be all Edith, I wish for a moment alone with my sister."

Edith bustled out of the room mumbling under her breath. Robin waited until he heard the door slam shut before marching towards his sister and swinging her around the room. She giggled joyfully as her long, auburn hair flew out behind her. Robin placed her on the ground and ruffled her hair affectionately. He nodded towards the door and warned, "You need to keep her on side until you're old enough to demote her to kitchen duties."

The young girl spat on the ground in a most un-ladylike fashion and screamed, "I hate her!" Her eyes widened as she begged, "Take me with you. I can learn to fight."

"The Crusades is no place for a little Lady and like it or not, you are a Lady."

"If I wear boy's clothes and cut my hair short, I look just like you and William. I could pass for a boy," she insisted.

Robin stroked her beautiful hair, twisting one of the delicate tiny plaits between his fingers. "Make me a promise, you'll never cut this beautiful hair off. Wear it as a crown. Your hair is just like Mother's was."

She swatted his hand away and exclaimed, "You always say that."

"Because it's true. You're a lot like her, she didn't follow the rules either. She always snuck me pudding to break my fast and she loved playing hide and seek, when I was supposed to be doing my Latin lessons. Now run along and go play with William he's outside."

"Is he playing with Alaric still?" She whined.

"Yes I think so. Why what's wrong with that?" Robin queried.

"They gang up on me," she complained stomping her feet and crossing her arms, "They make me be the princess who needs saving. I want to be the knight not the damsel in distress!"

"Then lock one of them in the tower and save them. I'm sure with your wily skills you can wrap them around your little finger. Run along, it's time I better be going."

Outside the sun was shining bright and our wanna be heroine found the two young boys pretend sword fighting with wooden swords. She ran towards them shouting, "Robin said you have to let me be the knight," as she wretched the wooden toy sword from Alaric's hand. "Now stand by that tree and wait to be rescued."

"This doesn't stand to reason, why don't I just run away? I have legs," Alaric complained.

"Would you prefer I tie you to the tree," offered William.

"No," moaned Alaric, "I'll pretend, or else this might take all day." He sighed as he held his hands around the tree, pretending to be tied to it.

The fake battle began and William was surprised with the force his twin sister was attacking him with. He would claim he was going easy on her, but in all honesty she was surprisingly agile and skilful with the wooden sword. She forced him backwards and he tripped over a large stone. He fell abruptly on his backside and before he could complain of unfair conduct, he had a sword pointed at his jugular.

"Do you concede?" She shouted.

Embarrassed and frustrated William replied, "Yes, but I've really hurt my ankle I think I need a doctor."

Skipping towards Alaric with the largest grin she pretended to untie him. "I have come to claim my prize," she announced, as she bowed dramatically.

"Prize, what prize?" Alaric asked confused.

"A kiss, the knight always receives a kiss." She puckered her lips and closed her eyes as she leaned forward.

"I'm not kissing you!" Argued Alaric as he dodged her embrace. "It's time to switch roles," he demanded, "I want to be the knight again, William it's your turn to be the damsel."

Ten years later

The heir and oldest son of the Lord of Loxley returned home from imprisonment during the Crusades to find his father murdered. His home destroyed and his siblings nowhere to be found. His land and titles had been forfeited. Rumours across the countryside said his father had been a devil worshiper, but Robin knew that to be a falsehood. He had set off south to Nottingham to accuse the Sheriff of murder. The fastest route

HANNAH HITCHCOCK

was through Sherwood Forest.

CHAPTER 1

A whistle sang through the large oak tree canopy of Sherwood Forest. It sounded like a skylark's mating call, but a trained ear would spot it was man-made. It was the well-rehearsed whistle, which signalled that a stranger of interest was riding through Sherwood Forest. A coordinated attack was about to take place. One that this band of vagabonds had rehearsed well.

A sheep's horn sounded and the attack began. Eight men and one woman jumped down from the trees into the affray. They startled the mare and the rider faltered, struggling to keep himself composed on the horse's back. The mare reared and threw the gentleman to the ground, where he landed in the mud. The skittish horse galloped off into the distance and the nobleman was left alone and unprotected. Aldo and Eddie ran after the horse, to claim their prize.

The camaraderie amongst the group was strong and they jested at what the fruitful forest had provided. Aimery reached for the stranger's sword and drew it from its scabbard. He twisted it within his fingers and marvelled at the precision. His eyes lit up like a child's on its name day when he saw the exquisite craftsmanship.

"Fine sword this," he remarked.

Billy took a break from tormenting the clearly drunk man to glance in Aimery's direction. He noticed the pommel and marched forward, grabbing the sword with such force he knocked Aimery off balance. Aimery's footing slipped beneath him and he landed flat on his backside in a dazed huff.

Billy pointed the sword at the nobleman on the ground, directly at his jugular. "Where did you get this sword?" He demanded.

The man clearly winded from the fall held a hand to his chest and wheezed out a reply. His words slurred from being intoxicated. "It's mine, it belongs to me."

"Lies, this sword was my fathers!" Billy roared.

The young woman of the group, who had kept her bow and arrow fixed on the stranger, lowered her weapon a fraction. She strode over to the sword and inspected it with her own eyes. The pommel was indeed her fathers. Her fingers traced the intricate patterns that intertwined around the outside of a bronze circle, with a garnet gemstone in the centre. It was one of a kind and a prize to any thief. She raised her arm back, ready to shoot her arrow at the blasphemer's head.

Billy leaned down and wrenched back the liar's hair to challenge him to lie to his face. As the man's head was yanked backward his eyes flew open and connected with his captor's face. Recognition flooded through him. Chocolate brown eyes with flecks of amber stared down at him, as if he were looking in a mirror.

Billy froze, he opened his mouth but no words came out. Keeping her bow and arrow poised, the archer circled around to see what had her twin brother so spooked. As soon as she locked onto his eyes, she lowered her weapon and exclaimed in shock, "Robin, is it really you?"

The man pushed up from the ground into a sitting position, whilst staring back and forth between the siblings.

"Twin's?"

"Brother," they replied in unison.

Billy extended his arm and Robin reached up and grabbed it. Billy hauled his brother off the ground and they hugged tightly. When Robin let go, he took his brother's face in his hands and stared in amazement. Both had a grin from ear to ear. Robin ruffled his younger brother's hair and moved his gaze onto his sister.

He bent at the knees preparing to pick her up and fling her around like he always did. Only now she wasn't eight anymore and standing in front of him was a woman. Not that it was easy to tell that though.

Gone were the long fine dresses, the porcelain skin, and the long, straight, auburn hair with pretty plaits. The woman in front of him was dressed as a man, clothes covered in mud and skin tanned from the sun. Her hair was roughly plaited behind her back and she held a bow and arrow.

"I guess I can't greet you like you're eight anymore?" Robin questioned, as he looked her up and down.

"Aye, course you can," she replied and she pushed her bow and arrow into Billy's chest and jumped into Robin's arms. He staggered back slightly from the shock and then spun her around as she hung from his neck.

Several of the men surrounding them started to grumble until Thom voiced what everyone was thinking. "So, if this is your brother, why are you two not lording it up in a castle?"

Billy shot him daggers and confusion crossed Robin's face as well.

"Come brother," Scarlett said patting Robin on the back and retrieving her bow, "We have much to tell you."

Scarlett led the way to the campsite, deep within the forest. Robin marvelled at the scale of the makeshift homes, it looked like a mini village. High up in trees were fabricated tree houses, camouflaged within the canopy. Hidden traps and alarm systems warned everyone in the camp of people arriving.

"Why are so many of you living in hiding in the forest?" Robin queried.

As Aimery walked past towards the fire pit, he laughed as he replied, "Because the Sheriff says we owe him taxes."

"A lot's changed in the ten years you've been gone brother," Scarlett confessed.

The men dispersed and Scarlett showed Robin around the campsite, introducing people as they went about their tasks. She continued towards a group of men sitting around a fire, sharpening blades. As they approached, Robin could see the frame of a large man with long scraggy hair sitting with his back to them. The other men around the fire nodded to him and the man turned around as Scarlett said, "John, I've got a surprise for you, look who's come back from the dead."

The surprise on his face as he laid eyes on the man next to Scarlett was heart-warming. Robin couldn't believe his eyes. Standing in front of him was John Petty, his father's old gamekeeper, the man who had taught him how to shoot his first deer. John stood up. He towered over the pair of them at 6ft 5, elation clear on his face. He dropped to his knee and bent his head as he proclaimed, "My lord."

"I'm no Lord. I'm just Robin, rise John. It's I that owes you a great debt for looking after my family."

John rose and Robin held out his hand to shake his as an equal.

"Join us around the fire," John offered, "Tonight we will feast under the stars to celebrate your rise from the dead." He showed Robin to the seating area and introduced him to the rest of the group. Scarlett disappeared momentarily and came back with three sheep horns full of dark brown ale.

"Thank you Scarlett," John proclaimed merrily, leading a toast in celebration.

Scarlett sat beside Robin on a large fallen log. He brought the horn to his lips and took a long swig of the ale. He pulled a face as Scarlet watched him wipe the dribbles from his unruly beard.

"You get used to the taste," she joked in merriment.

He leaned into her ear and whispered, "Why are you going by Scarlett?"

His sister shrugged beside him, "Because I ain't no Lady any more and Scarlett ain't a ladies name."

"Well no, Scarlett's a ..." But Robin was cut off by John

who chimed into the conversation.

"I tried to keep the twins hidden and safe, changing names helped with that. But I needn't have bothered, this one can protect herself. Best student I ever taught."

Scarlett beamed with pride, just as Billy marched over with a heavily pregnant young woman and introduced her as his wife to Robin. The siblings spent the rest of the night celebrating that they had found each other, against all odds.

CHAPTER 2

Scarlett woke early and quietly crept through the camp. Last night they had drunk a lot and she was feeling slightly worse for wear. She knew everyone would be nursing hangovers when they woke up and would be in need of sustenance. Nestled by the side of the lake, she could see a nest of sleeping ducks. She crouched low behind some reeds on the opposite side of the bank. Scarlett plucked three arrows from her leather quiver and laid them on the ground at her feet. She nocked the arrow to the string and drew back her arm to aim.

In a swift motion, she fired three arrows in a row, all hitting their designated targets. She jumped up and punched the air as she made her way down to the water's edge. In the centre of the lake, large boulders were hidden just under the surface of the water, visible only to those who knew where to look.

Scarlett slid her bow into her quiver and expertly jumped from rock to rock across the lake. When she made it to the other side, she retrieved her arrows and collected her prize. After tying the ducks to her belt, she checked the nests and grinned when she saw a clutch of twelve eggs. Carefully, she placed them in the bottom of her quiver and crept back to the water's edge. Bending over, she scooped up a handful of cool water and washed her face.

Seeing Robin again filled her heart with hope. She didn't hope for a different life as she loved her life. She did as she pleased and answered to no one. She was free from marrying for status and the pompous formality her noble rank demanded of her. The life she had been born into was one that she hated. Well not exactly hated, but now seeing what freedom was like, it was a life she could never return to. The hope it gave her was for a life of not having to live hand to mouth. Being hungry all the time and always being covered in mud were the biggest downsides to being an outlaw.

Scarlett scrubbed at her cheeks and grabbed a large dock leaf to dry her face as best as she could. When she returned to the camp, Beth, Billy's wife was boiling a large pot of water over the fire. She licked her lips when she saw the ducks swinging from Scarlett's belt. Beth was John's daughter, she was the same age as Scarlett and Billy and John's only family. The three of them had grown up together over the last eight years, after Lord Loxley had been declared a traitor and murdered.

John had smuggled them out of the castle and into the forest with his own family. John's wife had died two winters ago from a sweating sickness that claimed a lot of the camp. Only the strong survived and as a result, the group of outlaws were mostly men in their twenties. The young, the old and most of the women had died. It was no different in the towns, worse in fact. At least here in the trees, they had fresh air, away from the putrid smell of death and shit.

Scarlett unhooked the ducks and laid them on the floor beside Beth. Beth started plucking the feathers eagerly and Scarlett smiled, knowing that Beth was about to get even happier. "That's not all," she said as she lifted her quiver carefully from her back.

She took out the bow and arrows. Then reached carefully inside and pulled out an egg. "I've got twelve of these too. Get the frying slab on the fire."

"Will that be enough for all of us to have one?" Beth queried as she stood to fetch the stone.

Scarlett nodded and smiled. Beth had never been good at lessons. Scarlett often thought she should have done more to help her, but how good any of them were at counting and reading didn't matter anymore. Especially when there were many more important things to learn, like hunting and foraging, including which plants would kill you if you ate them. John had been an excellent teacher of survival skills and the twins owed him their life. The last eight years had involved a completely different education.

Since the death of John's wife, Scarlett, Billy and Beth had taken over the running of the outlaws. Beth had become the cook. Billy had become the lookout, with his wiry frame and aptitude for climbing, and Scarlett had become the brains. It helped that she was an excellent shot and the men looked up to her because of it. No one saw her as a helpless female and no one dared treat her any different than one of the men.

Beth cracked the eggs on the hot slab and Scarlett continued plucking the ducks. When the eggs were cooked, Scarlett rang the warning bell on the nearby oak tree. Panic erupted from around the campsite as men appeared out of trees, half-dressed and still drunk. Scarlett belly-laughed at the sight of them. As the men realised they weren't under attack, many groaned and complained of dull heads. But when the smell of duck stew and fresh, fried eggs hit their nostrils they followed the aroma to the fire. Greediness and starving bellies took over as Beth handed out the meal, with a noggin of the last stale loaf they had in camp.

Robin was one of the last to join the group and took a seat next to Scarlett.

"I'm sorry it's not more brother, but this is how we live."

"This is mighty fine versus what I've been eating," Robin replied and Scarlett beamed with pride.

Robin was ten years her senior and she had always looked up to him. When he left to join the Crusades she was so proud of him, but then as an eight-year-old, she had cried herself to sleep when he didn't come home that winter. She hadn't realised he would be gone so long, with no word.

When everyone had nearly finished, Scarlett announced, "That was the last of the bread, and last night you supped all the ale. Get ready men, it's time the Sheriff paid some taxes."

The men cheered in response and dispersed to load up with weapons. Scarlett patted Robin on the shoulder before instructing him to get ready, "You're with me brother, time to show you the ropes."

Scarlett placed her bow inside her quiver alongside her arrows and tied a cloak around her neck to hide them. A dagger was concealed in her belt at the back and another in her boot. She wrapped the cloak around her to hide her boyish clothes and pulled her hair out of its knot to flow down past her shoulders. Turning to the men, she ordered, "You know what to do. When I give the signal, attack from all angles so we appear stronger in numbers than we are." Turning to Robin she said, "Follow me, no one will recognise you."

The pair entered the village from the side and slowly made their way into the centre where the market was trading. Scarlett pointed ahead at a portly baker selling misshapen loaves to peasants. Next to him, Robin noticed a blacksmith selling horseshoes and non-lethal ironmongery from a wagon. To the right of them, a buxom wench sold ale, whilst her husband or father supped the profits, sitting on a barrel behind her. Robin pulled at Scarlett's arm and shook his head in disbelief as she turned to him. Is this what his family had become, thieves? He pulled her closer as he whispered into her ear, "I won't steal from these people, they don't have much more than we do."

Scarlett yanked her arm from his grasp as she replied, "We don't steal from the poor." Robin was confused and held back. Soon he heard hooves squelching in mud and the unmistakable sound of a wagon with a creaky wheel. Scarlett turned to him and mouthed, "Showtime," as she unlaced the top of her tunic to display her cleavage. He hung back but followed her into the village centre.

Three of the Sheriff's men were taking items from the merchants shouting, "Tax collection." Another was loading the wagon and the fifth was keeping the horses calm. Scarlett sauntered over to the guard holding the reins. Robin could hear her flirting with him.

When the wagon was loaded, the rest of the guards started to return to the horses. Noticing a woman speaking to the youngest guard, they shouted crude insults, insinuating she was a whore and the lad should pay her. Knowing she would be recognised, Scarlett took the guard's hand in her own and started to lead him in the opposite direction, away from the cart and the other guards. The lad went willingly and it was only when they disappeared from view into a home, that Robin heard a whistle. The same whistle he had heard before he was attacked.

Out of nowhere, the outlaws attacked from every angle. The remaining four guards drew their swords, but the outlaws outmatched them two to one. Robin joined in the fight and pulled a guard backwards from the wagon. Scarlett suddenly appeared and climbed into the saddle of the closest horse. She reached her hand out towards Robin's sword. He gave it without question and she cut through the harness attaching the horse to the wagon. She galloped towards the guards fighting with her men, her cape billowing out behind her as she waved the heavy sword high into the air. The guards threw their swords to the ground and raised their hands. They pleaded for mercy, knowing they were fighting a losing battle.

"Tell the Sheriff, no more taxes. Now strip!" Scarlett shouted.

With blades to their throat, the guards stripped to their undergarments, leaving their shoes, armour, clothes, and weapons on the ground. Scarlett pulled the young guard from where she had tied him up and forced him to walk blind folded with the rest of the group. As ordered, they began walking back to the Sheriff's castle. Five of the outlaws went with them until they got to the main road. Then they tied them to a large tree for passing traders to release them if they were feeling charitable.

Scarlett climbed down from the horse and handed Robin back his sword. The rest of the outlaws were handing back the goods that had been taken by the guards. Robin watched on in amazement as Scarlett bartered the guards clothes and shoes to the baker for bread. She negotiated that the ale merchant to drive the wagon to the edge of the forest for them before he was free to take the horses and the wagon.

"Two horses and a wagon for six barrels of ale isn't much of a trade on our part," Robin warned, concerned.

"Not much use for a wagon without horses, and horses need feeding which we can't afford. Don't worry brother, this is a slow day." Scarlett pulled out her bow and nocked an arrow ready should the merchant try to double-cross them.

As promised, at the edge of the forest he stopped to allow them to unload the wagon and then he disappeared in the opposite direction. Rolling the barrels on their sides the rest of the way, the men joyfully sang as they traipsed back to camp.

John had remained in camp with Beth, who was hovering over the stewing pot, adding in wild, edible berries. Billy brought up the rear and made a beeline for Beth. He kissed her on the cheek and she giggled happily.

Licking his lips, Robin declared, "That smells pretty good, whatever's in that pot."

"It's duck, my lord. Scarlett caught them this morning," Beth replied sheepishly. She was only seven when Robin left for the Crusades and she had only ever seen him from a distance, they had never been introduced officially until last night.

Robin smiled before shaking his head, "I'm no Lord Beth, and besides I'm your brother-in-law, you can call me brother."

She frowned as she replied, "I ain't never had a brother, not one that lasted past being a babe, don't seem right calling you brother."

"Then call me Robin, it's my Christian name after all," he replied kindly, as he watched Billy gazing dopily at her. She nodded in agreement.

Aimery passed around horns of beer and as the daylight started to fade, Beth ladled out fresh duck stew to the band of now merry men around the fire.

Robin sat quietly in contemplation after finishing his

food. Through the flames, he spotted Scarlett sitting close to the fire with her boots off, warming her feet. He made his way to sit beside her and warmed his hands from the heat of the fire.

"Has this been your life since father was murdered?" He asked rhetorically, knowing the answer. "Are you happy?"

Her eyes gave him the answer before she even spoke. "Here we're free. We have air in our lungs and right now, food in our bellies. What more is there to want?"

Robin smiled, he didn't realise his little sister would be the one teaching him the true meaning of a happy life. Age had made her wise and humble.

"Nursemaid Edith would beat you for wearing these clothes and getting so dirty, not to mention being around all these men when you're unmarried," Robin said in a jokey manner, reminiscing about what was deemed inappropriate in noble society.

Scarlett didn't hold her tongue when she lashed out, "Well, nursemaid Edith was a bigoted old witch, who knew nothing."

Robin was taken aback by the tone of anger in her response. He held his hands up in surrender as he replied, "You won't hear me defend her. I still have scars from the whippings she gave me as a small boy. I just want you to be happy. Living day to day, hand to mouth, is a hard life."

Looking into her brother's soulful eyes, she knew his questioning came from a good place, he wasn't mocking the life she had built. "I would be lying if I didn't want more," she admitted, "But nothing is worth trading our freedom for. Those in the towns have less than us and they play by the Sheriff's rules."

"But if I played by the rules," Robin offered, "If I got our estate back, you could marry a nobleman, this hardship would be over for you."

As she laced up her boots she replied, "And another type would begin. I have no interest in being a breeding mare." She grabbed her bow from the ground beside her and walked away from the fire, without waiting for a response.

Robin wasn't prepared for her to walk away, believing the only choice she had in life was to starve or be enslaved. He had had enough of injustice during his time in the Crusades. He chased after her and stood in front of her, cutting off her path. Grabbing her by the arms to force her to listen to him he declared, "Then by the grace of God, we take the life we want. We take from the rich and we give to the poor. We overthrow the system. Together, we can do this."

Scarlett looked at her brother in disbelief, but his enthusiasm was captivating. The twinkle of hope in his eyes was so enthralling. A grin broke across her face as she mocked, "Robin of the Hood, I think I might just believe you can do it."

"Only together sister. Scarlett the princess of thieves, will you join me in overthrowing the tyranny of the Sheriff of Nottingham?" He bowed before her as a court servant would for the Queen. She held her hand out for him to kiss, which he did. Then she helped him rise up from the ground. She spat on her hand and held it out for him to shake on the deal.

"Then together brother, we'll do it."

Robin looked down at her hand, thinking how far from a young lady his sister now was, but he shook her hand with the same force he would any other man. She shook it with a tight grip that matched his own. Staring at the determination in her eyes he was certain together they could do it.

CHAPTER 3

It was dark when Scarlett was awoken by a rustling sound above her head. It startled her and she sat bolt upright. She grabbed her dagger from beside her and held it out in front of her, poised for an attack. She listened intently, filtering out the rustling of the trees, the distant sound of snoring, and her own heavy breathing.

She pinpointed the out of place sound coming from above her head. She reached for her boots and laced them up tightly. Stepping out of her treetop home, she climbed stealthily onto the straw roof and squinted in the moonlight. She saw movement as two squirrels fought over a fallen acorn. One bounded away up the tree trunk with the acorn in its cheeks and the other gave chase.

Scarlett sighed, a mixture of annoyance at being woken up when it was not yet daylight and relief that it was just squirrels that had woken her. She returned to her makeshift bed of fur pelts, but couldn't get back to sleep. The ale had worn off and it was unusually cold for autumn. She wrapped her cape around her neck and then grabbed her quiver. Scarlett hung out the rope ladder and climbed down. Now safely on the ground, she took out her bow and nocked an arrow onto the string.

Scarlett crept out of camp and went to check her rabbit traps. Not one rabbit had been snared. The ground was hard with frost and she hoped that this wasn't an omen of a cold winter approaching. Not willing to give up on providing the first meal of the day, she wandered down to the lake but the ducks were all gone, a layer of thin ice was visible on the surface. It broke apart easily as she tapped it with her arrowhead. She had never really liked fish but beggars couldn't be choosers, so she scanned the water for any signs of life. She shook her head in disappointment when she realised the water was too murky to see anything.

Defeated and hungry, she returned to camp for a meal of stale bread. Beth was awake tending to the fire. Billy nodded as he passed Scarlett on his way to the lake for water to boil. Everyone had their jobs in camp and Scarlett felt useless that she had failed in hers. She shook her head as Beth looked optimistically at her. Beth sighed and rubbed her swollen stomach as she focused back on the fire.

Scarlett hated the thought that she had let everyone down and marched towards the warning bell, ringing it forcefully. A chorus of yawns and men scrambling out of bed could be heard in the canopy above. Aimery shouted down, "Are we under attack?"

Scarlett shouted into the sky, "Yes from starvation, now get your ass down here. Robin's got a plan."

"I have?" Robin queried, as he stretched out his aching muscles.

"Well, you gave me an idea. Do you care to hear my thoughts on how we start this rebellion?"

"Always," he chuckled, "Advise away."

Several hours later, Scarlett was squeezed into a full-length, emerald dress she had borrowed from Beth. Beth only owned two dresses and the one she was currently wearing had been adapted to allow for her growing belly. Billy had purloined this one from a wealthy cloth merchant and given it to her as a wedding present. Beth had offered it without hesitation, but Scarlett knew how much it meant to her, so she felt added pressure to keep it intact. She hoped she would have no cause to get blood on it, as she knew from experience how much that stained.

The swishing of the excess fabric around her feet was incredibly irritating. It was constantly getting in her way and she felt like she was going to trip up. She had grown accustomed to marching everywhere at full pace, but in this dress it was impossible. She had to restrain her instincts to ensure she walked slowly. For good measure she swayed her hips. It felt unnatural but looked seductive.

Her shoulders felt naked without the weight of her quiver on her back and her exposed skin felt cool. Her hair now loose behind her did nothing to protect her shoulders from the chill of the wind. Scarlett pushed her shoulders back to raise her breasts, as the curve of her ample bosom was now on display. She licked her lips to make them glisten, as she sauntered through the gates to Nottingham castle. Dressed like this she was certain no guard would recognise her.

Scarlett headed for the door to the flanking tower. She had traded Robin's gold belt buckle to get the name and location of the head guard from the local madam. A guard on duty was blocking the door. She batted her eyelashes seductively, pulled a grubby white handkerchief from her bosom, and waved it at him. The madam had told her that signal along with her client's name would grant her access inside. She approached him and whispered the name into his ear. He gave her a coy look and a wink then opened the door for her to enter.

"To the end of the corridor, up the stairs and turn right," he shouted after her. She proceeded as instructed until she was sure he had gone back to his duties. She glanced over her shoulder and seeing that the coast was clear, she searched the corridors until she found what she was looking for.

Spare guard tunics with the Sheriff of Nottingham's crest were hanging up in a boot room. She grabbed a set along with a helmet and chainmail. She scanned the room for a way to walk back through the castle freely with them and saw a basket of firewood by the hearth. She stacked the logs neatly by the fire and folded the uniform in a way that hid what she was actually carrying.

The basket was heavy but she had good upper body strength and she managed to carry the weighty basket down the corridor. The instructions from the madam only got her so far. She followed her instinct to get to the chapel to rendezvous with Robin. As luck would have it, she spotted a monk and followed him. He led her to the chapel where she saw Robin praying on the front pew.

Scarlett made a beeline for the same row and knelt in prayer. When she rose she left the basket on the pew and hurried out of the house of God. Robin took the basket into the confession box and proceeded to change into the uniform.

He barely recognised his reflection in the shiny church silverware. He headed for the watch tower, hoping there might be some loose-lipped, bored guards up there. As he entered the turret, three guards were manning the windows above, focused on different angles of attack. They heard him ascending the stairs and one shouted out, "Have you come to relieve me?"

Hearing only one voice Robin answered, "No, I was just told to tell you to head to the gatehouse."

When he made it to the top of the stairs, he realised his mistake, there were three guards in the tower. The other two grumbled and quizzed him about why he wasn't staying and why only one guard had to leave. "I don't ask questions, I just follow orders," Robin confidently confirmed.

"Well orders are orders," said the one who had been eager to be replaced, "I'm going on that run tonight to Sandal Castle. I told Eldridge I wanted to sleep before we leave or I'll be fit for nothing by morning."

"Sleep? Is that what you call it?" Mocked the eldest of the three, "I call it shagging that wench in the ale house before her father has her serving dinner." The three guards roared with laughter.

"Some men get all the luck," moaned the youngest.

"Luck? Travelling through Sherwood Forest in the dead of night, you've got to be joking," admonished the eldest guard.

"Why are you going at night?" Queried the youngest

guard; confusion written all over his face.

"Because that treasure needs to get to the Baron of Loidis quickly and the Sheriff only trusts his best guards to get it there in one piece, without any bandits stealing it." The guard felt suitably proud of himself and after over-inflating his own ego, he descended the stairs. Robin followed closely behind. Scarlett's plan had centred on him forcing a guard to show him the way to the treasury, but with this piece of information, there was no need to rob the treasury. It was coming to them tonight anyway. Robin slipped away when he could and rode straight through the front gate on a stolen horse.

As Robin approached the camp, he set off one of the alarms. An arrow landed inches from where he had dismounted the horse and within seconds he was greeted with a fierce welcome party. When he removed the helmet and they saw it was him, they relaxed. Running up behind them Scarlett approached the group, her bow and arrow cocked ready.

On seeing Robin's face she slowed and caught her breath. "What are you doing back here already?" She angrily shouted through deep breaths.

"Change of plan. A whole chest of money is coming to us tonight," he smugly declared.

"How?" Questioned several men in the group.

"Sheriff's sending money to old William de Blackwater, the Baron of Loidis at Sandal Castle."

"Why's he doing that?" Asked Billy, with a perplexed look on his face. Robin shrugged as Scarlett stepped closer.

"There's only one reason to send money to someone and that's to buy something."

"But what could he possibly be buying that warrants a secret wagon delivery in the middle of the night?" Billy queried.

"Loyalty, silence, support, take your pick," Scarlett declared, "King John hasn't been ruling long, he hasn't built up the same alliances a first born son would. The Barons were divided in support of the Crusades, wars cost too much money. That's what father always said. It's obvious isn't it?" Looking at puzzled faces staring back at her, Scarlett's astute intellect over her companions was clear. She answered her own question with, "The Sheriff is after the throne for himself."

The old crone stroked a long, crooked finger down the large ravens back as it perched on her shoulder. After years together they had a mutual understanding. When he visited her she knew it was time to use her dark magic. Morgana shuffled her deck of tarot cards and pulled six at random from the deck. She lay them face down on the altar table in front of her. She hovered her ageing hands with long, black fingernails over the deck until she felt the urge to flip one over. Pressing her hand on the card it stuck to her palm and she rotated her wrist so the card could present itself.

The Wheel of Fortune card lay upside down in her palm, a sign of bad luck and a lack of control. Her long fingers placed the card on the table face up and she repeated the exercise. This time an upright tower presented itself, the card to signify an awakening. This prediction was rare. The tower card had never presented itself upright to her before. She took her time choosing the final card. As she rotated her wrist she stumbled backwards as the King on the throne flashed before her eyes. An upright King on his throne meant only one thing, judgement was coming.

She reached for the potion she concocted every full moon and hastily drank the contents. Wiping the dribbles from her mouth she made her way to her bed for the lucid dreams depicting the new future to arrive. The raven flew to the window sill and kept watch, whilst the potion took effect.

The old crone woke with a start, when Oionos squawked loudly from the window sill. Her eyelids shot open and following the direction of the noise, she glared menacingly at the bird. Her eyes took several moments to adjust. It was still dark out, so she knew that she hadn't been asleep long, but it was long enough to have a vision. Her irises remained unnaturally dark from the aftereffects of the potion. She grabbed her walking cane and hobbled her way to see the Sheriff of Nottingham.

A secret staircase and passageway led directly to the Sheriff's quarters from her own. She slid through the concealed entrance and appeared in the living quarters. As quickly as she was able, she made her way to the Sheriff's bed chamber. She could hear movement so she entered without knocking. The Sheriff was grunting, as he reached climax inside a whore who had joined him for the evening.

The whore screamed as she saw the old woman approach the couple. The Sheriff reached for his dagger concealed within the fabric hanging from the four poster bed and turned quickly to face the intruder. His muscles relaxed when he saw who it was.

"Morgana, do you mind I'm a little busy," he remarked rhetorically.

"I have grave news. I need to speak to you and the boy now, make haste." Morgana shuffled out of the room back to the large fireplace in the living quarters. The Sheriff took a deep breath and let out a loud sigh, before turning his attention to the wench he was still inside of.

"Duty calls," he gibed.

As he started to get dressed, the whore asked, "Should I stay here or leave now sire?"

The Sheriff glanced over his shoulder, irritated that he would have to pay her when he didn't get his money's worth. "Leave. Now!" He barked. The whore gathered up her clothes and hurried to leave the room. She stalled at the door and the Sheriff threw her a silver coin. She caught it in her outstretched hand, bowed her head in respect, and left; relieved that her work was done for the evening.

The Sheriff exited his bed chamber and marched down the corridor to the last door on the right. He banged his fist loudly three times followed by the order, "Alaric, get dressed now.

Morgana needs us by the main fireplace." He heard the boy inside reply, "Ok," before he made his way back to his visitor.

"You have a knack for your timing Morgana," he muttered in a disdainful tone.

"I do not control the future, only interpret it. I had a vision," she replied.

"Yes, well you could do with telling the future to wait until I am done with the present. The boy will be along momentarily," the Sheriff retorted in response.

Alaric entered the room moments later, still lacing up his shirt. He addressed the occupants as he entered the room, "Rather late, is it not?" Nodding at them both, as a form of address.

"Quite," the Sheriff remarked. "Morgana do begin," he instructed.

"I had a disturbing vision," she spoke hauntingly and Alaric couldn't help being disturbed by her eyes which were almost all black. He had always been wary of Morgana. In truth she had terrified him as a child, but as he grew into a man he understood his father's reasonings for keeping her around. She had a knack for predicting the future and she had helped him rise in strength and standing. His father was now one of the most influential men in England.

Morgana continued, "I have seen a man rise from the dead this night.' A cold shiver ran down Alaric's back and he shuddered. "If he is allowed to ascend from hell he will steal your legacy and become a legend," she warned, "You must accelerate your plans. He bears you a grudge and will seek justice tonight."

The Sheriff slammed his fist on the mantelpiece over the fireplace. "Tonight," he repeated, "Tonight I ordered my men to send the money to the Baron of Loidis. Will he try to steal it from me?" He spat.

"Yes," she replied, "I saw his ghost ride into Sherwood Forest."

The Sheriff forcefully kicked a stack of logs by the fireplace, causing them to fly over to the other side of the room.

"I will go father," Alaric offered, "I will take a few of my best men and ensure the money gets to the Baron."

"Don't fail me," the Sheriff warned. Alaric nodded and strode out of the room.

Alaric ordered the first guard he passed, to ready three horses immediately. He marched quickly to the barracks of his men. He found the men he was looking for playing draughts by the fireplace. They stood to attention as he approached.

"Men I have a special mission for us tonight. Arm yourselves, we leave immediately."

The threesome galloped at full speed into Sherwood Forest, following the route the wagon would have taken.

That night, the group of righteous bandits split into four groups and lay in wait. They had been busy all afternoon laying wind chime traps to give them warning of the convoy arriving. Sure enough, a little after midnight the chimes started to sound. Shortly after the sound of the wagon being pulled through the thick undergrowth and the skittish whine from a nervous horse raised the alarm that the Sheriff's guards were approaching. The echo from the forest at night made it hard to know exactly what direction they were arriving from, but Scarlett knew they would be safe in the hiding spots she had chosen.

Aimery and Billy were the best climbers, so they were hidden amongst the trees, ready to swoop down and kick the front riders from their horses. Thom and Benedict as the youngest of the group had drawn the short straw and were lying in the mud, camouflaged by fallen autumn leaves. Scarlett and Aldo were the best archers, so they had flanked either side of the main path. Robin was leading the other three, who were lying in wait, hidden behind trees and bushes.

The sounds of the approaching cart increased in volume and when Scarlett gave the signal her plan was executed perfectly, until a strong gust of wind whistled through the forest bringing an unnatural chill. The sound of hooves speeding towards them followed and filled the air with an unprecedented dread.

CHAPTER 4

It all happened so quickly. Alaric and his two knights charged towards the outlaws as the sound of a wagon crashing to the ground rang through the forest. Escaping horses galloped past them dragging tied up guards behind them. The wagon had tipped over and a rope around the wheels anchored it to a large oak tree. Bandits were greedily filling sacks with the treasure, which had spread across the forest floor.

Charging into battle, Alaric wielded his sword and swung at the closest thief. He heard a man bellow out in pain and the edge of his sword was red with blood. As he pulled on the reins to turn the horse back around, an arrow pierced the horse's flesh close to its mane. The horse reared up in response and Alaric struggled to keep his balance. His companions had already dismounted and cut the other guards free from their restraints. Another arrow landed inches away from the first and this time Alaric was thrown from the horse as it galloped as fast as it could away from the affray.

Alaric had lost his sword in the fall but he used his training and his armour to defend himself when a bandit attacked with a stolen sword. The outlaw had little training and it was easy for Alaric to gain the upper hand. If it wasn't for the arrows raining down on him, he would have easily killed the brigand.

Alaric howled as an arrow made contact with his boot. The leather prevented the arrowhead from lodging in his foot, but the point had broken the surface. His reaction gave the bandit just enough time to run past him and he heard a man yell the order, "Back to the trees!"

The sound of steel clacking on steel stopped as sword-on-sword combat ceased. The sound was replaced with jeering from his men and a hostage struggling to break free. Alaric pulled the arrowhead from his boot and cursed at the pain. He could feel blood oozing down his foot and past his toes. He stood tall and tried not to show his weakness to his remaining men, as he walked over to the prisoner.

The guards had wrestled Scarlett to the ground as they cut her quiver from her back and prised her bow from her hands. Her legs and wrists were bound so tightly they stung every time she attempted to move them. Her face was covered in mud, but her eyes glared with pure hatred as she was brought before Alaric. Even with mud covering her face and dressed in male clothing, her ample bosom and womanly curves were evident. Alaric pulled at the rag within her hair and her long, dirty, mudded hair cascaded down her shoulder.

"What do we have here then?" He asked rhetorically, "Are the outlaws so desperate they are using women to defend them," he jeered. The men laughed and Scarlett seized her moment to spit in her captor's face.

Alaric stopped laughing and ordered one of his men to bag her head. The rest of the men including Alaric heaved the wagon upright. They collected as much of the money as they could find in the dark forest, hitched the remaining horses to the wagon and Alaric gave the order to return to Nottingham castle. They forced the captive to walk along behind, goading her and kicking her when she fell.

By the time they returned, the sun had risen and birds were tweeting. Alaric ordered his men to throw their prisoner into the dungeon, ready for his father's instructions.

The Sheriff wasted no time ordering his most skilled torturer to obtain information from the prisoner. The Sheriff and Alaric returned to their personal quarters, where Morgana was still sitting by the fireplace, eager for news.

"Did you see the ghost?" She asked with trepidation.

"No, nothing," Alaric confirmed adamantly, his tone giving away his disbelief in her credibility.

Morgana eyed him up suspiciously, "Don't look at me like that boy. Do you doubt me? Did I not tell you about the attack on the money?" She rose from her seat and approached Alaric. He stood his ground and puffed out his chest, but his heart rate rose. He disliked the old crone and didn't believe in witchcraft, but there was something about her that he couldn't explain. He couldn't deny she had predicted the attack and if he thought hard enough about it, he couldn't work out how she had foreseen that without witchcraft.

Morgana stood in front of Alaric and poked a long finger into his stomach. "You boy will have your loyalty tested soon enough. Choose the right side or die."

"Enough of that," snapped the Sheriff, "We will soon have answers when the prisoner gives up how they knew about my deal with the Baron."

Alaric excused himself to go to bed and the Sheriff continued staring into the flames of the roaring fireplace, entranced by the amber glow.

Alaric waited patiently at the end of the long banquet table for his father to show for dinner. He was growing impatient, salivating over the suckling pig in the centre of the table. He heard the clacking of boots on flagstones as his father entered the room. He gave no apology for being late and proceeded to the other end of the table. His personal guards stationed themselves around the walls of the room.

A serving wench poured them both a goblet of red wine. The Sheriff had it imported from France and served it at meal times even though he preferred ale. It was a symbol of status and he had always taught Alaric that the appearance of wealth and power was just as good as actually having it.

The two of them ate in relative silence. Alaric was

officially an only child with his mother dying in childbirth when he was a child. He suspected that he had a number of bastard siblings, but without the Sheriff's declaration of their existence, their lives had no consequence. His father had seen no reason to take another wife. His mother had been a second cousin of King John. It was no secret his father had only married her for wealth and status.

Alaric barely remembered her now. The only memory that remained clear was her laughing when having a picnic with her best friend Lady Lucy, in the grounds of Loxley estate. He spent the summer there every year when the stench of Nottingham was overwhelming. His mother was her happiest when with her best friend.

After his father switched to drinking ale, he started regaling old stories that Alaric had heard a hundred times over. As his words started to slur, Alaric asked to be excused. He rose from the table but he stopped in his tracks as his father started hysterically laughing and almost choking.

"Why don't I help you back to your room Father?"

"Yes, maybe it is time for me to retire," he confessed. Alaric put his father's arm over his shoulder and helped him to their private quarters. As he unlaced his boots, his father drunkenly slurred, "Pretty girl that prisoner you bought me, have her brought to me, looks just like Lady Loxley. I want to imagine nailing her and Loxley turning in that shallow grave I dug him."

Alaric froze at the coincidence that he had just been thinking about Lady Lucy and his mother over dinner.

"Boy, did you hear me?" His father spat, "The wench, bring her to me."

"Yes Father," Alaric replied on autopilot, interested to see for himself if the bandit looked like Lady Lucy. Those summers had been the happiest of his life, playing with Lady Lucy's children. He tried to picture Lady Loxley. She had beautiful, long auburn hair and a kind face, full of freckles. She had died shortly before his mother, from what he wasn't sure, but he had still been allowed to go every summer until his father had declared Loxley was a devil worshipper.

He had been too young to understand the details and he had never had cause to ask. It wasn't until this moment that he realised he didn't know what happened to his friends. He assumed they had been taken in by a relative, but surely they would be of age now, they were twins and a couple of years younger than him. Surely he should have seen them or heard about them by now. He mused they had probably travelled further North, to Scotland perhaps.

He descended the stairway down to the dungeon and made the guard open the cell the bandit was imprisoned in. She had been isolated from the male prisoners for obvious reasons. Alaric wrinkled his nose up in disgust, as the smell of urine hit his nostrils. The woman was strung up by her arms against the dark, damp back wall of the cell. Her right ankle was shackled to an iron weight and the tension on the rope had been set so she was dangling with her bare toes just touching the floor.

She didn't open her eyes at the sound of the cell door opening and he wondered if she was conscious. He ordered the guard to fetch him a pale of water and a rag. His father's most skilled subjugator loved water torture. It was evident the water had cleared her face of mud but it had swiftly been replaced by dried blood. After the guard returned, Alaric dipped the rag in the water and gently cleaned the blood from her face. He held a candle close to see her features clearly. He couldn't be certain that he recognised her. He brought the candle closer to her hair and saw the flecks of auburn reflected from the flame through the mud. He twisted it over it in his fingers and she started to stir.

"I order you to tell me your name." He stated forcefully.

Her eyes shot open and connected with his. Staring at him with pure hatred, her big chestnut eyes with flecks of auburn, this close up made him instantly recognise her. She was Lady Lucy's daughter. He stumbled backwards, as if he was seeing a ghost.

Was she the ghost the witch had foreseen? What path in life had she taken to end up living in Sherwood Forest with bandits? She was supposed to be a Lady, but she was dressed in rags, about to be forced into prostitution by his father.

For the love of his mother and the memories of those summers, he knew he had to free her. He took the keys that hung up outside the door and removed the weight around her ankle. He took out his dagger and cut through the rope suspending her from the ceiling. She collapsed into his arms, too weak to stand. He tucked his dagger in his waistband and cradled her in his arms. Then he carried her out of the dungeon.

As he walked across the moonlit courtyard, he was trying to formulate a plan when he felt her move in his arms. He looked down at her and the next thing he knew, her teeth had clamped down on his left ear. A sharp, pain seared across his face as he felt a blade slice through his flesh. He immediately let go of her, his hands rising to protect his face as he yelled in pain.

Scarlett took the opportunity to knee him in his privates and knowing she was in no position to outrun any cavalry, she ran back through the door they had just come through. She ambled down the corridor, trying not to look out of place. She spotted a servants corridor and found herself in the kitchens. Her shoulder was in agony and she was sure it was dislocated. She took a deep breath and using her working arm she slammed her shoulder back into place. She bit down so hard on her bottom lip to keep herself from screaming, that she tasted blood in her mouth. She had endured hours of endless torture, but now she had hope she could escape. That hope gave her the drive to strive on through the pain.

Dagger in hand she crept through the room in search of the sleeping quarters. She found a young scullery maid asleep on a dirty, thin bed of straw. She held the blade to her throat and threatened the maid to remove her clothing. Petrified, tears sprang from the maid's eyes, but she did as instructed. Scarlett ordered the maid to turn around with her hands on the wall whilst she swapped her tunic for the simple, woollen dress. She stole her footwear and rammed her feet into the boots. They were at least one size too small and pinched at the heel, but it was better and less conspicuous than being barefoot. She removed a shoe lace and twisted her hair into a messy updo. She frightened the young girl into staying in bed until first light, then disappeared into the night.

Scarlett passed several guards looking for an escaped criminal, but her disguise gave her the freedom to move about the castle. She found a place to hide until morning and allowed her eyes to close, seeking rest. It was a risky move, trusting the maid would do as she ordered, but she was too weak from being tortured to escape the castle walls.

She rubbed her sore wrists and ankles, flinching at the wounds the ropes had made. Her head was pounding from dehydration and every inch of her body hurt. The sadistic bastard, who had tortured her by nearly drowning her, had warned her he would be back later to collect her for the guards to get their pleasure. She was so relieved she had managed to escape, with her virtue still intact.

At first light, she lifted a wicker basket under the guise of collecting eggs. As soon as she was free of the castle walls, she made her escape and headed for the forest.

Billy was keeping watch and signalled her arrival before she made it to camp. Robin ran to her and she collapsed in his arms. He carried her to the fire and made her drink water from the stew ladle.

"I'm so sorry," he exclaimed, "By the time we knew you were missing, there was nothing we could do. We've just been planning on how to break you out. How did you escape?"

Her voice was weak when she responded, "I fought my way out, then laid low until first light. Now I need to rest, let me sleep a while." Robin carried her to the makeshift bed he had made for himself on the forest floor and covered her with fur pelts.

Alaric sat painfully still on a wooden stool, as the top physician in Nottingham sewed the laceration on his face. He was seething with rage, mentally calculating all the ways he could seek revenge. He didn't need the surgeon to tell him that this gash would leave a lasting scar across his handsome face. His ear lobe had been bitten clean off and to prevent infection, the wound had been cauterised. He refused the same method on his face.

When the physician was done, he ordered a mirror to be brought to him. Alaric built up the courage to look at his reflection by downing a tankard of ale. He looked hideous. His once boyish good looks were marred by a diagonal scar stretching from his forehead, across his nose to his opposing cheek. He was devastated by his appearance and smashed the mirror in disgust. He grabbed another tankard of ale and went marching off to his bed chamber to drown his sorrows.

Morgana was waiting by the fireplace. She didn't even turn to look at him as she asked, "Something vexes thee?"

"Look at me!" He shouted, "You dare to ask me what's wrong?" His words were slurred and he swayed as he spoke. Morgana turned towards him. No reaction registered on her face, not even surprise.

"If it's revenge you seek, I can help," she offered.

Alaric was in no fit state to think rationally, but he sat down by the fireplace opposite the witch and demanded, "Tell me how."

Morgana grimaced and leaning forward to touch Alaric's hands, she asked, "Do you know the name of the one who attacked you?"

Alaric recoiled in his chair at her touch but wearily confirmed, "Yes, Lady Loxley."

Morgana made an unbecoming noise as she grunted in recognition, "How the mighty have fallen, from a Lady to a common thief." She rose from her seat and grabbed her cane. As she reached the concealed entrance, she turned and confirmed, "Before the next full moon, you will have your vengeance."

CHAPTER 5

The old witch made her way through the castle and down to the dungeons clutching a lit candle. Dark shadows danced across the walls from the flickering flame as she descended the stairs. The guards on duty were scared of her and gave her free reign to wander whenever she came around. Her spells often required human offerings. Hair, toenails, blood, urine, even the odd toe and she often visited the dungeons to stock up her supplies.

Morgana ordered the guard to show her to the cell where they had held Lady Lucy's daughter. She held the candle close to the ground as she searched for the ingredients for her spell. By the iron chain, she saw what appeared to be recently spilt blood. She took a damp rag and wiped it. Turning it over in her hand to expect the cloth in the light she couldn't be certain it was the offering she needed. She jutted out her tongue and tasted the sample. The unmistakable iron taste confirmed it was blood. She smirked, pleased with her find.

Morgana cast the candle glow onto the walls and a fleck of amber caught her attention. She reached up as high as she could and pulled a strand of hair from the wall. It was auburn in colour. She had often heard the remarks about Lady Loxley's beautiful auburn hair, it made sense her daughter would have inherited the same. She wrapped the hair in the blood-stained cloth and left the dungeons.

Back in her chambers, Morgana brewed her spell. When the potion was bubbling, she added the rag containing the hair sample and blood. Then she added a piece of parchment with the name, *'Lady Loxley'* written in her scratchy scrawl. When it entered the potion the bubbling stopped and the liquid turned black, releasing a foul odour. She carefully ladled the liquid into a goblet and raised it to her lips.

Oionos was perched on the window sill waiting. She ran a finger over the raven's wing. "Be my eyes Oionos, make sure the curse holds true." The raven bent its head as if to nod. Morgana raised her cup and toasted the bird, followed by the full moon, before drinking the contents in one gulp. The taste was vile and she reached out to steady herself. Unsteady on her feet, she made her way to her bed and lay down as the effects of the potion took hold.

When Scarlett woke her head was pounding, she felt like she hadn't slept. A bird was making a raucous noise in the tree canopy above. She suddenly had the urge to vomit and scrambled up to wretch out of the tree house onto the forest floor below. When the purging stopped, her headache subsided slightly and she lay back down. Inconsequentially, noticing that her boots were on her feet and caked in dried mud. She closed her eyes and drifted back off to a troubled sleep.

By nightfall, Beth had convinced her to join the others and share a meal, but she retired early and stayed off the ale. The whole night, she was tossing and turning. She felt like she had a fever. The sun rose and she felt the same urge to vomit. She looked down at her muddy boots and frowned. Scarlett was sure that she had taken them off to sleep. Her skin felt clammy and her head was foggy, so she dragged herself to the nearby lake for a wash. She didn't dare stray too far from the camp. She had a constant feeling of being watched, but there was no around her.

When night fell, she was certain to remove her shoes and as it was a clear night she hung them up outside on the tree.

That night, Beth was relieving herself behind a tree just outside of camp when she heard the crunching of twigs behind her. She turned around quickly in anticipation of an attack, but saw Scarlett walking slowly through the forest.

She whispered, "You scared me, are you feeling ok?" But Scarlett didn't answer. It was then she noticed Scarlett didn't have any shoes on, her bare feet were covered in mud. Beth caught up with her and noticed her facial expression was vacant, like she couldn't see her. Her eyes looked glassy and Beth waved her hand in front of Scarlett's face, but she didn't even blink.

Beth wondered whether she should shake her, but thought against it. Scarlett had the strength to easily over power her if she felt threatened and she clearly wasn't in her right mind. So instead Beth followed her. She had never seen anyone possessed before, but she had heard enough stories to think that's what was happening now.

Scarlett stopped by a large oak tree and started frantically foraging in the fallen leaves. She uncovered a cluster of small, white fungi. As she plucked one from the ground, Beth could see it had a funnel-shaped cap with a white underside. She recognised it instantly as fools funnel, a poisonous toadstool that you should never eat. She watched as Scarlett raised it to her mouth as if to eat it. Beth stepped forward and violently knocked Scarlett's hand away from her mouth. She shook her by the shoulders and shouted her name.

Out of nowhere a large, black bird dived towards Beth. It halted mid-air as if to change course, but instead it flapped its wings and pecked at her. Beth threw her hands up to protect her face as she screamed. The movement of air on her face and the sound of screaming woke Scarlett from the trance. Her eyes returned to normal and her face suddenly came alive. The bird flew off squawking loudly.

"What's going on?" She exclaimed in shock, "Where are we? Are you ok?" She asked looking all around.

Relieved that Scarlett appeared herself again and the crazed bird had flown away, Beth explained what she had just witnessed. "It's like you were sleep walking, have you done that before?"

With a puzzled expression, Scarlett shook her head, "Not

that I know of. It's so strange. I have no recollection of any of it." She looked down at her feet and saw they were covered in mud. "I think I've been doing this every night since I returned from the castle. It's why I've been sick." She tried hard to remember, but the only evidence she had was the muddy boots she had been wearing every morning.

She looked Beth in the eyes, as she ominously asked, "Have I been cursed?"

"Witchcraft doesn't really exist. Story's about witches are just to scare naughty children. Witches are just lonely old women that have good knowledge of herbs and berries. You've just got a troubled mind. You need to clear your head. Let's get back to camp." But beneath her statement, Beth was afraid for her sister-in-law. She didn't believe in magic, but she knew what she saw and she believed in the devil.

For two days the Sheriff dined alone as his son was sulking. Finally, he was fed up. He ripped a turkey leg from the carcass in the centre of the table and marched upstairs. Alaric was slumped in front of the fireplace with a tankard of ale resting on his lap. As the Sheriff entered the room he didn't even look up.

"Enough of this sulking boy, scars are battles you won, wear it proudly, even if it was a woman who bested you. Go put her head on a spike if you want vengeance and when you've done that, I still need that gold taking to Sandal Castle."

Alaric remained by the fireplace, seething for the rest of the evening, but by morning he had adopted a new outlook. He was going to take his revenge. He ordered his men to spread the word of a reward for her capture. He wanted her alive.

The next morning when Scarlett woke, she felt sprightly and more herself. Her bruises were starting to heal and her skin was now various shades of purples and greens. It was a clear morning and the breeze was pleasant. She grabbed her quiver and set off in search of food. As she passed the tree with the toadstools from last night, her body gave an involuntary shiver.

Determined to put the episode behind her, she nocked an arrow on her bow and went on the hunt. It allowed her to forget her troubles and she returned triumphant to camp later that morning, with three pheasants and two rabbits. Beth set straight to work on plucking and skinning the catch. Aldo approached Scarlett as she sat by the fire. "Are we still having our archery tourney tomorrow? I've been practising, I reckon I've got a good chance this time."

"Good chance at what?" Robin interjected.

"At beating Scarlett," Aldo replied.

Robin raised an eyebrow at Scarlett before returning his attention to Aldo. "Can anyone join this tournament?"

Aldo smiled, "Course, fancy your chances against Scarlett, do you?"

Robin chuckled, "I sure do, who do you think taught her?"

Aldo's expression grew downcast as he realised his chances of winning had just got slimmer. He removed his bow from his quiver and stood to leave. Turning back at the siblings, he remarked, "I better go off to practise."

Both siblings smiled. Scarlett had agreed to the tourney as a fun way to train. She reasoned that a little bit of competition was healthy. A lesson her father had taught her, when he regularly pitched her twin against her in physical and mental pursuits.

The morning of the tourney arrived. Scarlett set out early, marking out the targets on trees. She measured the distance using her own steps. The furthest was 288 steps away. She had her father to thank for her advanced mathematical education. Lord Loxley didn't differentiate his affection, or expectations between his children. When the tutor had objected, Scarlett remembered hearing her father sternly dictate that he was paying the tutor to teach, and whether the room had one or five children in made no difference to his fee, or his task.

Scarlett carved out several other targets on her way back to the starting line, that she had drawn in the mud with a sharp twig. The rules were simple. Each round, they lined up to take one shot. If they hit the target, they advanced onto the next round, each time the distance increased. If there were multiple contestants still in the tourney by the last target they started again, but this time hitting the bullseye became imperative. The remaining archers had to hit the bullseye on every target or they were out, starting at the closest and working up to the furthest away.

The last time Billy and Scarlett had gone head to head, but Scarlett won by striking bullseye on the fourth target whilst Billy's arrow missed entirely. He had claimed he was distracted by hunger after seeing a rabbit in the distance, but the men had laughed at him all the same, winding him up further for being a sore loser.

Once Billy had heard that Robin was entering, he declined taking part, claiming Beth had asked for his help, he didn't want the evitable humiliation of going up against both his siblings. This made Aldo even more nervous about how good Robin actually was.

Several of the men including old John lined up to take a shot. Edmund was the first to miss, quickly followed by Thomas. John bowed out next, claiming his shoulder was sore and tourneys were for youngsters. The competition carried on until only Aldo, Robin and Scarlett remained.

They were on the third target of the bullseye round. Scarlett cracked her neck and then relaxed her shoulders as she stood on the line. A slight breeze swept past her face from the east, she knew how to correct her aim to account for it. She positioned her feet in the most comfortable stance. Then, she drew a large breath as she nocked her arrow. She held her breath for a split second as she took aim.

As she released the arrow, she exhaled. Scarlett didn't need to watch to know her aim was true, but it seemed cocky to turn before it hit. Cheers erupted as her arrow made contact with the centre of the target. She made a flamboyant courtesy for the merry men on the sidelines and even John wolf whistled his applause.

Thom had offered to retrieve the arrows and he sprinted out from behind a tree. Next, it was Robin's turn and his arrow sailed through the wind and landed right on target. He smugly winked at Aldo, who was lining up for his turn.

Aldo was visibly sweating and Scarlett felt for him. He had been practising constantly and he had developed into a skilled archer. He took his shot and although he hit the target, it was far from the centre. He bowed out with his head down, clearly upset, but the cheer from the men lifted his spirits and he smiled. Scarlett playfully shouted out, "Don't worry Aldo, I'll spread the rumour at the tavern you're a fantastic lover and you'll have women fawning all over you."

Scarlett watched the reaction and couldn't be prouder to call this bunch of misfits her friends. They were an odd bunch, but they were supportive and together they kept one another alive. Scarlett thought of each one of them as brothers, but she knew when it came down to it would they follow a woman into war? Would they be prepared to die behind a woman? She stared up at Robin and had an idea.

No one would question a Lord leading them into battle. Hell, half the villagers would probably join the revolt behind a Lord, in the hope that when they won, they would be granted land.

Scarlett set herself up on the line and took her shot. She missed. She hit the target of course, but missed the bullseye. The men's mouths dropped open and they jokingly offered her ale to drown her sorrows.

Robin eyed her up suspiciously, but he took his place on the line. If he hit the bullseye, then he won; if not, they would take turns again. He hit the bullseye. The men howled and hollered as they congratulated him. He lapped up the praise and they walked back to camp to celebrate properly.

Just as they were approaching camp Benedict sided up to Scarlett and asked, "You know what you offered Aldo," Scarlett stared at him blankly insinuating she didn't understand what he was referring to. Benedict continued, "Offering to spread a rumour about him. Could you do that for me?" Several of the other men were close enough to hear as Benedict had forgot to keep his voice low. A roar of laughter sounded and Scarlett playfully put him in a headlock. She messed his hair up until he shoved her off him. His face was bright red from the embarrassment, although she knew he would claim it was from the headlock. When the men dispersed upon their arrival to camp, Scarlett whispered in Benedict's ear, "Of course I will." Then she winked as she walked away.

Scarlett marched toward her tree house to store her bow away safely and as she climbed down Robin cornered her. "I know you let me win, why?"

Scarlett shrugged as she sidestepped past him. Robin pulled her arm to turn her to face him.

"If you don't tell me why, I'll tell everyone you lost on purpose. You could have made that shot."

Scarlett glanced over her shoulder to make sure no one was in earshot. Then she dragged Robin behind the nearest tree. "Look at them," she whispered, signalling behind her. "They respect you now. When the time comes, they will follow you into battle."

Robin understood her reasoning and sighed. "I think you underestimate their respect for you."

Scarlett smiled at the compliment from her eldest brother. She conceded, "They respect me, I know that, but would they happily march to war behind me? I wouldn't want to test their loyalty that far. Please don't say anything. Take the win."

Robin nodded in agreement and then gripped his sister's head in a playful arm lock. Scarlett squealed and fought her way free as Robin belly laughed. The night was spent in merriment with far too much ale.

Whilst everyone was gathered for the first meal of the day Scarlett shared her latest plan. Addressing the group she announced, "We need a way inside the castle, to hear when they plan on moving money again so we can intercept it. We're all to recognisable so I think the best option is to pay a tavern wench to report back."

"My cousin works in the tavern near the castle where a lot of the guard's go," piped up Thom. "She can be trusted and she could do with the extra money, she's got five siblings to support."

Thom was interjected by Aldo who queried, "Where are we going to find the money to pay someone?"

"The Sheriff will need to pay more taxes won't he," declared Scarlett in response.

Robin shook his head and stood up. "We still have the guard's uniform we stole and no one will recognise me. I should be the spy and pose as a solider," Robin proclaimed.

"That's risky. What if you're recognised?" Scarlett protested.

"I won't be. I can leave you notes to alert you to what's being planned so I don't have to break cover," Robin insisted.

"But you speak too proper, you need to dull it down the guards are not known for their intellect," Scarlett advised.

"I can play the part, don't worry about me."

"This is not just about you," Scarlett admonished, "I'm worried about all of us if this goes wrong."

"What's worse, trying and failing or never trying?" Robin countered.

"That sounds remarkably like something Father Fletcher would quote at mass, proving my point, dull it down or you'll get caught out." Even though she was chastising him, she agreed with him. He was right, they needed to do something and him playing spy was the best way to the get first-hand information. They were sitting ducks in the forest and whilst they were free, could she really admit they were living life? Her niece or nephew would be born shortly and she wanted more for that little soul than the hand-to-mouth life they could offer. Robin was the only one who stood a chance of not being recognised, given the number of altercations the group had had recently with the guards.

Later, as Robin redressed in the guards uniform Scarlett had commandeered for him he joked, "Are you going to offer any words of wisdom before I depart little sister?"

With a smirk, Scarlett yelled back, "Don't get caught!"

Robin waited until a group of the Sheriff's men marched through the entrance to the keep and he tagged along. He followed them through to the guard's quarters, where a guard with a slightly different uniform took charge and gave them new orders. Robin did as instructed and joined in the subsequent moaning at the new task with the other guards. No one questioned him and when night fell he settled to sleep in a spare bed in the guard's quarters.

The next morning, Robin was crossing the courtyard to his new posting when he spotted the elite guards training. He watched intently, assessing the sword skill and footwork. Only two of the six looked to have any real skill and the taller of the two, made quick work out of pinning a fellow guard to the ground by his black cloak.

The winner sheathed his sword and extended his arm to aid the fallen guard to his feet as he remarked, "Bloody liability these cloaks. No chance I'll wear one in a battle."

"Aye, but they're a clear sign we're a cut above the rest and not to mess with us," replied the fallen guard, as he collected his own sword from the ground several yards away.

Robin had lingered in the courtyard longer than he should and forgot his place when he scoffed openly in response.

The group suddenly noticed him and he turned quickly to walk away.

"Hey you!" one of them shouted, "Think you can do

better?"

Robin put his head down but another guard goaded him and he turned around to respond. Never one to back down from a fight, he replied, "I'll give it a go."

The men cheered and hollered, offering to teach him a lesson but the winner from the previous match pushed his way to the front of the group. He removed his helmet and cocked his head to the side. "You look familiar."

Robin shrugged and tried to place him. The scar on his face looked recent, but it had messed up his features pretty badly and whilst Robin agreed he did look familiar, he couldn't place him.

"You wanna fight? Then show me what you're made of. Don't hold back." His words were met with a chorus of laughter from the group.

Robin knew that it was a bad idea to single himself out, but he wasn't going to get the inside scoop if he remained on duty guarding the castle walls. Maybe if he displayed enough skill, he would get to join the elite ranks and find out useful information he could pass back to Scarlett, or at least get close enough to the Sheriff to end him. He hadn't been completely truthful in the forest, his plan A would always be to take down the Sheriff as vengeance for his father if he got a chance, no matter the personal sacrifice.

The guards dispersed and left the two men to face each other. Alaric, the previous fights winner circled his opponent with his sword drawn. "First one to yield or draw blood, no one needs to die today," he ordered.

"Agreed," Robin responded as he lunged forward to make the first move.

Alaric pre-emptied the move and batted his opponent's blade away. He launched a counter-attack and Robin deflected the sword. The fight continued this way for a few rounds until Alaric changed his foot pattern, forcing Robin backwards. Robin knew if he continued fighting this way he would be backed up against the castle wall in no time, so he quickened up his pace.

He attacked over and over again. Each time Alaric matched his move, but Alaric was now on the back foot, being schooled across the courtyard by his opponent.

Alaric's jaw clenched as he brooded on how evenly matched this guard was to him. He was determined not to lose to a lower-ranked guard and began to wield more blows. Alaric was pushing him back again across the courtyard when a broom was thrown across the floor behind his opponent.

Robin stumbled over it, lost his footing, and fell backwards onto the hard stone ground. The fall had winded him and he was panting for air.

Alaric seized his opportunity to knick his opponent's chin, carefully enough to draw just a bead of blood. Robin wiped it with his fingers. He had been defeated.

Alaric held out his hand to aid his competitor up as he addressed him, "I haven't had a fight that close in skill for years. What's your name?"

"R…," Robin stopped himself just in time and managed to get out the name, "Richard."

Clapping him on the shoulder, Alaric addressed the rest of the men, "Richard here is being promoted. I want him behind me when we take on those bandit scums again. Aengus, get him a black cloak," he ordered as he picked up the broom which Robin had tripped over. He snapped it half over his knee in a display of strength.

"And Conrad," he continued, marching over to a man pressed against a pillar. He held the broken broom handle to his throat like a javelin about to be thrown. "If you ever interfere in a sparring match again, I'll challenge you to a fight to the death and we both know who's winning that fight." Conrad's body language and appearance did little to hide how scared he was, as he apologised profusely. Alaric threw the broken broom to the ground and clapped Robin on the shoulder.

"Time for a well-earned drink I think, let's go raid my father's private stash." The men cheered as Alaric led the way. Robin ground his back teeth. Of course his opponent looked familiar. He was the Sheriff's bloody son, who had spent every summer with them as a boy. He clearly hadn't recognised Robin, most likely because he believed he was dead. At least he was in a good position to get access to the Sheriff, or at the very least be in the know about the movement of money across the county. Robin followed the group, contemplating his next move.

Later that evening, the drinking session had moved to the local tavern. Several of the men had wenches bouncing on their knees but not Alaric, he shooed away every maiden that made a beeline for him. When a fresh round of ale made it to the table, Aengus asked, "So when are we making that trip back to pompous, old William de Blackwater?"

Robin's ears pricked up and he listened intently. He had been faking being as drunk as the rest of the men, which was easy to do after the first few rounds and the men's words began to slur.

With his words slurring, Alaric confirmed, "The witch says tomorrow will be a clear sky, that's when we go." Without notice, he slammed his tankard on the table and stood up. "I need a piss," he declared, as he meandered through the crowd to the door, his hands already unfastening his breeches as he drunkenly swayed.

CHAPTER 6

Robin seized his opportunity to sneak out of the tavern. He disappeared into the night, back to the castle, and headed for the Church. Guards were on duty outside blocking the entrance, but one look at his new black cloak and they stepped aside. Robin's face was smug as he entered the church. He immediately searched for an obvious place where he could find parchment, or fabric he could use to send a message to Scarlett.

He found a torn piece of parchment on the pulpit, but there was no ink or quill anywhere to be found. He took the dagger from his belt and pierced the skin on his index finger. Blood instantly rushed to the surface and Robin used his own blood to write a one-word message. He blew across it to speed the drying and then he folded it in a small square. He marched out of the Church, past the guards, and back into the cold night air.

As Robin slunk past the tavern, he could still hear the loud, ruckus cheers of drunken men. In the distance, he could see guards on duty at the stone wall. He had been banking on them being drunk or asleep by now. He slipped back inside the tavern and looked for Thom's cousin. He had described her as a petite maid with long golden hair and a prominent birthmark on her chest.

Robin had thought it an odd description for one's cousin, but Thom assured him he couldn't miss her with that portrayal. He scanned the wenches serving, ruling out any that didn't have fair hair. He spotted a petite blonde with her back to him leaning over a table. He made his way over and lurked nearby, trying to get a glimpse of her chest.

She must have felt the heat of his gaze on her because she turned and Robin's eyes immediately glanced down to inspect her chest. Right above her breast was a port-wine stain birthmark in the shape of squashed love heart. It must have been the size of the lass's clenched fist and half the size of her ample chest. Thom wasn't joking when he inferred, 'You won't miss her.' Surveying him gawking at her, she hollered, "Like what you see?"

Robin's eyes immediately lifted to her face, embarrassed at being caught. She was a pretty lass and the birthmark didn't detract from that. He gave her a half smile as he stepped closer and leaned into her ear.

"Thom said I could count on you for a favour." Her gaze grew serious. She looked up at him and nodded. "Deliver two tankards to the guards on the wall out there. I need to sneak past them."

Playing up for the other patrons, she feigned a flirtatious smile like Robin had just propositioned her and patted him on the chest. "Two ticks love and I'm all yours."

Robin played along and waited near the door. A few moments later, as promised, he saw her heading towards him with two full tankards. He slipped out the door and held it open for her.

"When do I get paid?" She whispered as they headed towards the guards.

"When I get a chance, I'm good for it."

"If Thom sent you, I know you're a good man."

Robin moved towards the shadows, holding back as Thom's cousin delivered on the favour.

"You hard-working men never get a break, I don't know how you stay up all night and keep us all safe from those outlaws with no sustenance." As she offered the ale, she said, "Here's a treat lads, on the house. Make sure you come visit us once your shifts over."

Robin could hear the guards propositioning her and making lewd remarks as he snuck around in the shadows, trying to make it look like he wasn't skulking. He wondered if he had put her in danger and hesitated about whether he should step in. However, seconds later, he heard her roar with laughter and saw her returning back to the tavern.

Using the shadows to hide, he got close to the wall. He had mentally calculated ten large strides from the entrance, so now he was adjacent to the wall he took a further five strides. Robin found a loose stone and placed the note underneath it before placing the rock back into position. He took out his dagger and made a mark he hoped would last on the ground, then he stealthily returned to the sleeping quarters to rest. Tomorrow was going to be a long day and he needed to be in top form.

Scarlett was apprehensive about whether the plan would work without Robin being discovered. Nevertheless, she was eager to get to the hideaway spot to see if the mission had already been fruitful. As Scarlett left the forest, she concealed her identity with a head scarf. She carried a basket laden with mushrooms and mint as her excuse for travelling on the road. It was early and the sun had barely risen when she set off. The morning still held a lingering chill and she hastened her step. The night watch didn't stray far from the castle walls and as she anticipated, the day shift were still asleep, so she didn't encounter any guards.

Scarlett ensured her face and recognisable hair were fully hidden by the scarf as she slipped behind a wagon and followed it though the castle perimeter. They had agreed to fifteen paces along the wall from the entrance. She estimated fifteen large strides of Robin's would be about double that of hers. As she moseyed around the market stalls, she stayed close to the wall and counted to thirty.

She placed her basket on the floor, making it look like she was stopping for a rest. Her eyes scanned the surrounding area and she noticed an indent on the ground that looked intentional. She took another few steps before leaning on the wall, faking the need for support as she tested the rocks with her fingertips, trying to locate the loose stone. A medium-sized one wobbled at her touch, so she applied more force, trying to pry it free. As the rock budged under her forcefulness, she saw a folded piece of parchment fall. Scarlett quickly bobbed to the ground and snatched the parchment from the dirt.

She was desperate to open it, but she didn't want to draw too much attention to herself. Instead, she shoved the note into her cleavage and traded the mint and mushrooms for two loaves of bread.

She kept watch for a moment to sneak past the guards again and noticed two young farmer lads unloading eggs and poultry nearby. They didn't look familiar, so she made a beeline to get their attention.

"Hello there," she addressed the closest to her, using her meekest voice and touching her fingertips on his bare forearm. The lad turned immediately and smiled when he saw Scarlett in front of him, acting coy and biting her lip.

"Hello," he replied, resting on the empty crate he was loading onto his wagon.

"Would you be my knight in shining armour and let me catch a lift with you?" She batted her eyelashes for good measure, catching the attention of the second lad, who was now listening to the exchange.

He ran his hands through his thick chestnut-coloured hair as he replied, "Sure, hop up front."

"Oh no, I'm fine in the back. I don't want to trouble you."

"Suit yourself," he responded and held out his hands to lift her onto the wagon. Scarlett had to stop herself from jerking backwards. With a forced smile, she allowed him to lift her by the waist onto the back of the wagon. They finished loading the empty crates and set off. The wagon was covered in dirt, smashed eggs and feathers. Scarlett tried not to pull a face in disgust, as she crawled through the filth to nestle herself behind some crates.

They passed the guards without complication and when they were clear of view, Scarlett crawled back out of her hiding spot and sat on the back of the wagon with her feet dangling off the edge. It was turning into a pleasant day as the sun was beginning to warm the air and one of the lads started singing a merry tune.

When the road grew quiet and the thicket on either side of the road grew thicker, Scarlett chose her moment to jump down. She ran for the cover of the greenery and made sure they hadn't noticed, before she headed in the direction of Sherwood Forest.

It wasn't until she made it back to camp that she took out the folded parchment and read the note. The only word written was, 'Tonight'. Scarlett had been expecting a bit more instruction than that, but nevertheless, she gathered the band of outlaws and gave her orders.

Once all weapons and traps had been checked, she insisted they rest up as it could be a long night. As the sun set she stationed the men in pairs to the key watch points, where the tree coverage was sparse and would allow for a wagon to be pulled through the forest. Then they waited.

It was a harsh night. Heavy rain was pouring down from the sky. The tree canopy barely protected them and Scarlett was soaked to the bone. Large droplets of water were falling on her from her loose hair and she shoved it back out of her eyes so that she could see better.

The distinct call of an owl sounded in the distance and Scarlett nocked an arrow to her bow, waiting for further instruction. Bird calls were their secret language in the forest. A second cry from an owl filled the night air, sounding closer. She slowed her own breathing to listen for the unnatural sound of a wagon being pulled, or the trotting of hooves from a guard on an advanced scout, but the weather was playing havoc with her senses.

Then, she heard the rhythmic sound of a flattened wheel on a wagon, followed by a horse's neigh. A third owl hoot, sounding even closer than before pierced the air and Scarlett shook her head. That was definitely Aldo, he needed to practise his owl call more. It sounded too much like a skylark. Then Scarlett thought back to where she had stationed everyone and realised the travelling party were closer than she thought.

Within seconds, she heard a familiar voice shout, "HOLD! Stay together men. Something's not right."

"How can you tell?" Came back a gruff response.

"Can you see any owls out in this weather?" Alaric retorted in frustration.

"I can't see a damn thing in this weather." The second man to speak remarked, although noticeably quieter than the first time he spoke.

"Shall we send a scouting party ahead Sir?" offered another guard and Scarlett instantly recognised the voice as Robin's.

"No, we should stay together. Everyone move forward as one."

Robins's plan to split the numbers had been foiled and Scarlett was about to give the signal when Robin spoke again. "Whilst we've stopped Commander, can I just go for a piss?"

Scarlett tried to make out the facial response that must have followed, but she was too high up and their helmets prevented her from seeing.

"If you must, get on with it," came back the response and Robin jumped down from his horse, leading it by the reins to a shaded tree. Several other guards did the same. The group dispersed and the men were more vulnerable now that they were off their horses. One of the men who remained in the saddle jeered to Robin, "Are you sure you need a piss? Could be the clap. He was with that barmaid Marian last night."

He started singing a crude song when Alaric silenced him by snapping, "If I knew you were all going to go, I would have just said piss whilst you ride. It's not like we can get any wetter."

Scarlett seized the opportunity. She gave the attack bird cry as she aimed her arrow for the arse cheek of a urinating guard. She released the arrow and hit her bullseye, which was met by a shrill scream. Chaos erupted as she nocked another arrow and took aim. This time, the arrow pierced the hand of the guard unsheathing his sword.

Robin's stalling tactic had given the bandits enough time to circle the group. Horses were rearing and several fled as the outlaws struck from every angle. Scarlett noticed that Robin had removed his helmet and was fighting against the guards, much to their surprise. The mesh of bodies made it too hard for her to aim, so she climbed down from her branch to join the affray.

Between the two she had injured, the two Robin had wounded, and the one who had loudly shouted, "Fuck this!" as he deserted, the rest of the men had taken down the three guards in standard uniform. This left just one who was circling Robin as if it was a sparring match for sport, not a battle.

"If you have any honour, you will make this a fair fight, one on one," he shouted and Scarlett recognised him as the one Robin had referred to as Commander.

"I'll beat you fair and square. You don't need to worry about that," Robin replied.

They circled a couple of times and their boots were laden with thick mud. The outlaws had formed a makeshift circle and were cheering Robin on. Scarlett thought the whole thing was ridiculous. So what if this guard won? She wasn't about to let him go without a bash on the head and the confiscation of the wagon of money.

Both men hurled insults at one another as they lunged to take a shot. The clanking of steel on steel rang in her ears, followed by grunting at the exertion of wielding a sword. Scarlett surveyed her surroundings for something to use to stop the fight. Her eyes lingered on the remaining horses in the clearing tied up to the wagon. She marched towards them and cut off the reins with her dagger. Then, she joined the circle behind where Robin's opponent was standing and gripped the ends of the reins poised to strike.

At the opportune moment she looped the reins around the guard's throat and pulled hard. He stumbled backward and fell to the ground, flat on his back. Robin made his move quickly, standing on his right wrist so he couldn't raise his weapon.

From the flat of his back, covered in mud, the guard spat, "You said you would fight fair."

"He did; I didn't," answered Scarlett as she loomed over him.

"What now," asked Thom as he looked at Scarlett, "Do we kill him?"

"No," replied Robin sternly, "He's too important to kill. Remove his helmet."

Scarlett looked intrigued as Aldo held a knife to their captive's throat and Thom removed his helmet. The bandits stepped closer to get a better look and Scarlett turned her head to see his profile. An angry, not yet healed scar marked diagonally across his face and she recognised him as the guard she had escaped from. That scar was her doing. She stared at the man, but was still none the wiser as to why Robin said he was important.

Robin signalled to Billy to approach, and he stepped forward to take a better look. Billy's eyes widened as he realised and he turned towards Scarlett.

"It's Alaric, the Sheriff's son."

CHAPTER 7

At the sight of the three faces staring down at him, he was hit with a realisation. The long-lost Loxley siblings were alive and living as bandits. He should have recognised Robin when he first laid eyes on him, but with no word of him in a decade he had assumed he died overseas.

Alaric felt a pang of guilt when he thought of his friendship with William growing up. He should have asked questions years ago about his whereabouts. Their family was a noble one and now they were reduced to living as peasants. Worse than peasants, outlaws. As his eyes flicked to Lady Loxley's, burning rage took over him and he snarled at her like a trapped predator. She was the reason his face was so hideously disfigured now and all he had been trying to do was help her. If his arms and legs weren't restrained he would have taken his revenge there and then.

The two brothers left to check out the wagon, leaving Scarlett with Alaric. As she turned her attention away from him, Alaric swung around his bound legs and swept hers out from under her. Scarlett landed in a crumpled heap on the ground. "Paybacks a bitch," Alaric spat, as Scarlett glared at him. The sound of their altercation made heads turn to look at the pair.

Scarlett pulled a small dagger out of her boot and stood back on her feet. Brandishing the blade at Alaric she kicked him in the stomach hard as he tried to roll. He recoiled onto his back in pain and Scarlett crouched low, holding the blade at his throat. She straddled his body and sat on his torso.

"Don't think your name saves you, in fact, it condemns you. I told you long ago I wasn't suited to being the damsel in distress. I quite think it rather suits you," Scarlett mocked him as she held the blade to his skin.

She could see the rage in his eyes and she goaded him, "Give me a reason. I dare you."

"I remember it a little differently," he replied darkly, "I remember me letting you have a turn to be the knight and then you begging me for a kiss. Claim your prize if you like, but don't be surprised if I don't bite off that lippy mouth of yours."

Scarlett huffed before retorting, "I wouldn't kiss you if you were the last man on earth. Now, how about I remove one of those pretty eyes for you?"

Alaric's jaw tightened and his body stiffened underneath her as he desperately tried to think of a way out of his predicament.

Scarlett was tempted to hold true to her threat, but Robin appeared at her side and held out his hand to help her to her feet. Keeping the blade pointed in Alaric's direction and not taking her eyes off him, she took Robin's hand.

"If you've finished toying with him Scarlett, what would you like us to do with them?" Robin pointed to the injured guards.

Alaric cocked his head to the side, his assumption was wrong. She was in charge of this bunch of bandits, and she went by the name Scarlett. As two men tied him to the back of the wagon by his wrists and cut his leg restraints, he had a sudden thought. The witch had been right. A cold shiver ran down his spine. A man had risen from the dead and he did bear his father a grudge.

Alaric tried to remember what else the witch had foretold. It was some caution about the man stealing his father's legacy. Alaric swallowed, he was his father's legacy. Either the witch had predicted this very night and his kidnapping, or worse was yet to come. Stealing his father's legacy could be a permanent position, or a temporary one and Alaric knew he needed to play it smart if he wished to get out of this alive.

It sounded like they planned to exchange him for something, but he had no confidence his ruthless father would take kindly to being forced to do anything. He wasn't even certain how much his father valued his life. Just because he hadn't chosen to legitimise any bastards didn't mean he couldn't, or he could just remarry and make another heir.

Morgana's eyes shot open and she took a deep breath as she reached for a mug of water. She sat up and realised her night clothes were soiled and wet through. Clutching her cane, she hobbled over to the closest small window and peered up at the moon. It had turned from a full moon to a waning gibbous since the last time she had looked up into the sky. After drinking the potion, she must have been in and out of consciousness for days.

The witch stumbled over to a wooden table and retrieved her iron and flint to light a torch. She lit the others around her chambers, they cast an eerie glow about the room. She stared into a pale of water at her reflection. The effects of the potion were still lingering. Her eyes were completely black. She barely recognised her reflection anymore.

When she was younger, she had been above average in height, with soft, fair skin. Some may even have said beautiful. Now her spine was so bent that she had to walk hunched over with a cane. Her weathered skin was wrinkled and marked with age spots. The amount of dark magic she had been using in recent years was taking its toll, along with the brutal inevitability of time.

When she was a young girl she had a merry disposition, until her father sold her to an old and cruel merchant to be his wife. She had been a dutiful spouse and done her best to please him, but he was merciless. He beat her for pleasure and made her life a living hell. For years, she suffered mentally and physically. She prayed at her window each night before she slept for the suffering to end, but no relief came just the occasional visit from a black raven. It seemed to study her, occasionally cocking its head to the side as if trying to understand why she was crying.

Then she noticed an old woman in the village would stare at her without saying a word each time she collected water with fresh bruises. One day, when she sporting a particularly nasty purple bruise around her eye, which was so swollen it barely opened, the old woman spoke to her for the first time. She placed a parcel of cloth into Morgana's hand and cupped her own hand over the top.

In a raspy voice, she instructed, "Have him eat the berries, but don't eat them yourself."

Morgana remembered the intensity of her gaze and the darkness of her eyes. Foolishly, she hadn't realised the berries were from the deadly nightshade plant. She did as instructed and her husband was dead by morning.

Again the raven visited her and she started to associate its visits as an omen of fate. She was glad to be free of her husband, but single life didn't come without its hardships. She vowed never to live in fear of another again and she sought out the old crone to thank her for her kindness, when everyone else had ignored her struggles.

She ended up forming a friendship that led to an apprenticeship, so to speak. From the old witch, she learned the power of the dark arts. She learned how to trade part of her soul to the Devil so that he could work his magic. Morgana had learned the hard way that one's sacrifice did not always result in the desired outcome. The Devil had his own plan.

Morgana had become a master of alchemy under the old crone's tutelage. Reading the tarot cards came later, as if the gift passed onto her when her tutor died, but the most important lesson she learned was the power of persuasion. To influence others opinions and feelings took practise and skill. A skill Morgana was now an expert at.

The raven was a frequent visitor, so much so that she named him Oionos, the Greek for omen. He allowed her to stroke him and often perched on her shoulder.

When her mentor passed, she decided that she was fed up with living in squalor, meddling in the boring lives of village folk, so she had sought out a wealthy benefactor. In the Sheriff of Nottingham, she had found a man full of greed, who was willing to stop at nothing to possess power. She had moulded him and guided him over the years to the powerful man he was today. Their relationship was one of mutual respect. Her fate was tied to his, so she did everything in her power to keep him in good standing and thus herself.

She unlocked the door to her chamber and climbed the stairs. She shouted for the serving wench who was staring out the window at the top of the stairs. She came running immediately, her face was horror-stricken when she set eyes on the witch. "I need to bathe. Fetch me warm water," Morgana demanded.

The young servant nodded and scurried away.

Once Morgana was washed and dressed in clean clothes, she ordered the petrified servant to clean up the mess in her bed. She heard the girl retching as she left the room and she cackled menacingly. Life was about influence and status. The sooner the young girl learned that and made peace with her status, the easier she would succumb to the mundane existence her life would become. There was no time for daydreaming out of windows unless she had the stomach to sell her soul to the Devil. From the sound of the retching, quite clearly she didn't.

Morgana hurried up the secret stairway to check in with the Sheriff. She needed an update on what she had missed. As she reached the living quarters, she saw the Sheriff asleep in a chair by the fire. She approached the fireplace and took an iron rod to stoke the wooden logs. Then, she gazed upon the sleeping Sheriff and took a moment to unashamedly lust after him.

Her tongue darted out of her mouth and moistened her lips as she quietly approached him. She leaned in close and breathed in his scent. She reached out with her thumb and touched his lips. A grunt followed by a snort, escaped from his mouth and she froze. Then, when he didn't stir, she leaned in closer and pressed her lips to his.

It had been a long time since she had been kissed. He was the forbidden fruit and that made him all the more desirable. She had coveted him in secret for years, always watching from afar or the crack of a doorway. His wife had known. She had tried and failed to drive a wedge between them. That was why she had to die. It was not how she had planned, but so many women die in childbirth that no suspicions were ever raised. The Sheriff hadn't even asked Morgana to save her, not that she would have.

She stepped back and the empty tankard on his lap fell to the floor with a thud. He was startled awake and the old crone tapped her cane loudly on the floor as if to signal her arrival.

The Sheriff stretched out his arms above his head and yawned as he greeted her. "Crone, what are you doing here? I've not seen you in days." Realising his tankard had fallen to the floor, he looked around for another and saw one on the table by the door. He walked across the room to retrieve it, taking a long swig.

"I was helping the boy with his revenge," she replied. "The power it took consumed me. What date is it? What news is there?"

"Revenge?" Queried the Sheriff, puzzled, before he remembered the laceration on Alaric's face. He gesticulated a diagonal line across his own face and the witch nodded. "Boy needs to move on and be a man about it. Don't waste your energy on his foolish quests."

Morgana nodded and stepped back to take a seat in the high-backed chair opposite.

"Is there any news to update me on?" She asked, intrigued about any new developments in their plan for power.

"The Barons in the South are proving more difficult than the North to secure alliances with. At least the northern Barons just wanted money."

"How so?" Queried the witch.

"They squabble over land, wanting bigger private estates and more titles. I have a mind to kill them all and just take their lands for myself." The Sheriff was getting more animated and angrier as the conversation progressed.

"Calm yourself. I've seen your future. With me by your side, you will not fail."

"Don't tell me what to do old crone. I will be King!" He shouted but his words were slurred. Pointing at the witch, he thundered, "You will make sure of it!"

Morgana realised that there was no point in speaking to him further tonight. He was drunk and in a mood. Rising from her seat and making sure he knew she did not fear him, she looked him dead in the eyes as she dictated, "Stick to the plan." Without waiting for an answer, she descended the stairs to her quarters.

Alaric misplaced his footing for the third time in as many minutes, but this time, his ankle rolled and his leg gave way. Both knees smashed to the ground as his bound wrists meant he was unable to reach out to brace his fall. The blindfold they had tied around his head was making it impossible for him to navigate the forest floor. His left knee stung more than his right and he could feel it was bleeding.

"Whoa, STOP!" He heard bellowed close by. "He's fallen again, I'm removing the blindfold. He won't recognise the way from here."

Alaric recognised the voice as his old friend William. Moments later, he felt a strong hand under his arm pull him up. The blindfold was removed and the torches on the wagon in front of him made spots appear in his vision. He blinked repeatedly as he tried to adjust to the light level. He looked down at his legs to see a rip in his trousers and blood oozing out. He walked the rest of the way with a limp, as he tried to memorize his surroundings.

It took a while longer before the dense forest thinned to reveal a clearing. The stars shone extra bright through the night sky lighting up the forest floor. No doubt by now they were close to the centre of the wood. The shadows cast by the moonlight and the torchlight were enough to turn any man petrified. However, the sounds of animals in the quiet, dead of night were worse.

Alaric could hear scurrying and scratching all around him as he scanned the forest floor for vermin. Above him in the trees were squeaks, hoots, and knocking. The rustling of leaves and the howling of the wind sounded like ghosts. He had never been this deep into Sherwood Forest before. The sounds were so different from his comfy castle bed chamber. A lesser man would have been scared witless but not Alaric. He grew up with the witch lurking around every corner, the sight of her was enough to creep anyone out.

As the wagon slowed to a stop, he told himself to pull it together. He didn't want his face to give away any insecurity he had, even if his mind was letting him down.

A voice he didn't recognise shouted, "What do we do with him?"

Alaric's head spun just as Scarlett yelled in response, "Tie him to a Beech tree and keep his hands tied. We don't want him escaping."

A guy he loosely recognised from an altercation in a market a few months ago untied him from the wagon and led him to a tree. Seizing his opportunity, he asked the man, "Any chance you could let me go for a piss with dignity?" He raised his bound hands to signal he wanted to be untied.

The man had a gormless expression and seemed puzzled with the request. Rather than doing as Alaric had asked, he yelled, "He wants to go for a piss, what should I do?"

Scarlett left inspecting the contents of the wagon and stood in front of Alaric. She looked him up and down before turning her attention to the lad she had instructed to incarcerate him.

"Benedict, don't listen to a word that comes out of his mouth. He will try to trick you. He can piss himself for all I care. He is not being untied."

Alaric rolled his eyes as she thwarted his plan. He caught her eye and her expression was enough to make him smile. If it wasn't for the fact that her orders were against him and in direct violation of his freedom, Alaric was impressed with the command she wielded. He remembered her as a spoilt and whiney child, but now when she spoke, men listened.

The lad did as she instructed and try as he might, Alaric couldn't escape from the rope tying him to the tree. He wondered what lay in store for him.

As time ticked on, his eyelids grew heavy. He slumped forward into the clutch of the rope and he drifted to sleep.

CHAPTER 8

Everywhere ached as Alaric stirred awake. His rear was numb from the cold mud and in an attempt to stretch out his toes, he got cramp in his foot. He grimaced in pain. Without the use of his hands, he was unable to massage out the spasm. It felt like his foot was being hacked off with a blunt axe. He sat in agony, taking deep breaths until the pain passed.

It was only then that he took in his surroundings in the morning light. He had to admit it was like being in a different world. The colours of the forest were so vibrant in the daylight. There wasn't a cloud in sight and the early morning chirps from the birds, sounded like they were singing to the sun about the glorious day they were having. It was in direct contrast to the morning he was having and his desperation to get out of his current situation took hold of him.

He brought his gaze back down to his immediate surroundings. He could see a fire across the clearing with a pot stewing on top. He was too far away to benefit from any of the heat, but he could smell the tantalising aroma of stew. He couldn't help but lick his lips. A woman was tending to the fire on her own and Alaric seized the opportunity to escape.

"Fair maiden," he called over to her, "Could I trouble you for some water?"

The young woman looked perplexed at the request. She looked over her shoulder as if checking if there was anyone else around. When she had confirmed there wasn't and he had been addressing her, she rose from her crouched position by the fire.

She took an empty tankard and filled it with rainwater that had been collected in a water butt.

As she approached Alaric he could see that she was heavily pregnant. His heart sank. He had questionable ethics. He didn't abide by many of the Lords Commandments, but he had principles that governed his moral compass and he couldn't hurt a pregnant woman. He needed to change tactics.

She looked wary as she neared him, subconsciously rubbing her belly. She kept her distance, stopping a metre away, clutching the tankard of water. He decided that a charm offensive was the best approach.

"I promise I won't hurt you. In truth, I couldn't, even if wanted to with how tight these ropes are bound." Alaric gave a shuffle to show he had very little movability.

The woman took a couple of steps forward but remained apprehensive. She looked about seemingly checking if anyone else was about, then surprised Alaric by starting a conversation.

"You probably don't remember me, but I remember you. You and Billy used to play together."

"That's right. Me and Billy are friends," Alaric confirmed, assuming Billy was a nickname for William. He tried to place the young woman and where he might have seen her before, but try as he might he couldn't remember her. "If we'd met before I would have asked for your name." He gave her a smile and maintained eye contact to exaggerate his interest in her. She looked to the ground first, embarrassed by the attention.

Still looking at the floor, she mumbled, "We never met, I just used to watch you both from the scullery."

"Ahhh, that explains it then. What's your name? Please tell me."

Just then an arrow landed inches away from Alaric's thigh. His body went rigid and on high alert as he scanned around for the archer. In a split second, the shadow of a person came into view as they marched towards him. His new companion didn't even turn around to acknowledge who the arrow was from. She clearly already knew.

She lifted her head and confirmed, "My name's Beth, I'm Billy's wife." Then she proceeded back towards the fireplace, rubbing her lower back.

Alaric barely had time to register what she had just said as Scarlett came into view. Upon the sight of her, his rage boiled to the surface again. She seemed to be everywhere and yet nowhere. Her interruption had thwarted his plans again and made his new friend run away. He had serious reservations about her aim. It was sheer luck the arrow hadn't speared his dick. He glowered at her, hoping the manifestation of his hate would transcend into physical pain.

He swallowed and realised how dry and painful his throat was. Ignoring Scarlett approaching he shouted back to Beth, "I'm happy for you and Billy, you make a great couple. But I'm incredibly thirsty and I'm sure when I get a chance to speak to Billy this misunderstanding can all be resolved."

Beth faltered in her steps and turned around. She started walking back towards him less apprehensive than before, but as she reached him Scarlett was by his side.

"So, sleeping beauty's awake then," Scarlett mocked, as she reached out her hand towards Beth, signalling for her to hand over the tankard. "Beth, don't be taken in by his charming smile. Whatever he says is poison. Don't get too close."

Alaric saw Beth's eyes widen in fear as she handed over the tankard. She ambled back to the fireplace, which left Alaric and Scarlett alone. "So you think my smile is charming then? Shame I can't say the same compliment back," he said with a smirk.

Scarlett didn't bat an eyelid at the insult and her lack of emotion disgruntled him. Going straight on the offensive Alaric demanded, "What have you done with my men?"

"We've sent them on their merry way. You should be pleased. They're completing their mission and are on their way to William de Blackwater. Although, it may take them ever so slightly longer, naked, bound, and on foot." This time she gave him a smirk in response.

Alaric pulled on his restraints but roared when his

attempts were futile. "My father won't stand for his!" He threatened.

"I hope not, I'm counting on it," Scarlett retorted.

"What more could you possibly want? You already have the wagon full of gold. What are you planning to do with all that money?" He challenged.

"This is the people of Nottingham's money, they deserve it back," Scarlett proclaimed adamantly.

"I'll believe that when I see it. You're just common thieves." Not one ounce of him believed that bandits, who lived hand to mouth would give away all that gold.

"It's your father who steals from the poor, not us."

"My father is the Sheriff. People rely on him to protect them and that costs money. Not all of us can run and hide in the forest, playing make-believe," Alaric snarled.

"Your father has done nothing but line his own pocket and persecute innocent people."

"My father keeps the peace and protects people from thieving outlaws," Alaric said indignantly.

"It's easy to keep the peace when you're the one starting the trouble," Scarlett snapped back quickly.

Alaric glared at her and they engaged in a standoff, neither backing down. She held out the tankard of water to his lips and tipped the mug. Water spilled down his chin but she could see from his throat he was lapping up what he could. When she removed the tankard, he still had water dripping onto his chest. Scarlett didn't want Alaric to take her pragmatism for weakness and continued, "There's no point trading you if you're dead."

"So you plan on keeping me alive then?" Alaric sneered. His demanding and arrogant persona shone through, "Because if you are, I could do with some food."

"If I intended for you to be dead, you'd be dead already," Scarlett said matter-of-factly.

Scarlett went to walk away when Alaric shouted out, "There's one issue with your plan." Scarlett turned to face him, but made no attempt to walk back to him.

"Which is?" She challenged.

"You don't know my father as well as you think you do. You think him cruel and evil, yet you think he cares for his son. I've got news for you, he doesn't. He taught me to be strong and get out of my own messes." Alaric said it so matter-of-factly that Scarlett did pause for thought.

"But you're his heir, surely he cares about that?" The tone in her voice turned the statement to a question. Her own father would have moved mountains for his children.

"There's no need for an heir when you think you'll live forever," Alaric said bluntly.

"That's insane. No one can live forever," she argued.

"With a witch by his side, he thinks he can do anything."

Scarlett stepped closer as she assessed Alaric. "So the rumours are true, he consorts with a witch. Well, I don't believe in witchcraft."

"Then answer me this, how else does a peasant boy become the Sheriff of Nottingham, rising to be one of the most influential people in England? I've seen things that can't be explained by any other means but witchcraft."

Scarlett couldn't answer him, her mind whirling over everything he had just divulged. In truth, she might have to rethink her strategy. She had been banking on the Sheriff being willing to trade anything for his son's life. Perhaps she had been naïve in her plan, but there was no going back now.

Alaric had seen their faces and seen the camp. She couldn't just let him go. Then again, she had never killed a man in cold blood with no just cause. She decided she needed to test the theory, she was going to stick to plan A.

Without responding, she simply turned and walked away. Scarlett placed her catch of four pheasants down beside Beth, who immediately started plucking the game birds. Scarlett returned to Alaric with a chunk of bread and held it to his mouth.

Alaric took a bite and pulled a face. He spat it out on the

ground. "That's rock hard and stale," he complained.

Scarlett rolled her eyes in response. "I'm sorry Your Majesty, what do you think poor homeless people eat?" Scarlett mocked him but continued to hold out the bread. "Eat it or starve. Your choice."

Alaric scowled but took another bite. Scarlett took satisfaction in his repugnance. When he was down to the last few bites and the noggin of bread was close to her fingertips, she rammed the remains into his mouth. She slapped him on the cheek saying, "Good boy." Then she returned to the fireplace to help Beth prepare the stew.

Beth was breathing heavier than normal and Scarlett looked over concerned as Beth winced. "Are you ok?" Scarlett asked.

"I've been having back pains since yesterday but it's getting worse. I think the baby's coming." Scarlett could tell by the waver in her voice that Beth was scared.

"Have you told Billy?"

"No, I didn't want to worry anyone. He's gone to town to get more bread with my father," she replied.

"Beth, you should have told him. Someone else could have gone to get the bread."

Beth continued to wince and breathe heavily. It was obvious she was in a lot of pain. "Scarlett, I didn't think it would be this painful. Can you help me up, I need to walk about."

Scarlett went to her aid and helped her up. As Beth stood, a gush of liquid splattered the ground over her feet. She let out a harrowing scream. Scarlett froze as she continued to hold up her sister-in-law. Beth clung to her as waves of pain flowed through her body.

"What do you need me to do?" Scarlett asked, trying to remain calm. Beth's face was stricken with panic.

"Can you get Billy?" She pleaded, as tears rolled down her cheeks. She let out another ear piercing scream and grasped Scarlett's hand tightly.

"I don't want to leave you, not in this state." Scarlett

looked around the camp but it was empty. She had sent half the men to escort Alaric's guards out of the forest. The rest were hunting and going about their daily tasks. They were alone.

Alaric had heard the screams and was watching the drama unfold. It was clear Beth was in pain and given her situation, he deduced the birth had started. The thought of being forced to witness it turned his stomach. He still had vivid nightmares of his mother's screams echoing down the stone castle hallway the night she died.

Guttural cries were now emanating from Beth as she clung to Scarlett. He heard the panic in Scarlett's voice as she exclaimed, "I don't know what to do!"

Beth clung to Scarlett as she led her inside a wooden hut. Alaric tried to block out the cries but they only seemed to get worse. Scarlett reappeared as she collected water and Alaric shouted over. "How's she doing?"

Scarlett's face said it all, she didn't need to reply. She was worried.

"I know a good remedy for pain," he blurted out. He wasn't even sure himself why he had offered to help.

"What is it?" Scarlett demanded. She didn't trust him but she was running out of options.

"Do you have any white willow trees around here?"

Scarlett looked puzzled but replied, "I know a place but it isn't nearby."

Just then, another scream pierced the air. Without thought, Alaric blurted out, "Untie me. I'll stay with her whilst you go."

"I'm not untying you! How foolish do you think I am," Scarlett scoffed at his suggestion.

"Do you want to ease her suffering or not?" Alaric demanded.

Scarlett was torn. "Someone will be back soon. You can tell me what I need to collect and I'll go then."

An hour later, no one had returned. Scarlett was anxious and Beth's screams were heartbreaking. Beth was bright red in the face and panting. She was soaked in sweat and neither of them had a clue as to how long this was going to last.

Scarlett made a snap decision whilst cursing Billy. She exited the hut and marched over to Alaric. "What do I need to get from this willow tree?"

"The bark," Alaric confirmed.

"What do I do with it once I've got it?" She fired back.

"She needs to chew it. It relieves pain."

"How? Are you sure it works?" Scarlett demanded. She had never heard of anyone chewing tree bark for pain relief.

"I've no idea but I've seen it work. The witch uses it."

"The witch?" Scarlett questioned frantically. "I'm not doing witchcraft on her!"

"I thought you didn't believe in it?" Alaric snapped back.

More bloodcurdling screams came from the hut and Scarlett made a split decision to trust Alaric, she had no other choice. She took out her knife and cut the rope around his feet and then cut the rope binding him to the tree. He gestured his wrists forward but she shook her head. "You don't need your hands free to stay with her and keep her calm. Just tell her I'll be back soon and so will Billy. Keep this cloth damp and pat her brow."

He looked like he'd rather be anywhere else but he agreed.

Scarlett ran through the forest as fast as she could. She jumped over fallen trees like they were hurdles, dodging traps the outlaws had laid and animal burrows. When she made it to the tree, she used her dagger to pry off several pieces of bark and then ran back towards camp.

Her mind was racing, how could she be so foolish as to trust Alaric not to run at the first chance? Beth could be all alone and it would be her fault. If something happened to the baby she would never forgive herself. For all she knew the bark did nothing. She was more and more convinced that she had been duped by Alaric.

She could hear Beth's cries getting louder the closer she got and was utterly surprised to find Alaric had been true to his word. He was patting Beth's forehead with a damp cloth and speaking softly to her. Scarlett was unable to hear what he was saying but it seemed to calm Beth.

"I've got the bark," Scarlett panted as she waved it towards Alaric.

He grabbed it from her and broke off a piece.

Carefully, he placed it in Beth's mouth. "Chew this, it will help with the pain."

Beth did as instructed.

"Scarlett I feel like I need to push," Beth professed.

Scarlett and Alaric exchanged terrified glances and Scarlett pushed up Beth's skirts.

"Here," Alaric said as he offered Beth a larger piece of bark, "Bite down on this."

Beth bit down and started to push. Scarlett's face turned from being petrified to one of amazement as she shouted, "I can see a head!"

Just then, they could hear a commotion outside and Billy appeared. He raced toward Beth and grabbed her hand as Alaric made room for him to comfort her. Alaric kept wiping her brow as Beth continued to push. A new-born baby's cry sounded and relief washed over the group. A moment later, Scarlett passed a swaddled baby over to the happy couple.

The whole camp celebrated the new arrival. No one even seemed to question why Alaric wasn't tied up. Scarlett knew it was time to give the couple some space and signalled to Alaric to leave them to bond together. As they walked over to the fireplace, Scarlett remarked, "This doesn't change anything you know."

Alaric nodded, "I know."

Scarlett passed a tankard of ale to Alaric. He accepted and now free from the tree, he was able to lift his bound wrists to his lips and drink.

"Why did you stay?"

He looked at Scarlett for a long time and she wondered whether even he knew. Alaric simply shrugged and looked away.

Scarlett nodded and then downed her mug of ale. "You understand I need to tie you back up."

Alaric stood and then downed his drink, offering it back to Scarlett. She took it from his hands. His gaze shifted to over her shoulder and he lurched forward, barging past her. He knocked her to the ground before sprinting for the tree line.

Scarlett scrambled to her feet and headed after him. He was fast but she was agile. She knew the soft patches of forest floor and where the piles of leaves made the ground slippery.

Her hair whipped behind her as she ran and the tree branches pulled at her clothes. She gained distance on Alaric and she saw her chance as he ducked under a low-hanging branch. Scarlett followed and swung from it to cover more distance. Using the momentum, she booted him in the back with both feet and he fell forward onto the ground.

Pulling her dagger from her belt and holding it at his throat he relented.

Sounds of more footsteps followed and Aimery and Thom appeared. Scarlett climbed off his back but kept the knife to his neck and Alaric managed to stand.

He glared at Scarlett, reverting to his stoic demeanour.

Scarlett nodded to Aimery and Thom and they dragged Alaric back through the forest.

The party of four soon reached the camp and Aimery tied Alaric back onto the tree and bound his feet like before.

Alaric's little escape didn't deter from the evenings celebrations, which carried on into the night. Alaric watched on from his confines and found himself studying the group. He was intrigued at the camaraderie. They acted like they had no cares in the world. Like they had everything, yet they had nothing. He couldn't remember a time his father had ever looked as happy as John Petty did.

When Scarlett headed toward him with a bowl of stew and spoon-fed it into his mouth, he could tell she was merry from the celebrations. He noticed a softness to her happy face he hadn't seen before.

"What name did they decide on?" He asked, feigning disinterest.

"Susanna, it's from the Lord's book, means pure and beautiful."

Alaric simply nodded, not displaying any form of emotion.

Alaric stayed awake long into the night. His mind wandered and he couldn't help but think about the new life he had helped enter the world. Scarlett had asked him why he stayed to help. He could rationalise it was in memory of his mother and the happy summers he spent with them. Or simply justify it was to face his fears surrounding childbirth. The truth was, he didn't really know, it was just the right thing to do.

He had been studying the band of outlaws all evening. He lived a privileged life compared to this group of people yet they seemed happier. His friends were guards that his father paid. He had no one close to him that had his back just because they cared for him. He tried to imagine his future bride, but the thought was soured when he remembered his facial scar. No woman would want to look at his face every day. He doubted whether he would ever experience true love from a wife.

The babes cry filled the silent night and envy took over this thoughts. It reminded him that the Loxley's were his enemies. He couldn't afford to let his guard down again. Next time, he would ensure his revenge.

CHAPTER 9

It was still dark when Alaric heard the crunching of leaves. He opened his eyes and tried to focus past the shadows of the trees to make out where the sound was coming from. He saw a dark silhouette walking towards him and he braced his legs up towards his chest, in case he needed to use the one tactical move he had available to him; his ability to double leg kick.

As the figure approached him he could just make out that it was Robin. He was swaying from the effects of ale and Alaric watched him observantly, to see if he would make it to wherever he was going without falling over his own feet. He heard him hiccup before the sound of a thud as he tripped over and landed in a heap on the ground. Alaric sniggered. He heard a few slurred profanities as Robin rose to his feet and continued walking past him into the thicker bushes. Robin stopped and burped loudly before Alaric heard him relieving himself.

Alaric relaxed his legs and tried to settle back to sleep, when he felt the presence of someone else nearby. His eyes flew open as Scarlett crept past him, almost silently, with a dagger raised in her hand. She looked like she was hunting prey through the camp. The moonlight illuminated her face and he caught a glimpse of her eyes. They seemed glazed over and unfocused. He knew immediately that something wasn't right.

He was enthralled watching her as she headed towards the bushes where Robin stood. She raised her arm back, like she was preparing to strike and Alaric blurted out, "Behind you!"

His warning came just in time.

Robin spun around quickly and blocked Scarlett's attack. Alaric heard grappling sounds as Robin fought Scarlett to the ground. Scarlett didn't make a sound but Robin shouted, "She's gone mad!"

The disturbance drew Billy and Beth into the night air. Billy rushed to intervene, unsure of what was happening and who he should be helping. Billy managed to take possession of the dagger and Robin was shouting Scarlett's name repeatedly as she fought against him.

Suddenly, Scarlett stopped fighting and blinked away the glazed expression. Her eyes returned to normal and her face turned to bewilderment as she yelled, "What are you doing?"

Robin looked utterly shocked as he responded, "What am I doing? What were you doing?" The whole exchange seemed to have sobered him up rapidly. He slowly let go of his hold on her and rose to his feet. Scarlett pushed herself further away from him and looked up at him from the ground. They remained cautious of one another as Scarlett slowly stood.

Alaric was watching the whole exchange with fascination.

Scarlett looked to Billy for answers, but he looked as bewildered as she felt. "I just saw you both grappling on the ground. I don't know who started what," he confessed.

With pure indignation, Robin remarked, "You came at me from behind with that dagger," pointing at the weapon in Billy's hand. Continuing, he professed, "If Alaric hadn't warned me. I might not be alive right now."

Scarlett was shocked, but it was clear from her expression that she believed him. She stuttered out an apology and rubbed her face with both hands as Beth came closer. Baby Susanna was now closely swaddled to her chest.

Beth scoured Scarlett's face for clues. "This isn't the first time she's been sleepwalking. I caught her eating fools' funnel in the dead of night. She had no recollection of how she got there, or why she was doing it then either."

"Fools' funnel; that's poisonous. Is that why you kept

throwing up?" Robin asked, alarmed.

Scarlett nodded. "I don't know what's wrong with me. This seems more serious than just sleepwalking."

"No shit!" Billy exclaimed. "I've never heard of anyone poisoning themselves, or killing someone when sleepwalking. It's like you've been cursed."

Alaric had listened to the exchange with intrigue. The last words the witch spoke to him replayed in his mind. *'Before the next full moon, you will have your vengeance.'*

The witch had promised him revenge; Scarlett had been cursed. It was the only answer that explained her bizarre, nocturnal behaviour. Without much forethought, he revealed, "You've been bewitched."

All four heads swivelled in his direction, their expressions a mixture of confusion and disbelief. "I don't believe in witchcraft," Scarlett declared bluntly.

"Oh yeah," Alaric said smugly, "Yet on my word, you untied me and left me alone with Beth, whilst you went in search of a magical, pain-relieving tree bark."

"Herbs and plants have natural healing qualities. Knowledge and old wives' tales are not magic," Scarlett adamantly professed.

"Why are you so certain she's been bewitched?" Billy asked inquisitively.

Alaric swallowed hard. He was hoping that question wasn't going to come up. He thought about lying, but then didn't fancy being on the receiving end of one of Scarlett's murderous sleepwalking escapades tomorrow night. They needed to take him seriously and put precautions in place. He figured the blame was written all over his face as Scarlett pushed him for an answer.

"Well?!" She said sternly.

"Because my father's witch offered me revenge for my scar and I took it."

In a split second, Scarlett had yanked the dagger from Billy's hand and straddled Alaric's legs. Her free hand grabbed hold of his jaw and was holding him tight, whilst her other hand had the dagger pointed firmly at his jugular.

"So, rather than fight fair, you enlisted an old woman to do your dirty work. Did I wound you that severely you can no longer fight a woman, or was it just your vanity that couldn't handle looking at your own reflection?"

He laughed, remembering her dirty tactics when he fought Robin. She clearly didn't believe what she preached. "Do it!" He goaded, "You lecture me about fighting fairly, yet I'm tied to a tree. Untie me and give me a weapon. Let's see who would win in a fair fight."

The pair glared at each other with such intensity that the hate was palpable.

Alaric had hoped that she might actually be enraged enough to untie him until Beth spoke out, breaking the tension. "If you've been cursed, we should go to see a witch about breaking it. I've heard rumours in the villages. I know where we should go."

All eyes diverted to seemingly naïve Beth. Billy looked shocked and Robin was concerned.

"Beth, what rumours?" Scarlett asked in disbelief. Beth didn't like being the centre of attention and she looked at the ground when she replied. "I was worried about the pain of childbirth and when Billy let me go with him on supply runs, I asked some local women about pain relief."

"And..." Scarlett prompted when Beth wasn't forthcoming.

"There are rumours of a travelling party of oddities in Ledecestre. They have a powerful witch amongst them, but I knew it was too far to go alone, and I didn't want to worry Billy by telling him why I wanted to go. So, I didn't mention it." Beth looked up at Billy, her eyes pleading for forgiveness because she had not shared her worries. Billy said nothing but he took a step closer to her and kissed her forehead. They exchanged a silent apology to each other, Billy for the guilt of not realising how scared she was and Beth for keeping secrets.

"Well, no time like the present. If we leave now, we can be there before nightfall," Scarlett announced.

Her siblings stared at her in shock. "You're entertaining this?" Robin asked, looking puzzled.

"Do you have a better idea?" Scarlett retorted, "Or would you prefer I murder you in your sleep tonight?"

Robin gulped before pointing to Alaric. "Well, what about him?"

"I'm more than happy to fuck off. Just point me in the right direction and I'll be out of your hair," Alaric said facetiously.

Scarlett whipped her head around with a disdainful glower. "Robin, you stay here, I'll go with Billy."

"Can we come too?" Beth asked mirthfully, just as Susanna made herself known.

With compassion in her eyes, Scarlett turned to Beth. She didn't have the heart to say no when Beth looked so happy. So, instead, she nodded. Beth's eyes lit up and she hurried back to her hut to gather provisions. Billy followed her and Robin yawned as he walked away, leaving Scarlett and Alaric alone.

Alaric jerked his legs up and alerted Scarlett to their proximity. Her blade had very nearly pierced his skin. She resumed her scowling as he rolled his tongue and bit his bottom lip. Suddenly, she was very aware of her position, straddled over his legs and her thighs burned. A tingling sensation at her core made her hesitate. Noticing her delayed reaction, Alaric smirked, "You appear to be getting comfortable on top of me. If you intend on staying, you could at least make it interesting."

Scarlett pulled a disgusted expression and a dark smile appeared on Alaric's face as she scrambled to her feet. Scarlett couldn't think of anything clever to say back. Eager to hide her flushed cheeks, she turned and fled.

The party of four made it to a settlement on the outskirts of Ledecestre before nightfall. Scarlett deduced the best place to ask questions would be the local tavern and they would need a room to stay in anyway. Scarlett took up the mantle and asked around for information. She approached a female barmaid first, who sheepishly confirmed she didn't get involved with anything like that and scurried away.

The next wench she asked turned white as a sheet and fled before saying a word. Scarlett was starting to feel foolish, like this quest had been a stupid idea. She returned to Billy and Beth who had secured seats and ordered three pints of ale from a passing barmaid. Susanna was getting fussy and Beth tried to soothe her. "I think she's hungry. Do you think we can get a room here for the night so I can go and feed her in private?"

Scarlett caught the eye of another server as she passed and she enquired about a room. She said she would check with the proprietor and come back. When she returned moments later with drinks, she confirmed that there was a room available. She offered to show Beth and Billy to it. Scarlett assured Billy she would be fine on her own and she remained at the table.

A group of men, merry from ale, were on the table next to her. When they noticed she was drinking alone, they hollered over for her to join them. She noticed that they had a jug of ale on the table, along with a leg of ham and a loaf of bread. She downed her tankard of ale and decided to join them. She was hungry from the long walk and they had only brought provisions for one small meal each. She saddled up next to the man closest to the food and joined in the conversation. She helped herself and the men in their merry state didn't seem to mind.

She hadn't had any luck with asking the barmaids about the travelling party of oddities, so she thought it was worth a try asking this group of men. She slipped it into the conversation with ease, trying to sound nonchalant.

"I've heard a rumour there's a travelling party around here, one with odd fellows. Have you seen them?"

"Aye," came a chorus of responses as one man topped up everyone's drink.

Scarlett tried to keep her face from looking too enthusiastic as she probed for more answers. "Where would I find them?" She asked, following up quickly with, "I like a good laugh."

The man to the right of her replied, "You're guaranteed that luv." He took another swig of ale as he pointed west. "Next village along. That's where they were this morning. Very odd folks. Poor bastards."

Scarlett didn't know what to expect. Her father thought public humiliation was cruel and never even allowed jesters on his estate. Her curiosity overrode any fear she had and she excused herself from the group to meet up with Billy and Beth.

Susanna was settled and sleeping peacefully against Beth's chest. Everyone agreed that they would walk to the next town in search of the witch and come back to the tavern to sleep. Scarlett followed the men's directions and they came across the village in no time at all. There was a buzz about the area and it didn't take long for them to find out why.

In the centre of the village, where you would expect to find the water well and sellers, they found a large number villagers. They were watching in anticipation as several displays were being performed.

Scarlett observed an extremely tall and beautiful woman with long dark hair, lift a man over her head. She proceeded to squat low to the ground whilst still holding him, before straightening back up to full height. Her face was red and sweat was pouring from her brow, but Scarlett was astounded at the feat she had just witnessed. Applause erupted from the group watching and another man offered himself up to be lifted.

Scarlett signalled to Billy and Beth to move on and the group approached the next crowd of people. A slender woman in the tightest of clothes was performing the most extraordinary contortions with her body. The crowd stood mesmerised as the performer stood on one leg and lifted her other leg up to her ear without bending it. After a round of applause, the performer placed her hands on the ground and swung her legs into the air;

she was perfectly straight, just the wrong way around. Slowly, she changed position so that her forearms were in contact with the ground. The performer's toes touched her forehead as her body bent over itself. Scarlett had never dreamed such moves were possible. Scarlett started to feel queasy, imagining herself trying to contort that way and tapped Billy on the arm to follow her.

She followed the sound of a flute being played and came across a smaller group watching a man sitting cross-legged on the floor playing a melodic tune. Next to him, a dancing snake was emerging from a crate. The creature swayed to the music as if slithering in thin air.

Scarlett had never liked snakes. She stepped back from the gathering and surveyed the area. She whispered in Billy's ear that she was going to look around and marched off in search of the witch.

Four or five people appeared to be queuing to enter a wagon. Scarlett made a beeline for it and joined the line. She tapped the woman on the shoulder in front of her.

"Excuse me, what's this queue for?" She asked politely. A young girl with a swollen belly turned around and gave a half smile. Anxiousness was written all over her face.

"They say she knows things; all you have to do is touch her hand and look into a magical ball. It's not evil."

A portly man exited the wagon and the next patron went inside. The queue moved forward one and Scarlett waited in line until her turn.

One by one, the patrons entered. Eventually, she was next. The door opened and the young girl descended the stairs with the help of the man guarding the door. The worry had left her face and her smile shone from ear to ear.

The doorman held his hand out towards Scarlett and grunted, "Contribution."

Scarlett pulled out a coin from her bosom and handed it over. The doorman closed his palm and entered the wagon. He returned moments later and held the door open for her to go inside.

It was cosy and smelt strongly of herbs. Fabric hung over the windows, blocking out all moonlight. Candles on the table were the only source of light and they cast a golden glow. A young woman with tanned skin sat behind the table. Her dark, curly hair, half up and half down. An unusual green feather that looked like an eye was sticking out her hair.

On the table was a globe that swirled with colours. The woman was wearing a shawl the colour of lavender and it was made out of a fabric that Scarlett hadn't seen before. It looked expensive. The bangles on the witch's wrist jangled as she moved and a shiny, black stone was hung around her neck. She beckoned for Scarlett to take a seat opposite her.

As Scarlett took the offered seat, she was spellbound by her bright green eyes. She had never seen anyone with eyes that shade, so bright and unblemished.

Up close, she could see that the woman's hands were wrinkled and aged, in stark contrast to her youthful face. Scarlett assumed that her aged hands were a more accurate indicator of her age. When she spoke, Scarlett was surprised to hear an unfamiliar, heavy accent. She had to pay extra attention to decipher the words she spoke.

"Why do you seek me out child?"

"Are you a witch?" Scarlett asked bluntly.

"My talents have many names," replied the mysterious woman.

Scarlett wondered if she would get any straight answers, or if the whole notion of a curse was just a clever ruse orchestrated by Alaric. She questioned whether the woman truly was a witch, or just a good con artist who spoke in riddles. It was probably the latter, but she was disturbed enough about her nocturnal activities to hear the woman out.

Not wanting to make it too easy for a con artist to read the answers she sought, Scarlett made a broad request. "I want to know my future."

"A popular choice, but I can only see the fate that has been decided already."

The witch moved the globe to the side of the table and started to shuffle a worn deck of cards that appeared on the table out of nowhere. Scarlett frowned and then deduced they must have come from under the globe, there was no other explanation. She wasn't about to be suckered in by a sleight of hand magic trick.

The witch fanned the deck of cards on the table in a horizontal line. "Pick three that call to you," the witch instructed.

Scarlett pulled a face. None of the cards were speaking to her. She selected three at random, pulling them out of the line, but not turning them over. The witch collected up the rest of the cards and moved them to one side. Then she flipped over the first card.

Scarlett was presented with an oddly dressed man displayed on the card, with the name magician written on the bottom.

Scarlett scoffed daring the witch to fabricate some falsity. The witch eyed her dubiously through hooded eyelids. "If you do not believe in my ability, I wonder why you took the time to seek me out."

Scarlett had to give it to her, she was calling her out for her blatant scepticism. "Call it due diligence on my part," Scarlett replied.

The corner of the witch's mouth raised in an amused half smile and she continued with the reading. "The upside-down magician signifies you have been touched, or have cast dark magic. Given your attitude towards magic, I would assume the former."

The witch flipped the second card over and even without the writing being visible for her to read, Scarlett could understand that card was the symbol of death. She shuffled nervously on her seat. The witch caught her eye as she said, "The card of death, signifying ends but also new beginnings."

Scarlett didn't speak, she just watched as the witch flipped over the final card. The image depicted a moon but once again it was upside down.

"An upside down moon is the sign of darkness and fear." The witch assessed her reaction before holding out her hand. "Let me see your hand, palm side up."

Scarlett held her hand out towards the witch. She took it and flipped it over. Her fingertips tickled Scarlett's skin as she traced lines etched into her palm.

Suddenly, she reached over the table and startled Scarlett as she grabbed her face. Her eyes bored into Scarlett's until she let go and removed a small dagger from her boot. Scarlett leapt up, away from the table and drew her own blade. The witch raised her hands in a non-threatening way as she exclaimed, "I merely need a drop of blood. You can prick your own finger if you would prefer."

Scarlett nodded but remained upright. She pricked her middle finger with the point of her blade and a bead of blood appeared on the surface. Scarlett held her dagger up as she offered her finger to the witch.

"Please sit down," she said as she gestured to the stool.

Scarlett took a seat but kept her dagger drawn. The witch took hold of her hand and then lifted it to her lips. She sucked the blood from Scarlett's finger as Scarlett grimaced, repulsed by the action.

For a moment, the witch kept her eyes closed. Then suddenly, they flew open. "You've been cursed child."

The hairs on the back of Scarlett's arms stood to attention. She couldn't explain how this woman would know her greatest fear. The shock must have been evident on her face as the witch asked, "Did you not know?"

"How can I break it?" Scarlett demanded fervently.

"This is a blood curse, it's not broken easily. A powerful witch cast this."

"Name your price."

The witch moved her hands over the globe in front of her. Staring into it, she replied, "There is nothing I can do to break this curse. The only way to break the curse is to die."

Scarlett's sarcastic nature kicked in as she responded, "Is that all you can suggest?"

The witch side-eyed Scarlett before resuming her focus on the globe. "I didn't say you had to die for long. Just a moment. A moment is all it will take for the curse to break." Returning her full attention to Scarlett, she asked, "Can you swim?"

"Yes," Scarlett responded truthfully and a little perturbed.

"Shame," was her curt response.

Scarlett didn't care for the turn the conversation had taken and pushed the witch for more answers. "So what future do you see for me?"

"I told you your future. Just because it's not what you want to hear doesn't make it not true."

Scarlett frowned, puzzled as she reflected on the conversation.

"Look into the sphere. What do you see?"

Scarlett felt foolish staring into the globe. She saw nothing but mist and if the witch hadn't shocked her by confirming her fear about being cursed, she would have walked out telling everyone what a load of rubbish the experience had been. "Nothing, I see nothing," she said with attitude.

Smugly, the witch replied, "Precisely. You have no future. Your future is death. Whether that be by your own hand or the curse. Death is your only future. Heed my warning, child. These types of curses are usually linked to the lunar cycles. I would say you have until the next full moon." She paused for dramatic effect and then stated, "Your time is up."

The witch gestured to the door and knocked on the wall with her fist. The door was opened by the doorman, but before Scarlett climbed down the steps, the witch had one final piece of counsel. "What is remembered lives on."

Scarlett walked down the stairs, baffled by the parting statement. She was still in disbelief about having no future and the only way to break the curse was to die. She decided not to share any of this information with Beth and Billy.

Night had fallen in the time she had been inside the wagon. Scarlett looked around for her companions so that they could return to the tavern. She spotted the couple over by a group and headed for them. As she approached, she saw how happy they were in each other's company. Both were laughing and smiling. Billy had his arm around Beth's shoulder and when he thought no one was watching, he gave her a kiss on the temple. Such a sweet gesture made out of love, not lust.

Scarlett had witnessed plenty of men succumb to lust, especially after alcohol. Love just seemed something completely different. Her mother and father had it. John Petty and his wife had it. Billy and Beth had found it with each other. For a brief moment, Scarlett wondered if she would ever know what it felt like. Then the witch's words sank in and she shrugged off her melancholy. If the witch was to be believed, she would be dead before the next full moon, so what did it matter?

Scarlett placed her hand on Billy's shoulder and signalled it was time to leave. The group headed back to the tavern and en route Beth quizzed her about her conversation with the witch. Not wanting to share the witch's predictions about her future, Scarlett shut down the questioning, insisting she was just a charlatan and it had been a wasted journey.

Not willing to take any chances when they made it back to their room at the tavern, Scarlett forced Billy to bind her wrists and ankles. It was uncomfortable, but after the long walk she was tired enough to sleep through the awkward position. However, that night her dreams were plagued by her conversation with the witch. Each time she asked about her future, she got the same response. She didn't have one.

CHAPTER 10

The group had set off at first light and after a long day of travelling, they finally arrived back at camp just as the sun was setting. Everyone was happy to see them return, none more so than John, who fussed over his granddaughter.

Scarlett had marched ahead on the last leg of their journey, not wanting to miss the opportunity to hunt. She had successfully shot four pheasants and as she walked into camp, she untied them from her belt. Beth made quick work of preparing them for dinner.

Scarlett had felt uneasy about leaving Alaric, when she knew how manipulating he could be, so she immediately checked that he was still tied to the tree. She smiled smugly when she saw the disdain on his face. Robin approached her and she pointed to Alaric, asking, "Has he caused you any trouble?"

Robin held his head in his hands and looked exasperated. "This is the first time he's shut up. He won't stop singing offensive drinking chants. He's driving me insane." Scarlett had to stifle a giggle when she saw the torment on her brother's face. "Well, he seems quiet now."

"You won't be saying that soon when he starts again. We need a plan to trade him and get him the fuck away from me."

Robin looked and sounded the most agitated Scarlett had ever seen him. Clearly, incessant noise was his Achilles heel.

"Don't worry brother, tomorrow we start the revolution."

Scarlett heard a loud scoff from Alaric's direction. "So, do you only stop singing to eavesdrop?"

Alaric ignored her question and instead spat, "Do you really think with an army of twelve ragtag misfits you can revolt against my father and win?"

Scarlett marched towards him with fury in her eyes. She bent close enough to be at eye level and stared into his eyes. Alaric stared back, unafraid. "You think it will be just twelve of us fighting?" Scarlett saw a flash of curiosity shift across his eyes and it was her time to scoff. "Tomorrow you're coming with us, to see for yourself." A smug smile broke out across her face and she laughed when Alaric had no witty comeback.

After dinner, Alaric started singing again. He was wildly out of tune and being incredibly obnoxious with the use of foul language. When he sang the line, *'Even monks who have nowhere to spunk'*, Scarlett had had enough. She searched around for some rope or fabric and found the horse's reins that they were planning to trade. She marched across the camp towards Alaric as he started the second verse.

At first, Alaric thought that she was going to whip him. He had been no stranger to whipping as a boy, but she pulled it taught in her hands and at the last moment, he realised what she intended to do. He clamped his jaw shut and stopped singing. Scarlett tried to force the leather into his mouth, but Alaric's jaw was like a vice and wouldn't open. She wrestled with him for long enough, to realise that she wasn't going to get him to open up without forcing him to. Not one to back down, Scarlett decided to offer him a choice.

"Open your mouth, or I cut your balls off." Scarlett took out her dagger and pointed it at Alaric's crown jewels.

Alaric's mouth fell open to protest. Clearly, he didn't believe the crime warranted the punishment. His eyes gave away how twisted he believed Scarlett to be. "You're obsessed with my manhood," he spat out. She seized her opportunity and rammed the leather into his mouth. She tied it around the back of his head and smirked in triumph.

"Of course I am; don't you remember how much I love a game of hide and seek!" She threw her head back and laughed.

Alaric's eyes darkened. He didn't make any further noise.

Scarlett marched back to the centre of camp towards Robin. He had been watching the exchange and as she approached, he rhetorically asked, "Why didn't I think of that?"

Scarlett shrugged and collected a tankard of ale to ease the pressures of the day away.

That night, Scarlett went to bed early and she asked Billy to tie her hands and feet together again. She didn't want the rest of the men to see her as weak or a liability, but she didn't trust herself. Discretely, Billy did as she asked and no one in the camp was any the wiser.

The next morning, camp was in full swing. The men that escorted Alaric's soldiers to the outskirts of the forest had returned. Alaric watched on from the sidelines as everything was prepared for their departure. Horses had been hitched to the front of the wagon, laden with the money Alaric had been transporting. Only when Beth and the baby were seated on the front of the wagon beside Billy, did anyone seem to remember Alaric.

Scarlett appeared out of nowhere and unravelled the rope that anchored Alaric to the tree. "Don't worry, little one. No one's leaving you on your lonesome."

Scarlett had wound the rope around her elbow and dragged him to standing by his forearm. Warning him like a child, in a mocking voice she offered an ultimatum, "Now I'll remove this rein from your mouth if you're going to be a good boy." She stared at him, waiting for recognition and he nodded curtly. Scarlett removed the leather rein and Alaric immediately stretched out his mouth and jaw.

Scarlet tied the rope to his wrist restraints and checked to make sure the knots would hold before attaching him to the back of the wagon. Alaric heard the horses neigh and start to trot, pulling the heavy load. Then everything went dark. A sack had been placed over his head again, blocking his vision.

Finding his voice, even though his throat was sore, Alaric complained, "Is this really necessary? One tree looks the same as any other."

He felt a foot hit him in the arse and it nudged him forward. Scarlett laughed. "Oh, it's necessary." Her comment was met with several laughs from the bunch of merry men surrounding them.

Alaric scowled, he would get out of this and when he did, he planned on humiliating and gutting every single one of them. After several near-misses and only one face-plant to the ground, the sack was removed from Alaric's head. He blinked profusely, trying to adjust to the bright light.

They were no longer in the forest. In fact, the settlement looked oddly familiar. He took in the houses and the stalls in front of him. He recognised this village. He had been here recently in fact. The smell of freshly baked bread flooded his senses. His belly growled hungrily and his mouth watered. He kept quiet but watched as the men were handing out purses of coins. In exchange, the wagon was loaded up with bread, eggs, and cheese.

Alaric watched the exchanges closely. The traders were gushing in thanks to the men. It was very odd to witness. He scanned the crowd, looking for Scarlett. She was close, just a few yards behind him. He turned to watch her. Scarlett handed a leather purse bursting with coins to the elderly lady, but she didn't receive anything in exchange. Alaric continued to watch the interaction, zoning out the rest of the noise and trying to listen to the conversation.

The elderly lady had pocketed the pouch and clasped her hands over Scarlett's. "God bless you dear, I'm sorry I don't have anything to thank you for your kindness."

"Don't worry about it. You take care of yourself," Scarlett replied.

As if sensing his eyes on her, Scarlett suddenly looked his way. Their eyes met. Alaric didn't shy away, it's not like he was doing anything wrong in studying his enemy. You need to know your enemy to defeat them.

Scarlett smirked smugly and it caught Alaric off guard. He didn't know what she had to be smug about. In fact, she appeared to be making some very bad financial decisions. Alaric had never heard of people giving money away. Only ever in church had he seen people giving away money for nothing and they were always coerced by the threat of eternal damnation.

Scarlett marched towards the wagon. Alaric watched as she stood on a wheel arch to clamber on top and stand on the roof. People in the area started to stare at her and she gestured for people to come closer. She shouted, "Everyone, shhhh." She used the universal symbol for people to fall silent and the gathering grew quiet.

"Good people of Nottingham, the Sheriff says we owe him taxes." The crowd booed loudly and Scarlett revelled in the chants. She gestured for the noise to die down again and continued. 'Well, I say the Sheriff can stick his taxation where the sun doesn't shine!" The people listening roared with laughter and Alaric heard several people holler, "Too right!"

Scarlett continued when the crowd died down. "This money was unlawfully taken from the citizens of Nottingham and I'm here to tell you. Whatever he takes, we will give back to you. The Sheriff's tyranny is coming to an end. Will you stand with us?" A deafening roar of support came back in response. Alaric was alarmed at the fervour of the crowd. Whether she had won them over with her words, or her bribery, one thing was evident, Scarlett was a charismatic leader. Even Alaric had been blown away by her passion. If she fanned these flames of discord and this mentality spread, his father might have a genuine issue with keeping the peace.

Alaric continued to watch Scarlett as a young man from the camp aided her in disembarking the wagon. The boy's face flushed as Scarlett's body came into contact with his. Alaric couldn't explain why, but he ground his back teeth. He had a newfound disdain for that bandit. Scarlett didn't seem to notice the exchange and instead she marched in his direction. Alaric's smugness at her disregard of the boy must have shown on his face, as Scarlett remarked, "Did you like what you heard?"

Alaric hocked up some phlegm and spat it on the ground an inch from Scarlett's boot. He didn't break eye contact with her and the disgust on her face pleased him. As she turned to leave, Alaric retorted, "What I saw was a fast way to get poor. What happens when you run out of money to buy their support?" This time it was Scarlett's turn to grind her teeth and stiffen her jaw. She walked away and Alaric did his best to watch her until he lost her in the crowd.

They visited three more small settlements and repeated the exercise. Each time, the crowd roared with support against the Sheriff. Thankfully, no one seemed to recognise him. The wagon was empty of gold, but now full of supplies given in gratitude. Alaric only realised they were heading back to camp, when his vision was blacked out by a sack being placed over his head.

After an hour of walking blind, Alaric had an idea. It would cost him a few unnecessary bruises, but the reward was worth the price. He staggered forward and faked misplacing his step. He landed on his knees and let out a staged cry of pain. He felt a large hand grab at his arm and yank him to his feet, followed by a gruff voice saying, "Keep moving."

Alaric put on an exaggerated limp and after a few stops, he did it again. After the third incident of throwing himself on the ground and wailing in pain, he heard Scarlett's voice approaching. "What's the matter?"

"He just keeps tripping over. It's because he can't see a thing with that sack over his head," the outlaw walking nearby replied.

Alaric could smell her as she stepped closer. She smelt nicer than any of the males around him. He couldn't place the smell but he recognised it. He was suddenly blinded by the instant light as Scarlett removed the sack from his head.

"We're close enough now. He can walk the rest of the way without it." Addressing the man rather than Alaric, Scarlett mocked, "I can't stand his whining. He sounds like a little girl." Alaric gave her a filthy look as the men close to him roared with laughter and Scarlett smirked.

A movement in the bushes over her shoulder caught his attention. Scarlett noticed his eyes shift and she spun around. Quietly, she asked, "What is it? What did you see?"

"I don't know. Something large moved," replied Alaric. If it was an ambush coming to save him, he didn't want to give the game away, however, it was more than likely a large beast and he didn't fancy being sacrificed.

Scarlett drew her bow from her quiver and nocked an arrow. All eyes were on her and she must have given a signal that Alaric missed, as the men all drew weapons but remained in situ. Then, she stalked into the undergrowth in the direction of the movement.

The entire group remained silent and poised for an attack. Seconds stretched into minutes and the minutes felt like hours. Alaric couldn't explain why but he stared at the spot where he had seen the movement, barely able to tear his eyes away.

Out of nowhere, a loud bird song sounded. Billy instructed two men to follow the way Scarlett had. Alaric recalled the evening his party had been attacked and hearing the owl noises. Bird calls were clearly a clever party trick to these bandits. It was a clever trick indeed, but he was pleased they hadn't hoodwinked him. He had been on to it before Robin used the opportunity to cross him. He mused that it was too clever a ruse for Billy. It must have been Scarlett's idea.

Sometime later, heavy footsteps and tree movement alerted the group to people approaching. Billy shouted into the forest, "Who goes there?"

With laughter evident in her tone, Scarlett shouted back, "Your big sister with a gift."

The sounds of them approaching grew louder as Billy mumbled, "By five minutes." Alaric sniggered, that had been an ongoing argument throughout their childhood.

Out of the bushes, Scarlett appeared with the biggest

smile. Alaric studied her face. He couldn't remember a time when he had seen anyone so full of joy. Even when the baby had been born, the anxiety and panic were still palpable in the air and it marred the joy, turning it into relief. This was pure, unadulterated happiness and it was breathtaking.

Movement behind her distracted Alaric's attention and the two men that followed after her came into view carrying a large, thick branch of a tree with a full-grown stag swinging from it. Alaric couldn't help but lick his lips, venison was his favourite. The rest of the group hollered and cheered in celebration.

Clasping her hand on Billy's shoulder, Scarlett rejoiced, "Tonight, brothers, we eat like Kings." The group cheered again and they continued on their journey.

Scarlett hung back and walked close to Alaric. Every now and again she glanced in his direction. Each time her eyes were met with his. Her agitation grew and she declared, "You're staring at me, why?"

Alaric shrugged his shoulders, but Scarlett swore she saw the side of his mouth smirk upwards. "And you were smelling me earlier. I saw your nostrils flare. Why?" She demanded, growing more perturbed.

Alaric shrugged his shoulders again and this time Scarlett definitely didn't imagine his smirk. Scarlett turned away from him and discreetly tried to smell her armpits. She had to admit personal hygiene had not been on her priority list. She did like to enjoy a weekly bath in the lake and if she was honest with herself, that had fallen by the wayside recently. She may not be a Lady anymore, but she was still female.

The wagon caught on an uprooted tree root and Scarlett paused for a moment, long enough to realise where she was. They were close to the lake. It would be hours before the venison was cooked and she justified that she deserved some time alone to bathe. Turning to Thom, who was closest, she instructed, "Carry on without me. I've got an errand to run. Watch him. I'm leaving him in your charge." Thom nodded, clearly pleased she trusted him with the task.

Alaric studied Scarlett as she disappeared into the forest. Despite her bullish behaviour and fiery temper, she was stealthy and graceful as she merged with the undergrowth.

Alaric surveyed the rest of the group. Billy was cooing over the baby with Beth. The men carrying the stag had taken the lead and marched ahead. The guard who had hung back on Scarlett's orders to watch him was Thom. The young, dopey fool who clearly had eyes for Scarlett. Not that she was interested; that was quite evident by her lack of physical contact.

Alaric decided that now was the time to seize his opportunity to escape. He whistled over to Thom to get his attention. "Hey, you," he addressed him as he caught Thom's attention. "You need to untie me, I need to go."

Thom looked puzzled as he replied, "Go where?"

"You know, to relieve myself."

"I'm not stupid you know, you don't have to be untied to take a piss."

Alaric's hope that Thom was as gullible as he looked was fading, but he thought of his reply quickly.

"I don't need a piss, I need a shit. Scarlett has been letting me go for them in private. A man needs to do his business, you know how it is." Alaric was trying to appeal to Thom's compassionate nature.

The puzzled look on Thom's face deepened and he tried to recall if he had seen Scarlett allowing that. Alaric pressed him to make a decision by pulling agitated facial expressions and Thom rationalised that as long as he watched him, he wouldn't be able to escape.

"Ok, but I'm coming with you," Thom confirmed.

Thom untied Alaric's left hand first as Alaric teased, "Oh you're one of those, are you?"

He didn't manage to distract Thom, as he tied his loose right hand behind his back before un-attaching him from the wagon.

Alaric ground his teeth in annoyance. That had not gone

to plan. He had clearly underestimated Thom's naivety. Alaric tested the knot for tightness but unfortunately, the knot was strong.

"Move," ordered the young lad and Alaric scowled at being ordered around by someone younger than him. Nevertheless, he would think of a way to overpower him. He marched forward, keen to put distance between the rest of the travelling party. He spotted a large tree in the distance and headed for it.

"Just here will do, if you can just pull my breeches down I can take care of the rest."

Thom groaned but moved closer. "Well you could just untie me and I could do it myself. It's your choice," Alaric offered.

Thom pulled an unflattering expression and came closer still. Alaric seized his opportunity and head-butted him. Thom stumbled backwards before collapsing on the floor.

Alaric took several long blinks. His vision was blurred after the force of the skull clash. He heard a rustling in the bushes and he paused. Out of nowhere a wild boar came barrelling out of the bushes towards him, tusks first. Eyes wild. Alaric pivoted and ran blindly forward. He navigated through thick tree roots on the forest floor and headed for thicker undergrowth. As he ran through a dense patch he was too late to realise that the bushes were hiding a steep slope. He skidded down the loose dirt and landed in a heap at the bottom feet away from a lake.

Alaric spat the dirt out from his mouth and tried to put weight on his ankle, but it felt badly sprained. He couldn't get much leverage and only managed to pull himself into a seated position at the water's edge. He was lucky, if he had rolled much further he would have fallen in and he couldn't see from here how deep it was. Without the use of his hands he could have drowned. He cast his attention to the lake and saw movement on the water. He sat up straighter and then he saw her gliding through the water.

CHAPTER 11

Alaric stared unashamedly as Scarlett gracefully swam towards him. With each stroke, the water parted and brought her further into view. Her bare shoulders were visible above the surface of the water. Her skin was so pale that it almost shimmered in the sunlight. The swell of her breasts were a tantalising tease at what was concealed beneath the water. Alaric couldn't bring himself to look away as his thoughts spiralled.

She swam closer still and ducked her head under the water, when she re-emerged her auburn hair was sleeked back away from her face. The wetness created the illusion that she was a mysterious brunette mermaid that lived in the water.

Alaric barely registered that Thom was now standing next to him. Thom yanked him up into a standing position by his arm. The movement broke his gaze and he growled at Thom. He balanced the majority of his weight on his good ankle and caught sight of Thom's gaping expression as he spotted Scarlett. His intuition had been right. The boy had a thing for her.

Alaric returned his attention to the lake, just in time to see Scarlett pull herself out of the water onto rocks, that were hidden just beneath the surface. He couldn't look away as her naked body came into view. Her movement was fluid and precise. She effortlessly rose to standing. The sunken rocks gave the impression she was standing on the water in the middle of the lake.

Alaric had been with his fair share of whores, but he

had never seen anything let alone a woman look so majestic. Her breasts were in perfect proportion to her hips. Her slim waist providing the perfect hourglass figure. His mind had him imagining his hands on her hips, touching her skin, that he imagined was softer than any fabric he had ever felt. Her legs were slender and she appeared taller than he knew she was. He knew his bodily urges were betraying him as his cock grew stiff.

She was a vision. Utterly breathtaking.

Scarlett was startled when she realised that she wasn't alone. Seeing the two of them had her furious at Thom's stupidity. She had left clear instructions. Anger flooded her, she couldn't believe that he had allowed Alaric to hoodwink him into being untied from the wagon. It felt like she had to do everything herself.

She climbed out of the lake onto the hidden stones and squeezed the water from her hair. Both of them were gawking at her in silence. Thom looked like he had lost the ability to speak, or blink. Alaric looked dangerous. He had a glint in his eye and his mouth was curved into a smirk. He looked unrecognisable from the memory she had of the spoilt brat that stayed every summer. She had done him a favour by giving him that scar, he looked more interesting now, more mysterious and rugged.

She walked towards them, and neither of them reacted. A cold wind blew across her bare skin and her nipples peaked, reminding her that she was naked. So what? She thought to herself. They must have seen a naked woman before. It couldn't be that easy to subdue a man, or women would rule the world.

Neither man moved out of the way as she approached, so she was unable to jump from the stones onto the grass verge. She placed her hand on her hips and gave them an incredulous look. With vexation, she asked, "Have you never seen a naked woman before?"

Thom gulped and his skin started to flush crimson. He stuttered out nonsense whilst Scarlett was drawn to Alaric as he replied, "Just enjoying the view." He licked the corner of his mouth and over his top lip seductively all whilst maintaining eye contact. Now it was Scarlett who couldn't tear her gaze away from his moist lips. Suddenly she was acutely aware she was naked and aroused.

Alaric adjusted his stance and the movement had Scarlett dropping her gaze. The bulge in his breeches was blatantly obvious. Scarlett's mind was racing. She was disgusted by her own lustful thoughts, he was her sworn enemy and she should detest everything about him. Rationalising that it was a physical reaction, nothing more, she turned her thoughts back to the anger she had felt when she first spotted them.

"Shame I can't say the same," she retorted back, before snapping at Thom. "What were you thinking when you untied him?" Her question was rhetorical so she didn't pause for an answer, "Stay here while I grab my clothes. We're heading back to camp."

Gracefully, she crossed the stepping stones to her clothes. She dressed quickly and then rejoined them on the bank. Alaric couldn't put his full weight on his ankle, so Thom had to act as support so he could make it back to camp. Thom had found his voice again and apologised numerous times. Scarlett didn't respond and just shook her head. Alaric faced Thom as he mocked, "I'd quit whilst you're ahead. You sound like a pathetic puppy."

Scarlett rolled her eyes but didn't disagree.

After they reached camp, Scarlett ordered Robin to tie Alaric back up. Her trust in Thom was spent for the day. Alaric closed his eyes and allowed the scene at the lake to replay in his mind. The vision of her standing brazenly nude was delicious. At the mere memory, his cock joined in the fantasy and stiffened. He replayed the conversation, changing the words they spoke to illicit his preferred outcome.

In his fantasy, she took his cock in her mouth before straddling him. Her perfect breasts bouncing as she rode him into oblivion. The build-up of tension whilst having his wrists bound was truly punishing and frustrating in the most tantalising way.

Baby Susanna's cries snapped him out of his fantasy. He instinctively glanced around to ensure she was being attended to. Billy was trying to wind her, pacing back and forth, rubbing her back. He was impressed that Billy was playing such an attentive role in parenting. He didn't have a single memory of his own father until he was six or seven.

Alaric's attention returned to his own dirty thoughts. He started replaying the memory of Scarlett exiting the lake again, but this time fixated on her comment that she didn't enjoy the view. He replayed it over and over. She had seen his manhood stood to attention. The size and the promise of what was lurking underneath his breeches was evident. He didn't believe that she was that naïve that she didn't know a man's anatomy. He had been with several whores who had commented on how well-endowed he was compared to other men. He was convinced she had been lying to cover up her own arousal.

By nightfall, everyone had had their fill of venison and the ale was flowing. Alaric was desperate for a drop of ale, but he needed to be grateful that they were at least feeding him. Beth truly was a good cook. He would gladly offer her a job in the kitchens once his father killed the male outlaws. He felt a small pang of guilt for the baby at that thought. He didn't like the thought of any child growing up without both parents.

He was mindlessly watching the drunken interactions of the merry men when he saw Scarlett approaching him with Thom following. There was something about his gait and facial expression that made Thom seem nervous. Alaric watched intensely. Thom overtook Scarlett and stopped in front of her. Thom had his back to Alaric, but he heard Thom stutter out, "So next time you go hunting, could I come with you as a chaperone?"

Alaric let out a chortle. Thom was trying to court her.

Alaric saw Scarlett's puzzled expression as she remarked, "I don't need a chaperone, Thom. I go hunting all the time and I'm more than capable of looking after myself." Realisation of what he was asking dawned on her when she saw Alaric grinning from ear to ear. Now it was Scarlett's turn to look uncomfortable. Alaric could see her mind racing for a way to let Thom down gently. She stepped back from him, giving them space as she followed up with, "You know you're like a bother to me Thom, and I'm grateful for that."

Thom stepped forward, closer this time. He was invading Scarlett's personal space and she considered maybe he had got the wrong impression when she appeared naked in front of him earlier. He leaned in closer, as if to kiss her and Scarlett pushed at his chest to stop his advances. "Thom, no." She stated clearly, "I consider you a brother and I don't fuck my brothers." She sidestepped past him and marched past Alaric into the undergrowth. Alaric erupted into laughter, earning him a scowl from Thom.

Feeling petty, Thom took a piss on the tree Alaric was tied to. Alaric caught his breath from laughing and mocked, "You don't stand a chance with her."

"Neither do you, she didn't think much of your manhood earlier," Thom retaliated.

"She thought plenty of it. She just didn't want to say anything in front of you. You know fuck all about women and what they want," Alaric spat back. Continuing, he boasted, "She would take me to her bed in a heartbeat. I've got status, I've got power and I've got wealth, that's what women want."

Movement in the bushes averted both their attentions. Scarlett was returning to camp and from the murderous look on her face, she had heard their exchange.

"Thom don't listen to any of his lies, go back to the others," she ordered. Thom walked off wounded and humiliated. Scarlett turned her attention to Alaric. "If you think that's what I want, you're sadly mistaken."

Snidely, Alaric retorted, "The clock's ticking, you're going to be a spinster soon. You better work out what it is you want."

The truth in his words stung, not that she would let him know that. In response, she replied, "I don't plan on being anyone's wife, that isn't in the cards for me." Wanting to wound him with an insult, she continued. "What's your plan? To let Daddy and his witch pick a bride for you, or do you just plan on having bastards, that you don't need to acknowledge until you need an heir."

Alaric's eyes deepened. He knew she was inferring to his fathers rumoured bastards. He wasn't intending on following in his father's footsteps, but he didn't need to tell her that. He knew she was trying to deflect and her choice of words about her own future was odd and intrigued him. "What do you mean, isn't in the cards?"

Scarlett hadn't thought that he would call her out on that. Her silence gave her away, as Alaric pushed for more information. "You had a reading didn't you? You believe what that witch told you in Ledecestre. What did she predict?"

She responded without thinking. "She filled in the blanks about the parameters of the curse, that's all."

"Which are?" Alaric challenged.

Scarlett looked towards the moon, she took a moment to appreciate the beauty. Looking back down at Alaric, she wearily replied, "Why should you care? You're the reason I'm cursed."

The Sheriff stomped down the hallway en route to Morgana's chambers. He saw a young servant girl vacantly staring out of the window and he barked, "Find something to do." He descended the stairs, then opened the door and entered without knocking, making his presence known by yelling her name.

"Morgana! I don't appreciate being summoned. Do you have a valid reason at least?"

Morgana came into view and hobbled over to her chair. "My knee is playing up; that's why I sent the brat to find you."

The Sheriff rolled his eyes in annoyance and made a dramatically audible sigh before exasperatedly stating, "I meant, what is the purpose of my summons?"

"Ah yes, the boy, is he back yet?" Morgana enquired.

"No. Why? What do you want with him?"

"Should he be gone this long?" She asked, somewhat feigning concern and hinting at the reason for summoning him.

The Sheriff counted on his fingers the days since he had last seen Alaric. "He should be back today. Who knows, the Baron may have provided hospitality."

"Do you grow concerned for him?" Morgana questioned.

The Sheriff's demeanour changed as his anger grew. "Don't speak in riddles around me. Are you telling me I should be concerned?"

Morgana held her ground, unafraid of the Sheriff's temper. "Would you like me to ask the spirits?"

With a wave of his hand, the Sheriff confirmed, "Yes, do it. Get him back here." The Sheriff had turned to leave and had reached the door as Morgana vociferated, "I will need something of his for the spell, preferably a hair."

The Sheriff pulled a disgusted face and then stared into the corridor. "You there," he shouted as he pointed down the hallway, "Fetch the old crone what she wants from my son's room." The servant looked like a deer caught in a trap. He neither moved nor spoke until the Sheriff pointed inside Morgana's chambers and shouted, "Go!" The Sheriff marched off, leaving Morgana to instruct the servant.

The young servant scurried into Morgana's lair, clearly in a state of panic. She ordered him upstairs via her private staircase and explained what to fetch and from which room. It didn't take long for the servant to return with a comb in hand.

Morgana dismissed him and sat at her altar with her tarot cards laid out in a fan. She plucked the few strands of Alaric's hair from the comb and intertwined them between her fingers. She pulled six cards at random from the deck and then laid them face down. She took her time selecting, waiting for the fates to select one for her. When the urge to flip one intensified, Morgana pressed her hand on the reverse and rotated her wrist for the card to present itself.

Mid-twist, Oionos flew through the window and landed on the alter. The unexpected action startled her and the card dropped onto the table face up. Morgana shouted angrily at the bird, shooing it away from the table.

Focusing again on the task at hand, she tried to guess which way the card should be. It had landed horizontally in front of her, therefore telling her nothing about Alaric's future. She studied the card. It was the card of lovers. Upright, it would mean a passionate union, or even love was on the horizon for Alaric. Upside down, it foretold conflict and suffering. Morgana moved the card out of the way and repeated the exercise to see if the other cards would guide her on how to interpret the misplaced card.

The next card that presented itself was the upside-down Devil, a sign of resentment. Morgana was leaning towards believing the previous card should have been upside down as well. She revealed the third card to see an upside-down wheel of fortune. This was a popular card of late and she didn't like that one bit. It was a sign of bad luck and a lack of control.

Morgana stared at the three cards and considered their meaning. Usually, the full moon gave her the extra power she needed to interpret the future. She would need an extra strong potion tonight to decipher Alaric's fate. She set to work concocting the potion, adding Alaric's hair to the glass before she drank. Consuming his essence would help her connect to his fate.

The irony wasn't lost on Alaric. Scarlett had a point. He was the reason she was cursed but it was her own fault. All he had been trying to do was help her to escape and she had scarred him brutally for life.

He went to church. He listened during the never-ending

sermons, an 'eye for an eye' and all that. He worked in the justice department for his father. Crimes and wrongdoings should be punished. So what if when the sun went down she went a bit batshit crazy. Her husband would need to get used to tying her up.

She had threatened him more than once with severe punishment whilst he was her captive. He refused to feel sorry for her. Instead, he remarked, "I guess we're even then. You cursed me with a new face for all to see in the sunlight and I cursed you, so you always have to watch your back when the sun goes down." After a brief paused, he added, "So, when are you letting me go?"

Scarlett rolled her eyes but responded, "A messenger has already been sent. If your father values your life, you will be in your own bed by tomorrow evening."

A half smile graced his face before he sobered, asking, "And if he doesn't value my life?"

Bluntly, with no hint of a jest in her voice, she replied, "You won't be needing that bed."

CHAPTER 12

The next morning, Morgana woke with a start. Her eyes flew open and she took in the dark oval eyes staring back at her, inches away from her face. Her heart pounded with terror as she feared the devil had come to claim her. It took a moment for her to realise that Oionos was on her chest, staring at her. Her realisation brought her back into the physical world and she instantly started coughing. Her movement caused the raven to flutter off towards the window sill.

Morgana's coughing intensified and she felt like she needed to heave. She could feel something trapped in her throat. She sat upright and used her long, spindly fingernails to pincer out a strand of Alaric's hair from her throat. The hair lodged in her throat explained why no visions had come to her. The potion had been incomplete. Agitated and in a foul temper, she dressed. She was undecided on whether to come clean to the Sheriff, but before she came to a decision, there was a knock.

Morgana grabbed her cane and staggered to the door. "What do you want?" She rudely barked without opening it.

A feeble child's voice replied, "The Sheriff sent me. He wants you to join him in his chambers."

The witch slid back the bolts and unlocked the heavy wooden door. She stared into the young boy's eyes. He was the same height as her, so she had no issue staring him down whilst she found out the nature of the summons. "What mood is he in?"

The boy looked nervous to answer, he looked at the floor

as he mumbled, "Not good, ma lady."

"Speak up boy, I can't hear you," The witch demanded.

The boy repeated himself but louder.

The witch ran a long sharp fingernail, quizzically above her top lip. "Is he alone?"

Still looking sheepish, the boy replied, "He was last night, but soldiers arrived this morning. He's been in a rage ever since."

"Do you know who these soldiers were? Why did they speak to the Sheriff so early this morning?"

The boy nodded, "Aye, they're usually with the Sheriff's son but not this morning. I heard them mention an ambush."

The witch sighed and then grumbled. "Tell no one about this conversation, or I will gut you and use your body parts for my spells."

The boy stepped backward in horror and then ran away down the corridor. The witch closed the door and made her way up the private staircase to the Sheriff's quarters.

She was out of breath by the time she climbed the last step. The Sheriff was pacing by the fireplace and Morgana glanced at the three guards looking terrified to the left. None of them had shoes on. Their feet were blistered and bleeding. Their clothes were dirty and torn. All three had a sallow complexion and gaunt facial features. Morgana was more than capable of putting the pieces together. She had more than enough information to fabricate a story about her non-existent vision and deceive the Sheriff.

Morgana's breathing was laboured as she addressed the room. "I came at once. I have had a vision. Alaric is being kept against his will."

The Sheriff eyed her suspiciously. "Convenient timing, Morgana," he spat out viciously.

Morgana held her ground and met his gaze. "I would say rather inconvenient to find out after rather than before, but I am bound by the hands of fate and when they wish to impart wisdom."

"Quite," he remarked with a scowl. "Do you have any more

wisdom to impart us with? It appears these three couldn't find ale in a tavern." The Sheriff's wrath was palpable as he glowered at the three men.

"The wheel of fortune has been turning against us ever since I foresaw the rise of the dead man," Morgana prophesied, "He is hiding in plain sight, I am sure of it. He is the key. He must die."

The Sheriff rolled his eyes, he wasn't impressed. He wanted answers and actionable tasks, not theorising. "It's not so easy to kill a man without a name," he bellowed back in response.

One of the disgraced guards nudged forward. "Sire," he mumbled meekly. The Sheriff shot him an incredulous stare for daring to interrupt.

"Go on then, speak," he demanded.

"One of the guards was a turncoat. He was a new recruit who went by the name of Richard. Maybe he's the man hiding in plain sight."

Another of the guards interjected. "His name wasn't really Richard. I heard them call him Robin."

Then, the third guard spoke up as if he had only just pieced together the puzzle. "When Alaric was fighting Richard... I mean Robin. A girl cut into the fight and used horse reins to knock Alaric over. Foul cheat she was. She looked familiar, but I've only just remembered where from. She was the one to give Alaric that dirty great scar on his face."

The Sheriff's mind went into overdrive and he worked out Robin's true identity quicker than Morgana could voice it. "Robin of Loxley, a man truly has risen from the dead." He turned to Morgana as he gestured for her to join him in a chair by the fireplace. "Morgana, it seems you were right. Take a seat."

Staring back at the guards, he dismissed them with a wave of his hand, but he warned them, "It's a good job you just proved useful. It saved your lives. But if I find out you left my son to rot in the dirt whilst you escaped to freedom, your heads will be cut off and speared onto the castle walls." The guards hurried for the door, relieved they were being allowed to leave.

The Sheriff took a chair opposite Morgana. "You have my attention," he said. "Now, to keep it, tell me what we should do next to regain control. I am the law and the people need to realise it."

"Put up a reward for the villagers to turn Robin in," Morgana instructed. "We will have Alaric back in no time."

The Sheriff rubbed his chin and appeared to be contemplating Morgana's advice. Several moments passed before he clapped his hands together loudly and shared his plan. "I have decided. I must make an example out of Robin and his whole family. They do not cross me and live to tell the tale. I will offer a reward for their whereabouts, dead or alive makes no matter to me."

The witch was used to male egos and knew when to stroke them and when to pull back. Her eyes darkened as she replied, "Excellent idea, your lordship."

The Sheriff reclined in contemplation. If the bandits harmed his son, the entire forest would burn. He had put a lot of effort into moulding Alaric and it would be a pain to have to start again.

That morning, the order was given and errand boys were sent out with the official declaration.

Later that afternoon, the Sheriff was falling asleep in his large chair by the hearth when a knock at the door startled him awake. He yelled, "Enter!"

A young servant boy, the Sheriff thought looked familiar, was being shoved into the room by a guard. "Sire," the guard addressed him formerly "This scrote," using his head to indicate the lad he was holding by the scruff of the neck, "Says he has a missive about Alaric."

The guard snatched the parchment from the boy's hand and walked forward to give it to the Sheriff. He unrolled the parchment and quickly read it. It was from Robin of Loxley.

It was a veiled threat and an offer of exchange. He furiously scrunched the parchment up in his hand before snapping his attention back to the messenger.

"Boy, who gave this to you?" The Sheriff said, waving the screwed-up message.

"I dunno, never seen him before," the boy insisted.

"You wouldn't lie to me, would you boy?" The Sheriff said whilst studying his facial expressions for any signs of a lie.

The boy knew he was under scrutiny now and a simple errand was turning into a dangerous affair. "No, my lord," the boy insisted once again.

The Sheriff wasn't satisfied that the young lad was telling the truth. He questioned him further, hoping the boy would trip up in his story. "Where did he give it to you?"

"In my village, he was just there one minute and gone the next."

The Sheriff pushed his interrogation further, asking, "Why did you agree to bring this to me?"

"He paid me."

"Do you like money?"

The boy nodded and his eyes lit up. "I have lots of it," the Sheriff goaded him. "If you show my guards this man, I will make you rich. How does that sound?"

The boy was hesitant to respond, but the Sheriff could see the greed in his eyes. Eventually, the lad replied. "If I see him again, I'll point him out to the guards."

"Good lad, make sure you do." Then, the Sheriff turned to the guard and instructed them, "Let him go." The guard released him and let him run from the room. When the corridor was clear and the sound of the distant footsteps running down the stairway grew faint, the Sheriff gave his final instruction. "Follow him and report back. He knows Robin, I'm sure of it."

The guard nodded and left the room in pursuit.

The Sheriff took a long swig of ale as he mulled over the letter. The more he thought about it, the angrier he became. He would never bow down to these demands from an outlaw. After a second tankard of ale he marched to the door and bellowed for a servant. A young girl came quickly. He ordered her to bring Morgana to him immediately and then bring more ale. He went back to his chair beside the fire and continued drinking himself into a stupor.

It wasn't long before Morgana was climbing the last step up the secret staircase into the Sheriff's chambers. She knew instantly that he was drunk. His slouched position in the chair and the dribbles down his chin were a dead giveaway.

She cleared her throat to make her presence known. "You requested I visit."

The Sheriff looked up in a daze, he hadn't realised anyone had entered the room. He gestured for Morgana to take a seat opposite him. Slurring his words, he rambled, "That Loxley boy is trying to threaten me," he hiccupped mid-sentence. Morgana had to concentrate to understand his slurred words. If her knees wouldn't punish her for descending and climbing the stairs for the third time today, she would have returned with a potion to sober him up.

He continued, drinking ale between breaths, "Well, soon I will be King and we'll see what he makes of that."

"He's made contact. How?" Morgana inquired.

The Sheriff waved the ball of parchment in the air before throwing it into the roaring flames in the fireplace. The witch pulled a face. She would have liked to have read it, considering he wasn't likely to remember the contents in the morning. "What news of Alaric did it bring?"

The Sheriff sighed, "Stupid idiots own fault for getting imprisoned. Not my problem." The Sheriff continued drinking and Morgana pushed him for more answers before he fell asleep for good.

"Did they want to trade for his safety? What did they want?" She quizzed.

"Me, to give up being Sheriff. No chance. I will have more sons. I've probably got more somewhere. You will find them for me," he babbled in response, as his eyes started to close.

Morgana was frustrated that she hadn't had a chance to read the letter for herself. She hobbled over to the snoring Sheriff and pulled the tankard of ale from his grasp. She threw it over his face and the Sheriff's eyes opened wide in shock. Before he could accuse her of anything, she got in their first.

"You spilled your drink, my lord, let me put it down for you." Turning back to the Sheriff, but remaining inches away from him she asked, "Does Robin want money and his title back in exchange for Alaric?"

"What?" The Sheriff said in confusion before remembering the earlier conversation, "No, he wants lower taxes for the people and me to renounce my office." The Sheriff scoffed loudly at the audacity of the request. This was followed by a round of hiccups and then the Sheriff passed out in the chair. The sound of loud snores filled the room.

Morgana sat back down in the chair opposite him and stared at the man before her. She had always possessed a talent for reading people. Just by walking into a room, she could tell who the smartest and most powerful person in the room was, versus those who just thought they were. When she met the Sheriff, she knew she had found a power-hungry, ruthless individual whom she could mould. She had made the right choice and these last twenty years had been plentiful. Sitting in contemplation, she wondered if this partnership had run its course.

The cards had not been favourable lately. The wheel of fortune symbolising bad luck had cropped up a few times. Morgana knew the Sheriff wouldn't live forever, especially with the way he drank. The signs of liver failure were visible on his skin. He had dark spots on his hands, and a tinge of yellow to his skin. She had intentions of grooming Alaric to be her new benefactor. Befriending him recently and offering revenge for his disfigurement had been the start of forming that bond. She intended to live far beyond a normal lifespan, her potions would see to that.

Yet, staring at him in front of her, she still lusted for

that forbidden fruit she had always coveted. Wickedly devilish, sexual thoughts raced through her mind. Like the time many years ago when she had paid a prostitute who he had hired to tie him up and blindfold him. She had traded places with the prostitute that night. Or the countless times she had watched him from a crack in the door and imagined it was her he was with.

She resolved to stand by the Sheriff, but she would also do her best for Alaric. He was less easy on the eye now his face was scarred, but she had never been one for pretty boys. It was always wise to have a back-up plan and she had grown accustomed to her comfortable life in the castle.

She pushed herself out of the chair and leaned over the sleeping Sheriff. She ran her long fingers through his hair and then inhaled his powerful scent. His snores echoed loudly and she knew he was in a deep sleep. She leaned forward and licked the side of his cheek, savouring the flavour. Then she staggered to Alaric's room and surveyed his belongings.

She needed a personal item for a protection spell. His room was fairly sparse, but she found a pair of leather gloves, so she took them for the spell.

Later that night, Morgana hobbled with her cane through the castle to the walled garden. Oionos perched on her shoulder. She verbally chastised the young servants she had commandeered to carry her alter outside.

"Put your backs into it lads before I make you cripples for life," she warned.

Eventually, they positioned the altar in exactly the right place to harness the power of the moon. The walled garden was a private sanctuary maintained by gardeners but used very little since the Sheriff's wife died. It was the perfect place to perform witchcraft; away from prying eyes.

Morgana knew her magic wouldn't be at its most powerful as the full moon wouldn't be for several days. However, she intended to bind the spell with another's energy to intensify her magic. She laid the objects she would need on the altar.

Using her flint stone, she lit a red wax candle. Then, she went off in search of fresh rosemary. She found some growing in the herb patch that she threatened the gardeners to always maintain; herbs were useful for spells. Next, she lit a sprig of the fresh rosemary she had harvested and wafted it in the air in a ring to form a protection circle around the altar.

In a pestle and mortar, she ground together the leftover rosemary and a heap of salt. She rubbed the mixture into the gloves and then placed them next to the candle on the altar, in the centre of the protection circle. Carefully, she opened a jar of the remaining potion she had made to curse Lady Loxley. The potion was tied to her essence from her blood and hair. Morgana smirked at her own brilliance for having the foresight to keep the leftovers. She poured the contents of the jar over the gloves. The salt dissolved instantly.

Next, Morgana took out the last ingredient and prepared for her chant by clearing her throat. Oionos flew off and landed on a wall, where he had a clear view. As she poured on a vial of aqua fortis, the gloves started to perish before her very eyes, binding the components together. Through her chant, she bound the life forces of Alaric and Lady Loxley, with the aim of protecting Alaric from harm at the hands of the Lady's brother.

When her chant was complete, she stepped back out of the protection circle and immediately started coughing. She staggered backward, away from the altar, until she collapsed on a garden bench. She heaved the contents of her dinner onto the ground and she knew her spell was sealed with as much power as she possessed. Now, she only had to wait for Alaric to return unharmed. Oionos gave her a knowing look and took off into the night's sky.

CHAPTER 13

The smell of meat cooking on an open flame wafted into Alaric's nostrils. His mouth watered at the smell and he imagined a full banquet spread over a long table. Strange sounds echoed in his ears, sounds that didn't fit with the narrative of his thoughts. A loud belch nearby had him snapping back to reality and a moment later, after opening his eyes, he remembered where he was. He cursed, convinced that he had dreamt the delicious aroma. However, he grinned after inhaling deeply, the smell of cooking meat was real. He stretched his neck towards the fire pit and saw a haunch of venison skewered on a makeshift rotisserie. It was enough to have him salivating.

He brazenly shouted, "Beth, when's the food ready?"

Beth scrunched up her face in an attempt to be menacing and held her finger to her lips for the universal quiet gesture. She pointed at the babe swaddled to her chest. Alaric tried to convey a fake apology in the hope that he would still receive some food.

Sure enough, moments later, Beth handed him a noggin of bread and held a bowl of meat broth for him to dunk it in. He could just about manage to eat with his wrists tied.

Rustling from the bushes spooked Beth and Scarlett appeared behind her. Before Scarlett could speak, Beth raised her finger to shh her as well. Scarlett offered to take over feeding Alaric and Beth accepted, going back to the fire with baby Susanna.

"You've been up early," Alaric said, wondering what she had been up to and whether it would affect his fate. Scarlett raised a quizzical brow as if to infer 'what's it got to do with you?', but she remained silent.

"Not a morning person," Alaric continued on, "I get that. Me, I like rising with the sun. It allows me plenty of time to sharpen my sword." His eyes held an unspoken threat.

"Stop talking," Scarlett demanded as she scowled at him.

"It's a lovely morning, I'd love to stretch my legs," Alaric said. He was concerned that if he didn't use his legs soon, he would be unable to run when the next chance to escape appeared. His ankle seemed to have healed from the fall, but without putting weight on it he couldn't be sure.

Scarlett placed the bowl on the ground. She closed her eyes and massaged her temples, exasperated. When she opened them again, Alaric's mouth opened as if to speak but she cut in, warning him, "If you don't shut up, I will make you."

Alaric's plan was working. He was starting to get to her. It was only a matter of time that it caused her to make a mistake. Then he would get his revenge. However, he had to play his hand carefully as he didn't fancy the reins strapped around his head again. He merely nodded and without replying, finished off the last of his food.

The day continued and Alaric was left in solitary confinement. By late afternoon, he was beyond exasperated with his situation. He would gladly take the reins in his mouth all night if it meant he could have one conversation   He asked everyone that passed if they would speak to him to pass the time, but they ignored him. Finally, Billy walked past and Alaric shouted out, "Do you remember when we played that prank on old Friar Tuck?"

Billy stopped in his tracks and smiled, "Which one? He fell for them every time."

"My favourite was that time you convinced him your father had said he had to abstain from alcohol. His face was a picture." Alaric smiled at the memory. It had been too long since he had indulged in remembering his childhood.

"Aye, that was a good one. I liked it when you convinced

him you could turn water into ale." Both men started laughing and soon they were regaling tales from happy times long ago.

Beth enjoyed hearing the pleasant sound of her husband laughing, so she wandered over. Soon, a group had gathered and they sat in a circle telling mischievous tales from their childhoods. Robin had been gone for so much of his siblings' childhood that he wasn't familiar with any of their anecdotes.

The group were in such high spirits, no one noticed when Scarlett approached from behind a tree. She planned on chastising everyone for fraternising with the enemy. However, when she heard the tales being told, she couldn't help but laugh along with them. As the sky darkened, Beth returned to the fire to continue cooking. The wind had picked up and she was having trouble keeping the fire lit. Several of the men stood to shield the flames from the wind. The gathering dispersed, leaving Alaric alone again.

The tall trees swayed violently in the wind. Leaves whipped around the forest floor and the branches were shaking. The squawks of a frantic, loud bird pierced the air. Before Alaric knew what was happening, Scarlett had withdrawn her dagger and was cutting him free of the ropes which bound him to the tree. Within a matter of moments she was down to the last rope when an almighty crack overhead sounded. Scarlett's dagger cut through the last strands and she pushed him to the side, hurling herself on top of him.

Scarlett's arms and head were protecting his. Her breasts were pushed into his face and her legs were straddling his torso. His hands were being squashed between his chest and her groin. If it wasn't for the shock and the bound wrists, Alaric could have easily taken advantage of the situation.

Scarlett let go of him and scrambled to her feet as Alaric fumbled to try and get off his side. He gave up trying to right himself and Scarlett dragged him into a sitting position. "Not that I'm surprised at you falling over yourself to ride me, but a little notice would be nice." A hint at the natural boyish charm he had had as a youngster shone through his cheeky comment.

Scarlett rubbed her head more in confusion than from any pain. A large branch lay on the ground where Alaric had been sitting. Her eyes darting to it caused Alaric to notice.

"I guess I should say thank you. I didn't know you cared," he retorted.

Under her breath, Scarlett mumbled, "Neither did I," as she continued rubbing her head. In truth, she hadn't known what caused her to act. She had just felt an overwhelming urge to protect Alaric at all costs. Scarlett stood and grabbed her bow, she walked into the woods without looking back. She needed to clear her head and hunting was the best way to do that.

Two days had passed and no one had come forward for the reward. The Sheriff was in a foul mood and had summoned Morgana to his chambers. As she climbed the last few stairs she could see the Sheriff pacing the room. She immediately knew the mood he would be in from this action alone.

He acknowledged her presence with a clear accusation, "Well?"

Morgana cocked her head to the side, debating on how best to respond. "Patience is an ally, my lord."

"You sound like a priest." The Sheriff retorted with a snarl. In a tirade of anger, he bellowed, "I want my son back, I want Robin's head spiked on my walls, his whole gang of bandits strung up in nooses, and Lady Loxley as my slave. I'm not particularly fussed in what order. Is that too much for the future King of England to demand?" His question was rhetorical but Morgana eyed him up with reverence.

She shuffled closer to show him that his outburst did not scare her. In fact, she found his assertiveness arousing. He truly believed he would be King and Morgana knew that a man who believes in himself was a powerful force. She had created this belief in him, moulded him to be King. It was the next logical step for his ambition.

"You will be King. Show them that, lead from the front, as

a King does in battle. They need to see you, to be inspired by you, and then they will not only fear you but love you. They will then fall over themselves to serve you Robin's head on a platter." The Sheriff stopped pacing and relaxed into his chair, mulling over Morgana's words.

Scarlett saw the pot bubbling over the fire and sniffed the air. She couldn't smell any food cooking, so she went to investigate. She peered over and saw what appeared to be boiling water. This wasn't odd in itself, but Beth usually boiled the drinking water in the morning when Billy collected it from the lake.

Scarlett turned around to see Beth struggling over to the fire with a pail of water.

"What are you doing?" Scarlett enquired.

"Giving Susanna a bath, she needs to keep clean. It's not healthy for people to be dirty," Beth replied in earnest.

Scarlett hadn't realised you needed to bathe for health, she just washed because she couldn't stand the smell when she didn't. A strange feeling made her glance towards Alaric. It had been over a week since they captured him. He had been tied to that tree day and night in the same clothes.

Scarlett felt inexplicably drawn to him and she walked over. Alaric didn't feel her presence until she was leaning over him.

He cocked his head to the side and studied her face. "Are you," he hesitated, pulling a disgusted face before continuing, "Smelling me?"

Scarlett was repulsed by the smell and accidentally coughed in his face, he smelt rank. He had clearly urinated in his clothes more than once. "You stink!" She exclaimed, moving further away. She wondered how she hadn't noticed before.

Sarcastically, he replied, "Cheers, how about you tell me something I don't know."

"Challenge accepted," she replied, as she disappeared

behind the tree.

Suddenly, the ropes around his torso fell loose and Scarlett reappeared in front of him. She retied the ropes on his ankles to enable him to move slowly whilst his legs were still bound together. As she dragged him upwards by the armpit, she replied, "You're going to take a bath."

He scowled. "I am?"

"You are."

Alaric shuffled forward as fast as his restraints would allow, as Scarlett encouraged him forward with an arrow pressed into his back.

Scarlett warned, "Any funny business and I'll shoot you. I won't aim for your heart because, quite frankly, I doubt I could find it, but I could take out an eye quite easily."

Alaric sardonically replied, "Haha," as he continued forward.

He tried to imprint the route to memory, focusing on every distinct-looking tree. He ran through several escape scenarios in his head. Occasionally, Scarlett would knock him on the arm with an arrow to steer him in another direction and the weapon was a stark reminder that there would be dire consequences if he ran for it. As much as he hated to admit it, Scarlett was one hell of an archer. She had proved that with the shooting the deer.

They made painfully slow progress until he suddenly recognised where they were. They were standing at the top of a hill and beneath them was the lake where he had seen her bathing. Tantalising memories flooded back and he couldn't help mocking her, "Is this all a ruse so you can see me naked?" Looking over his shoulder to see her reaction, he winked at her as he added, "All you had to do was ask."

Scarlett was suddenly aware of how this looked and for a fleeting second, she did feel confused as to why she was entertaining this. She was tempted to walk back to camp and simply dump a bucket of water over his head. She suddenly wondered why she hadn't just asked Billy to bring him down here. She wasn't sure, but now that they were at the lake, she smirked at the turn of fortunes. He had seen her in all her glory, so it only felt fair he got to suffer the same humiliation.

She grinned and nudged him forward with the tip of her arrow. By the water's edge, Alaric turned to face her as he joked, "Would you care to untie me or at the very least undress me?"

"You're remaining tied up. I trust you about as far as I could throw you. Now turn back around."

Alaric obeyed, intrigued to see what Scarlett would do next. Suddenly, he felt her tugging at his shirt near his waist. With a huge heave, his shirt was free of his breeches and she roughly pushed it over his head. She left his shirt covering his bound arms and he felt her fingers brush against the small of his back, near his beeches.

He felt a sudden tingle rush up his spine at the feel of her skin on his. No woman had elicited this response from him before, but he rationalised it had just been too long since he visited a brothel. He reasoned it was just a bodily urge and nothing more. However, his carnal thoughts continued when she pulled on his breeches and they didn't budge.

"That's not going to work. You need to undo the fastenings at the front." His voice betrayed what she was doing to him and evidence of his arousal was growing swiftly.

"Not happening," she responded, "Can't you manage that yourself?"

"I can," he replied as he smirked to himself. With great difficulty, he managed to unfasten his breeches and Scarlett gave them a sharp tug downwards. They fell to the ground, trapped on his legs by the restraints binding his ankles. Completely exposed but still restrained, Alaric stood brazenly waiting for Scarlett's next move. He could tell she'd hesitated.

This was a game and one he was determined to win. She had taken control but he was determined to take it back. "I'm interested in what happens next. Surely you need to remove my clothes fully. I will surely drown if I'm bound."

Scarlett hated to admit it but Alaric did have a point. She

hadn't thought this far ahead, which was very unlike her. She weighed up the options. If she untied his ankles, there was a greater chance he might flee and she would have to shoot him. If she untied his restraints whilst she removed his clothes, he might use his strength to overthrow her. She couldn't perceive a scenario where untying his wrists wouldn't disadvantage her, so his hands had to remain bound. However, she knew she needed to remove his ankle restraints and breeches. Without a doubt, he would have a powerful kick and she couldn't afford to get kicked in the face trying to untie him.

Alaric shifted, trying to glance over his shoulder at her. He started whistling to agitate her, before jeering, "Still alive back there."

"Shut up, I'm thinking," Scarlett snapped back fiercely.

Scarlett made a snap decision to cut the rope binding his feet. In a fluid movement that she hoped he wouldn't anticipate, she pulled out her dagger, bent down, and cut the rope in one swift action. As she rose from the ground, she couldn't help noticing his long bare legs that led up to a muscular, pert bottom. The contrast in his skin colouring from his arms versus his bottom was laughable and a smile crossed her lips.

Alaric felt a slight tug on his legs from the rope binding them and he looked down to see frayed ends. The rope had been cut. He just needed to remove his breeches and he was free to run. He didn't care that he was naked; he was confident he could outrun her.

"Before you have any ideas about running away," Scarlett declared, "Remember I have excellent aim with a bow and arrow." Prodding an arrow tip into his back, she threatened, "And this one has your name on it. I promise that I will aim straight for your manhood. Now remove your boots and breeches. Then carry your breeches into the water with you and wash them."

Alaric did as instructed, even though his balance was precarious and he knew he looked like a fool, hopping about on one leg trying to remove his breeches.

As he entered the water, the cool temperature instantly made him shudder. The hairs on his arms stood to attention but once his body was half-submerged, the soothing nature of the water on his bare skin felt relaxing. It felt good to be clean after so many days of being held prisoner and tied to a tree in one position.

He rolled his shoulders back and swivelled his head from shoulder to shoulder. Even though his wrists were still bound, it felt good to stretch out and he lifted his arms above his head, showcasing his muscles. He could feel eyes watching his every move and he continued to put on a show.

Scarlett stared from the bank with her arrow nocked and pointed at her target. One move out of line and she was ready. He hadn't turned around and his back was facing her. The water only came up to his waist and she became fixated on the way his muscles moved. The way he stretched towards the sky showed off every toned muscle in his back. Scarlett's lips parted just a little as she watched in awe.

Desire was building within her core and her pulse quickened. She continued to stare as he ducked below the surface of the water. Five seconds passed and he didn't resurface. She started to mentally count how long he had been under when suddenly, he burst through the surface of the water. In one fluid motion, he flicked his head back and his now dripping wet hair sleeked back out of his eyes.

Droplets of water glistened on his skin and Scarlett had an insane desire to lick them off. The desire in her core was mounting like a highly wound spring ready to explode.

Keen to see how his display had affected her, Alaric turned around. Their eyes met and as he had hoped, she was transfixed by him. He could see a burning desire in her eyes that he hadn't seen before. She wasn't even trying to hide it, or be coy about it. His thoughts flashed back to the last time they were at this lake and their positions were reversed.

His cock had wilted in the cold water, but with her fixated on him it came to life. With his cock standing proud, he had a desire to show her every inch of himself. As his manhood grew harder and larger at his racing thoughts, he slowly walked towards her. The closer he got to the edge of the lake, the less water covered his body until he was on full display. Unashamedly, her eyes hadn't left his body. He watched with interest as her eyes flicked down to see him fully erect.

Scarlett's tongue subconsciously darted out to lick her lower lip.

The atmosphere was charged with sexual energy and as much as Alaric should run, he couldn't bring himself to look away from her face as she stared at him in wonder. No woman had ever looked at him with so much desire. The closer he got to her, the more he noticed the effect he was having on her.

Scarlett couldn't keep her eyes off him as he neared. His body was that of a toned Adonis. Of course, she had seen a naked man before, but never one so beautiful. And never one she wished to touch. Her eyes drifted downwards and the sight of him hard and ready did something to her body on a physical level that she had never experienced before. She lowered her weapon and it slipped from her fingers to the ground. The action caused Alaric's eyes to glance away, breaking the eye contact.

That was enough to break the spell he had over her and her brain kicked in. She reached for the dagger in her waistband and threatened, "Do not come any closer. Turn around."

Alaric did as instructed and he felt the tip of the dagger at the nape of his neck.

"Drop your breeches to the floor and step into them," Scarlett instructed.

"But they're soaking wet," Alaric protested.

"So, wring them out."

Alaric exhaled loudly but did as ordered. He bent down to pull them up and as he rose he took advantage of his feet being unbound. He spun on his heel and looped his bound wrists over Scarlett's head. He locked his arms in place, pressing her tightly into his body. Her arms were immobilised by her side, rendering her dagger useless.

The speed of the change in dynamics took Scarlett's breath away. She was pressed against his body and could feel every inch of him. His erect shaft pressed against the middle of her back. She felt his hot breath on her ear as he whispered, "I could crush you with my bare arms and run away."

She made an attempt to break free but it was useless. He was right about being able to crush her, but the hard length pressing into her didn't make it seem like he wanted to run away. She knew she should be scared but she wasn't. All she felt was desire at the touch of his skin on hers and the feel of his strong arms cradling her. His head hadn't moved and he whispered again, "I can feel your heart rate rising, but I don't think you're scared of me."

"I'm not," she replied forcefully.

Her defiance made him smirk and he added, "Then your body is betraying your desires."

"Or maybe I'm getting ready to throw you over my shoulder onto your ass."

His mirth was evident in his tone when Alaric responded, "I think you protest too much. More like you can't stop thinking about my ass."

Scarlett knew he was playing a game now. He had had ample opportunity to discard her and run, but he was still toying with her. She wiggled her behind into his crotch as she remarked, "It feels like you're the one who can't stop thinking about my ass."

Scarlett felt a twitch from his cock that was pressed up against her and it sent a tingle up her spine. The tension in her core was fit to burst. He took his time to respond, as if he was taking time to enjoy the friction she had just caused.

In a breathy response, he replied, "I'm always thinking about your ass and all the ways only I could pleasure you. You would be dripping wet for me before I even entered you. Only difference is I'm the only one willing to admit it. Admit you've thought about me when you're alone at night and your pleasuring yourself."

"Why?" Scarlett argued and she tried to wrestle free again. She wasn't willing to admit the salacious thoughts she'd had about him.

"You aren't in a position to deny me anything. Answer."

Embarrassment and anger kicked in. Scarlett knew he was toying with her and she wasn't going to give his ego any more satisfaction. He had bested her and that was enough. "I would never allow you to touch me," she cried enraged, "I would rather die."

Scarlett had been brought up with boys and had always been able to look after herself. She brought up her leg and kicked her heel back hard into his knee, causing him to crumple. As his arms loosened and he bent, she threw back her head, smashing it into his nose.

The couple toppled to the ground and she pulled herself free of his arms. As he lay writhing on the floor, his face covered in blood, Scarlett pointed her dagger at him.

"Now you have a broken nose to go with that scar. How many more times do I have to show you not to underestimate me."

When his eyes focused on her she pointed to a tree basking in the sun behind his head and snapped, "Walk towards that tree and you can dry out in the sun over there." She just wanted him away from her so she could clear her mind. She didn't want to give a moments more thought to his affirmation. Even now she could feel her treacherous core leaking with desire.

Without fighting or attempting to run, Alaric did as she requested, still trying to stem the bleeding from his nose. Scarlett tied him to the tree and then bound his ankles together again.

Alaric sat brooding in pain over his latest injury. Every time he felt like he was enjoying himself in her company, something reminded him of the laceration on his face, and his blood boiled, pushing his anger and self-loathing to the surface.

Neither spoke again. The moment they had shared had

passed and the tension which had been wound so tight had broken like a coil that had been overstretched.

CHAPTER 14

The Sheriff was dressed in his finest armour. The breastplate had been buffed, so the silver shone bright and reflected as well as any mirror. The chainmail was heavy and he felt sluggish in it, but he would be sat on a horse, so vanity won out over practicality. A guard handed him his helmet but he dismissed them. The point of this exercise was so that the people could see him, there was no point in wearing a helmet.

Down at the stables, it took two guards to aid him onto his horse. It was a mighty black Destrier. It was much taller and more muscular than an average horse. It had been extremely expensive and for someone who didn't much like horses, it was a pure status symbol. Its impressive size was matched by its beautiful, shiny coat, making it a magnificent beast.

The horse neighed when he sat in the saddle as if to complain about the excessive weight, even though such a horse was bred to handle the weight of a knight in battle. It was expertly trained and even for a novice rider, it obeyed all commands and knew how to behave.

The garrison proceeded in formation with the Sheriff displayed like a peacock in the centre. As they approached the first village, the Sheriff was appalled at the lack of interest he was receiving. He deduced that the villagers were so ignorant that no one was aware of who he was, so he had the guard leading the garrison announce a proclamation. A small group gathered to greet him, mostly made up of children, the old and the infirm.

He looked at his subjects from his great horse and announced, "These last few days, you have heard that my son has been kidnapped by bandits led by Robin of Loxley. I personally offer a reward for news that leads to his safe return."

An old cripple near the back of the group shouted back, "How much is the reward?"

"A purse of silver coins," he replied smugly. However, he was shocked by the reaction as several of the villages left the group and the cripple who had asked spat on the ground, then hobbled away. Confused, the Sheriff looked to his men. He grimaced and the guard marched towards the cripple.

The guard grabbed him by the scruff of his neck and took his cane away from him, preventing him from leaving. Waving it in the air, he jeered at the man mocking him. "Are you too rich that you sneer at a purse of silver?" The man tried not to appear intimidated, although he obviously was.

"Tell your Sheriff why you dismissed his gracious offer," the guard demanded.

"I didn't dismiss it. I don't know him, that's all. Hard to get excited about a prize you can't claim."

The guard grimaced at him but turned to the Sheriff for further instruction. The Sheriff gestured for the guard to let the man go. The guard struck the man's backside with his own cane, earning a jeer from the other guards, but then let him go on his way.

The garrison travelled to the next village and received a similar reception. At the third settlement, the Sheriff spotted the young boy who had delivered the missive from Robin. The Sheriff watched as the boy actively avoided joining the group of listeners. He delivered his speech, which was met with a lacklustre response, all whilst keeping the boy in his sights. He watched him enter a ramshackle tavern, only to exit moments later. He was followed by an older lad, not quite a man. The young boy pointed to the garrison and the older lad forced his hand down so as not to draw attention. The Sheriff signalled over to the nearest guard.

"See the young man with the kid by that doorway," he instructed and then boxed the guard's ear for making it obvious. "Be more inconspicuous," he ordered. "Follow him." The guard nodded and the Sheriff instructed, "Lose the armour, blend in."

The garrison moved onto the fourth village and the Sheriff's patience had well and truly waned. As he watched from his horse, something struck him as odd about all the villages they had visited. He had seen no beggars since leaving the marketplace by the castle. Even the cripples were not begging. His mind ticked over the day's events. Everyone he had met seemed content, happy even. He had to admit the sun was shining, but what was so great in life that no one was melancholy? This was England, complaining was a national pastime.

He pointed at the next woman he saw smile and instructed a guard to bring her to him. She looked concerned as the guard dragged her over.

"Answer me this question and you are free to go. Why is everyone so happy?"

The woman looked perplexed as she replied, "Happy, my lord? I wouldn't say everyone was happy but then again, what is there to be sad about?"

"I have people whining at my doors from noon until night about taxation and yet away from the town, everyone is thriving."

At his response, the woman's cheeks flushed and she was clearly hiding the truth when she replied, "I think it's the good weather and you gracing us with a visit. It's cheered everyone up no end."

The flattery was welcome but the Sheriff was still suspicious. He ordered the garrison to return to the castle after the visit to a sixth village, he was bored from the day's activity. He had a niggling feeling that he was being lied to. He ordered several guards to accompany him to his chambers.

"What did you make of today?" He enquired.

The first guard started by flattering him, praising his

decision for visiting and he put the villager's happy attitude down to his magnanimous presence. The second guard grunted that he hated the small-town folk and they were an odd bunch. The third guard did nothing more than shrug and agree with the other two.

"You're wrong," the Sheriff bellowed. "Something wasn't right. Go in plain clothes and find out what they weren't saying. The first one to bring me the truth gets a bag of silver and a promotion."

Scarlett sat in front of the blazing fire and stared into the flickering flames, lost in thought. She glanced over her shoulder towards Alaric. He had his eyes shut and she allowed herself to really look at him. He had been lucky her blade hadn't caught his eye and affected his sight. Even with the scar, he was still handsome. His eyelashes were beautiful like his mother's, thick, long, and dark. His lips were full and permanently blush-coloured; another of his mother's traits. His floppy, dark brown hair covered part of the raw scar. She followed the line of the laceration over his strong Roman nose, high cheekbone, and square jaw; all courtesy of his father.

Scarlett battled internally with her thoughts at the memory of his father ordering her own to die. Anger raged within her. Hatred for the Sheriff rose like bile in her throat and the feeling of being helpless engulfed her. It wasn't a terribly cold night but she wrapped her arms around herself, holding her own body together before it shattered. She fought back tears that she had kept down for so long. Then, lost in regret at being too scared and too helpless to help her father, she left the fire in search of solace.

Alaric stirred as he heard the distant sound of a baby crying. His eyelids were heavy and he could tell it was very early. He yawned and he opened one eyelid at a time. His vision was struggling to focus when he saw Scarlett standing over Susanna with a dagger raised, ready to strike.

He shouted, "No!" At the top of his voice. Scarlett didn't react. She just wiped what looked like blood from her lips and smeared it across her cheek. Dropping the pail of water he was carrying, Billy ran past Alaric towards Scarlett. He launched at her, knocking her to the floor. He grappled with her to disarm her. There was movement from the rest of the camp as everyone started shouting, asking what was happening.

Beth had run to Susanna and was now soothing her. Scarlett was now out of her trance and shouting for answers.

"Billy, what happened?" Panic was evident in her voice. Billy's face turned from anger to dumbfounded. Scarlett appeared to have no recollection.

"How can you not remember what you nearly did?"

"Billy, please tell me. What did I nearly do?"

Billy released Scarlett's wrists but stayed straddled over her, pinning her in place as he answered, "You nearly killed Susanna. You had a dagger drawn, ready to attack her."

Horror swept over Scarlett's face. She stuttered his name. "Billy, I wouldn't. I don't remember." Tears had formed now and were rolling down her cheeks. "Is she ok?" She pleaded desperately.

Billy shook his head in disbelief, "No thanks to you." His anger had turned to fear and his eyes had filled with tears that threatened to spill.

Robin had joined the siblings now and held his hand out to help Billy stand. Billy took it and rose, releasing Scarlett from the ground. She stood slowly and apologised to them both for her actions. She saw Beth cradling Susanna, but Scarlett kept her distance and shouted, "I'm so sorry." Looking back at Billy, who looked like he would never forgive her, she ran from camp.

She passed Alaric, now in floods of tears and he saw her truly vulnerable for the first time. It was the curse, it had to be. He looked back at her brothers, who seemed deep in discussion. No one was going after her and Alaric thought back to their conversation after she had visited the witch in Ledecestre. She had learned the parameters of the curse. The only sure way Alaric knew to end a curse was to die. Suddenly, Alaric had an overwhelming feeling that she was about to do something stupid. He shouted over to her brothers, "Are you not going to go after her?"

Neither brother acknowledged him. Growing frustrated and more irate Alaric shouted louder. "If you don't go after her, she's going to do something you'll regret." Still, they didn't respond. Alaric decided to tell the blunt truth. "You do realise she's going to kill herself."

That got their attention and both heads snapped towards him. Robin ran towards him shouting, "What direction?"

"That way," Alaric responded, gesturing with his head, "Towards the lake."

Robin ran as fast as he could. At the top of the slope, he scanned the lake and saw Scarlett walking into the water fully clothed. He shouted for her to stop as he ran down the hill.

Scarlett was submerged to her neck by the time he reached the water's edge. He waded into the water towards her, all the time shouting for her to listen to him and turn around.

As she submerged her head under the water, he reached her and pulled her out. She kicked against him, screaming, "Let me go!"

He dragged her from the water onto the bank and she continued to resist his help. He picked her up and threw her over his shoulder. He had to clamp her legs tightly to prevent her from kicking him. She pounded her fists on his back as he stomped back to the camp.

She was incensed with rage. Rage at herself and self-loathing. Robin did the only thing he could to restrain her and tied her to the opposite side of the tree Alaric was tied to. When he had finished, he warned, "You need to calm down. You can stay here until I can trust you to behave normally again."

Scarlett called him every profanity she knew before relenting and hanging her head in shame.

Alaric wasted no time before taunting her. He chuckled

before scoffing, "Oh, how the tables have turned."

"I don't see that your fortune has improved at all," Scarlett spat, "It's hardly a turn of fortunes when only one of our fates has changed."

"Oh, but my fortune has changed," he appeared to reply in earnest, before satirically adding, "I now get your scintillating company to keep me amused."

Scarlett screwed her face up in response, knowing he couldn't see her. The urge to stick her tongue out and fully regress to the indignant little lady that she had been in childhood was fierce. He brought the impetuous, childish side of her to the surface and she hated it. She hated the feeling of being helpless, of being classed as silly for the big ideas she had. In upper-class society, she was raised to be quiet and do as she was told without thinking for herself. Her father had always indulged her, giving her more freedom than society would and for that she was grateful.

Self-loathing over her recent actions took hold of her. Under a curse or not, they were unforgivable. She deserved to die. She tilted her head back and looked for the moon. If that witch were to be believed, she would be dead shortly anyway.

Alaric started whistling an annoying, repetitive tune. She took a deep breath and sighed. Death wouldn't come quickly enough and she had no intention of spending her final days tied to a tree with only Alaric for company.

Intensely overwhelmed, she shouted, "Enough! For the love of God, please, desist."

Her plea was met with a dark chuckle, before the whistling started again. Alaric knew what he was doing and he did it on purpose. He whistled the same frustrating tune over and over again.

"I would rather you talk than listen to that tune again. Talk to me, tell me anything. Confess your sins or retell a story from the Bible, just please STOP whistling," Scarlett pleaded.

Alaric just continued to whistle until Robin took pity on her and threatened Alaric with the reins. Alaric fell silent and Scarlett was left with her thoughts again. The silence was deafening and whilst she found the whistling infuriating, her own thoughts were much more lethal to her current wellbeing. Softly she asked, "Tell me about the witch. I know nothing about the woman who has cursed me."

Alaric could hear the vulnerability in her plea and he felt a twinge of guilt at her predicament. He wasn't sure why, but he felt a need to give her the answers she craved. "Her name's Morgana. She's pretty creepy, always hovering around in the shadows. Her eyes are dark, almost black and they bore into you like they can see your soul. She has a pet raven that sits on her shoulder and I've heard her talking to it when she climbs the staircase that leads to my father's private quarters."

Alaric was interrupted by a loud squawk when a large black bird landed on the ground in front of Scarlett. Its beady eyes stared at her and it ruffled its feathers. Scarlett drew her legs close to her chest in a defensive manoeuvre. The bird strutted towards Alaric on the other side of the tree. Scarlett watched it until it was out of her view. She heard Alaric gasp and Scarlett whispered, "Does it look like that?"

Scarlett heard the flapping of wings and she craned her head up to see if she could see the bird flying off. "That was him. Morgana will know where I am." His voice had emotion in it that she hadn't heard from him before. Throughout the whole time they had kept him captive, he had either been angry or jovial, but now he seemed different.

"How can you be sure? One bird looks like any other."

"Did anything about that seem like a normal fucking bird to you?"

Scarlett wasn't scared for herself, her days were numbered, but everyone's life in camp depended on them remaining hidden. Scarlett had a desperate desire to keep everyone safe, even from her. The witch clearly had a vendetta against her. If she could break the curse and kill the witch before she told the Sheriff, everyone would be safe. With desperation clear in her voice, she begged Alaric for more information.

"What powers does she have? Tell me everything you've witnessed."

"She has these dreams that tell her about the future, but she has to interpret them and they always seem to support her point of view. She harps on about the power of the full moon. I've watched her read tarot cards and when I was sick as a boy, my mother ordered her to mix a potion to restore me to health. It tasted foul but I suppose it did the job."

"So she can't move things with her mind, or shoot bolts of lightning from her hands?"

"She's an old crone, not a supernatural entity from a storybook."

"Right," Scarlett calmed her imagination, then asked, "How would I recognise her?"

"Old, ugly, wears black, hunched over, and walks with a cane. Usually hovering around my father dripping poison into his ear." Alaric described her as best he could. He was suddenly intrigued as to why Scarlett wanted to know. She was currently tied to the same tree he was, so it wasn't like she was in a position to hunt the witch down.

"Where would I find her?"

"What are you planning?" Alaric questioned.

"That bird's back, I'm not free to say, just answer the question."

Alaric was intrigued but also weary of the bird. "Her quarters are in the basement of the castle. On the left side of the building, she has slim windows on one side due to the lay of the land."

"Ok, got it. Don't tell me anymore until we're alone."

Alaric wanted to retort, 'we are alone' but if the bird was back, were they really alone? Alaric didn't know how much the bird could communicate with Morgana and he certainly didn't want to get on the wrong side of her. He had never given her due cause to be in her bad books. He had long since suspected she was infatuated with his father, but he didn't know if that meant she would extend kindness to him.

However, she had cursed Scarlett out of vengeance for him without even asking for payment. The fact that she lived with them and didn't have piles of gold showed that his father didn't pay her well for her services. He had always known his mother despised her. He had walked into many quarrels between his parents, where his mother begged for Morgana to be sent away, but his father wouldn't hear of it. He had continued his mother's weariness of her. He knew they weren't a couple, his father always took whores to his bed, but he had watched Morgana lust after him from the shadows for years and he blamed her infatuation for the reason she made no attempt to save his mother's life when she died.

The rest of the day passed in relative silence. Beth came over to offer food and she even showed kindness to Scarlett.

"Scarlett, I know it wasn't you. I'm trying to convince Billy to let you go. The curse seems to take hold at night, so if we tie you up at evening twilight, then you aren't a danger to anyone."

"Thank you, Beth. I'm so sorry." The sadness in her voice was evident in her apology.

As the evening meal was being served, Robin approached. He untied Scarlett and asked her to join them around the fire for supper. She glanced regretfully over her shoulder at Alaric, still tied to the tree.

Scarlett sat around the fire pit and watched everyone's eyes nervously glance at her every so often. Thom was noticeably absent and she wondered whether he was still sulking over her rejection. She watched as everyone interacted and she allowed herself to fade into the shadows. She turned to leave and caught Beth's eyes. She pointed to the bushes and mouthed, "Nature calls." Beth nodded and Scarlett held her breath as she escaped back to her tree house.

She grabbed her weapons and crept around in the shadows to Alaric. She placed her finger over his lips to gesture to be quiet. Then she hacked through the rope that bound him to the tree. Next, she cut the rope binding his ankles but she hesitated when he raised his wrists to her blade. She shook her head and signalled with her eyes for him to follow her into the thicket.

Alaric glanced back towards the fire to make sure no one was watching and then he followed Scarlett into the shelter of the trees. As he ran behind her, he couldn't decide whether to run off in the other direction or follow her. He continued to follow her and he couldn't explain why. He should be escaping or taking his revenge but he was too intrigued.

They passed a large oak that had cracked in half and he recognised where they were heading: the lake. It wasn't until they reached the water's edge that Scarlett turned to him, panting. "You get your wish. Kill me so I can't be a danger to anyone else."

Alaric cocked his head to the side wondering if he had misheard her. Then she continued, "The only way for me to break this curse is to die. I saved your life when that branch fell. A life for a life. Help me kill myself, but bring me back and I will kill the witch. It doesn't sound like you like her either."

Alaric stared at her blankly for a moment before he spoke. "That branch might not have killed me. May I remind you, the only reason I was in danger was because you've kept me prisoner, or have you forgotten that detail? I owe you nothing."

As a sign of faith with nothing to lose, Scarlett took out her blade and cut through the ropes binding his wrists. "I'm setting you free. You don't need to help me. But bring me back to life and I will help you get out of the forest and you'll be back in your own bed before morning. The forest is a scary place at night, any number of beasts could feast on you whilst you stagger about trying to make your way out."

Alaric mulled over her proposition. Killing her, he had no issue with and he didn't fancy wandering aimlessly through the forest trying to find his way home. Her offer was tempting, but how was he supposed to kill her and then bring her back?

"How do you envisage this going down?"

Scarlett looked out at the lake. The moonlight was glistening on the water's surface and a layer of fog was rising from it. Alaric cottoned on quickly.

"You want me to crown you?"

Scarlett nodded. "Then breathe air back into me," she instructed.

"You're putting a lot of faith into me. What if I want you to remain dead?"

"Then my family is still safe from me and I die a few days earlier than the curse will kill me anyway." Poking him in the chest, she added, "But more importantly for you. You will have to find your way out of the forest on your own. Many a person has died in Sherwood Forest. You know the stories."

Alaric stared at the woman before him. She was completely indignant about him debating whether to aid her in ending her own life. The fact that she was so ardent about such a topic raised a smile on his face. He lost nothing if he failed and if he managed to bring her back to life, he had a greater chance of being in his own bed by morning.

"You realise if this succeeds, I will still be your enemy again when the sun rises," he let his words linger ominously.

She nodded and Alaric was distracted when she bit her bottom lip. The coiled spring between the two was under tension again. They were talking about life and death, but his mind was drifting from enemies to lovers.

Scarlett reached for his wrist and she pulled him behind her towards the water. For a fleeting second, her hand slid into his palm. He wrapped his arms around her before she entered the water, holding her in place.

He leaned down and his lips touched her ear as he said, "If we go in the water fully clothed, we'll freeze when we get out."

He pulled her back slightly, then removed his grip and he started removing his boots. Scarlett watched him for a moment and a smile broke across her face. Alaric looked up as he stood tall to lift his shirt over his head.

"What are you smiling about?" He asked, confused by her expression.

"You said *we*. When *we* get out."

Alaric couldn't tear his eyes away from her smile, which even reached her eyes. They sparkled in the moonlight brighter than they had in the day. He continued getting undressed just so he wasn't staring wildly at her. His mind was racing. What a fucked up situation he was in. He was about to murder his enemy and yet his greatest wish in this moment was for her to survive.

CHAPTER 15

The Sheriff was taking a late supper in his room and Morgana was joining him, when a knock at the door had him intrigued. He shouted, "Enter," and one of the guards he had tasked with finding out what the villagers were hiding rushed inside. He was breathing heavily and held onto the wall. Morgana and the Sheriff eyed him with contempt as he tried to catch his breath.

"I don't have all night man, what's so urgent?" The Sheriff scolded.

"You were right," the guard started and then hiccupped.

"As I often am. Get on with it," he insisted, rolling his eyes in Morgana's direction.

The guard continued between hiccups, "The villagers on the outskirts of Sherwood Forest have been receiving money from the outlaws."

"What!?" Roared the Sheriff as he stood up. His tray of food clattered to the floor and he strode over to the guard, demanding answers. Morgana followed closely, hovering at his side. "Money?" He queried, "Why would thieves be giving away money?"

"It's not their money they give away," the guard insisted.

Dumbfounded, the Sheriff replied, "Then whose is it?"

The guard looked sheepish and his eyes darted back and forth from the witch to the Sheriff. He cleared his throat before responding, "Yours, my lord."

The Sheriff's expression turned to one of pure rage and

Morgana pointed a long finger at the guard. Threatening him, she declared, "If you're lying to us, I will feed your entrails to my bird and have you watch."

The Sheriff looked incensed as he picked up a chair and whacked it to the ground. Wood splintered as the chair smashed into firewood at the Sheriff's continued attack.

The fear in the guard's eyes made Morgana believe him and she dismissed him from the room. Face red with anger and too much ale, the Sheriff roared with rage.

"How dare they steal my money and then give it away!" Grabbing Morgana by the face and holding too tight, he spat, "I will make them pay, all of them will burn!"

Morgana stared him straight in the eyes without blinking until he came to his senses and released her from his grasp. "Calm yourself, this behaviour is unbefitting of a King. Vengeance will be ours."

The reference to 'ours' didn't go unnoticed by the Sheriff, nor did the veiled dig at his behaviour, but the look he had seen in her eyes when she stared into his soul, was enough to tell him he had overstepped the mark. She was a powerful ally and whilst he knew he was always destined for greatness, he knew the path had been smoother because of her. She had good ideas and her gifts of foresight were useful, although not of late, it would appear.

He allowed the rage in his heart to subside and drank the remains of his drink in one go. He paced by the fireplace, deep in thought. When he was feeling calmer, he turned to Morgana now sat back in an armchair. "When will I get my revenge?"

Morgana dipped her long fingernail into her drink and swirled the contents. She rose from her chair and hobbled towards the fire without her stick. She threw the contents of her drink into the fire and the flames roared. For a moment, the Sheriff watched as they turned jet black. Morgana grimaced at the reaction but soon the flames returned to amber, "It is already underway," she said ominously as she cackled in front of the flames.

The water was freezing cold as they both stood waist-deep in the water. Alaric couldn't help his gaze being drawn down to her perfectly pert breasts. He would have lost focus, if it wasn't so damn cold that his cock was buried deep inside his body.

Neither spoke.

The air was pregnant with anticipation.

Scarlett shivered as a wave of cold tingled up her back. Alaric's focus shifted to her face and she broke the silence.

"Ready?" She asked, seeking confirmation.

"How will I know when to pull you out?"

Scarlett shrugged, "I'll stop struggling, I suppose."

Alaric nodded, "Right, makes sense. Let's do this. I want to be back in my own, warm bed before dawn."

As Alaric stopped speaking, Scarlett let out a large and deliberate exhale and slowly lowered herself into the water. Alaric watched her intently as she slipped beneath the surface. He found her head with his hands and applied force, pushing her down.

A few seconds passed and he suddenly felt her hands grabbing at his. He could feel her trying to stand and push upwards.

He continued to apply pressure, to keep her under as she instructed. He had never killed anyone outside of battle before. He had always used a weapon. It was less personal. It was quicker.

At least he didn't have to watch, the water was too murky, the light from the moon too dim. Her force was strong against him. He continued applying pressure until suddenly there was no resistance.

He stopped applying pressure and brought his hands up. Her body didn't float to the surface like he expected and he froze. Then instinct kicked in and he dived into the water, finding her motionless body drifting. He pulled her up and threw her lifeless body over his shoulder. He waded through the water to the bank and laid her down. Her skin looked grey and sickly in the light. He didn't have a clue what to do next.

He rolled her onto her side and straddled her body. He used the flat of his palm to deliver strong blows to her back, using his other hand to keep her in position. Water sprayed out of her mouth, followed by coughing. Her body was heaving water whilst desperately gasping for air. She was shaking.

Alaric didn't realise he had been holding his breath until she rolled onto her back and her eyes bored into his. Her lungs were greedily taking in air and the colour was rushing to her cheeks.

He was suddenly very aware that they were both naked and he was straddling her. He still felt freezing cold and it wasn't his best look to be hovering over her this cold and naked. The damage was already done as he watched her eyes take in his entire physique.

He pushed off from the ground and rose, extending a hand to help her up. Her tongue protruded from her mouth and then her teeth sank into her lower lip. Her eyelids looked heavy and her gaze was intense, but she reached for his hand. He pulled her up and she seemed a little unsteady on her feet. He grabbed her around the waist to support her.

She tilted her head up and locked eyes with him. Her eyes said one thing, but her hands rose to his forearms and pushed him away. The moment was broken and Scarlett reached for her clothing.

"We better get dressed before we both die of a lingering chill."

Alaric grunted in response, as he bent down to retrieve his clothes.

As Scarlett sheathed her dagger, she hesitated. There was a strange mutual trust between the enemies now. At least until the sun rose, she didn't fear Alaric would hurt her. She had set him free, yet he hadn't run. He had helped her break the curse and he had brought her back to life when he could have let her stay dead.

She slung her quiver over her shoulder and carried her bow at her side. She glanced over at Alaric, who was just tucking in his shirt.

"Ready? Follow me."

Alaric nodded and Scarlett set off quickly through the hidden paths in the trees that only she knew. Alaric struggled to keep up, initially losing his footing on the tree roots that littered the dark forest floor. When the tree canopy thinned a little, more of the moonlight shone down and he started to pick up his pace. Now he was keeping up, he spoke quietly next to her.

"What was it like to die?"

Scarlett shrugged her shoulders.

"Is that it? I helped you to die, brought you back to life and you won't even share what it felt like."

"It didn't feel anything. I felt nothing until I started spewing my guts up and I was panicking as I tried to breathe."

Alaric watched as her focus seemed heightened and not on him. She slowed her pace and then reached for an arrow.

"What are you doing?" He asked, concern evident in his voice as she nocked the arrow.

In a barely audible whisper, she replied, "We're being hunted."

Alaric spun around, his gaze darting high and low, trying to see what danger he had evidently missed.

Scarlett was rigid beside him, her arm engaged ready to release the arrow at a moment's notice. He followed her gaze upwards and then he heard the faintest of flutters from a bird's wing. Then a flash of black in the canopy above as Scarlett released her arrow into the sky. A loud squawk followed and then a thud a few yards in front of them.

Together they raced over to see the bird. A large, black raven lay flat on its back with its wings spread and an arrow in its chest. It appeared to bleeding black blood.

Alaric looked amazed as he stared from the bird to Scarlett, but before he had a chance to speak, they both heard a rustling in the bushes behind them. Scarlett reached for another arrow and within seconds, had turned to face the danger.

Scarlett was dumbstruck at the animal in front of her. It was beautiful and majestic, with a small crown of feathers on its head and huge white feathers fanned out in a proud display from its rear. She had no idea what it was. It didn't look particularly vicious, but she couldn't be certain it wouldn't try to attack them. It was so white it looked like it could be ghost.

"Do you know what it is?" She whispered to Alaric.

"I think it's a peacock, but the only ones I've seen before have been blue and green."

Scarlett focused on the fanned display of feathers and recognised the pattern. The witch in Ledecestre had a feather just like it in her hair, but in green.

"Will it attack us?"

"I don't think so. It's like a fancy pheasant," Alaric responded. Looking at her bow and arrow, he added, "With your aim, I think you could take it."

Alaric turned his back on the majestic peacock and marched towards the raven. Scarlett's eyes lingered a little longer before retreating. Alaric was bent down, with his hand on the arrow protruding from the raven's chest.

"Leave it," Scarlett ordered and Alaric removed his hand.

Scarlett stabbed the arrow in deeper, spearing it all the way through the animal's chest. Then she picked the animal up using the arrow and jammed it into the nearest tree until the arrow tip was embedded in the bark.

With a stern look, Scarlett added, "I'm happy to sacrifice an arrow to make sure it remains dead. We both know things can come back to life."

A strange squawk filled the air and they both turned back around to see the peacock disappear into the bushes it came from, leaving behind a single beautiful white feather.

Scarlett felt an intrinsic need to pick it up, so she left Alaric's side and collected it. She speared it into her hair just as the travelling witch wore it and an idea crossed her mind.

The rest of the journey to the edge of the forest was done

in relative silence. She purposely took the long route with the least recognisable landmarks to ensure Alaric wouldn't be able to find his way back. After a few hours of weaving through the thick forest, the edge was in sight. When they reached the outskirts, Scarlett turned to Alaric and pointed. "Head that way and you'll eventually come to a road. Follow it and it will take you home."

Alaric nodded as he watched Scarlett turn in the opposite direction.

"Where are you going? I thought you wanted to kill the witch?"

Scarlett didn't even turn around, she just shouted her reply. "All in good time. The sun's nearly up and we'll be back to enemies, as it should be."

Alaric couldn't help but smirk, but keen to have the last word, he shouted back, "Until we meet again."

Quietly to himself, he added, "The greatest adversary to my happiness."

By the time Alaric reached the stone wall surrounding the castle, the sun was starting to rise. His feet ached and his belly groaned, begging to be fed. The guards at the gate were asleep. He used the last of his energy and pent-up frustration to kick them both in the stomach as she shouted, "Wake up you lazy arseholes."

The guards woke up furious and instantly reached for their weapons. As soon as they set eyes on the assailant, they lowered them. The shock was clearly visible on their faces, they looked like they had seen a ghost.

With an authoritative tone, Alaric threatened, "Act lively men, or you will have me to answer to."

Alaric strode past them and into the empty marketplace. An equally pathetic excuse for a guard was slumped against the side door that led to the guard's quarters. Alaric easily stole his dagger from his belt and, clutching the blade, he wacked the hilt into the side of the guard's head.

The guard's eyes shot open and his hands flew up to defend himself. Seeing it was Alaric, he started apologising profusely. Alaric pulled at the door handle and as he expected, it was unlocked. The force of the door opening caused the guard to fall on the floor and Alaric didn't even bother to glance at him. He strode through the halls, making his way to the quarters he shared with his father.

He spotted a young servant boy lurking in the halls and he pointed at him. "You," he ordered as he marched towards him, "Bring me bread, ham and cheese." The boy looked scared, like he had been caught doing something he shouldn't. "Do you hear me boy?" Alaric bellowed, "Do you know who I am?"

The boy nodded and started for the kitchen, when Alaric grabbed him by the scruff of the neck. Twisting the boy back to look at him, he ordered, "And don't forget the ale." He released the boy who then ran in the direction of the kitchen.

Two guards were outside his chamber, luckily for them, they were awake and alert. They nodded when they saw Alaric approaching, recognising him instantly. One guard opened the door for him and he stepped inside. He could hear his father's loud snores as he passed his room en route to his own.

As he entered the solace of his room, he lay on his bed and closed his eyes. He had dreamed of this moment for so long that it barely felt real. He drifted off into a deep sleep, filled with dreams he wouldn't remember when he woke.

The Sheriff broke his fast late due to the amount of alcohol he drank the night before. In truth, it was nearing midday. Someone had left bread, ham, and cheese in his quarters. He sat by the empty fireplace eating the meal to soak up the alcohol. He heard the lock of a door open and he glanced at the main door, but it was closed. He jumped up and looked behind him as Alaric swaggered out of his room like he hadn't been missing.

The shock on the Sheriff's face must have been evident

as Alaric felt the need to confirm who he was. "It's me, Father. Alaric. Did you miss me?" The cheeky glint in his eye was back.

The Sheriff composed himself and barked, "What the devil are you doing back here?"

"Am I not welcome?" Alaric responded as he swept past the Sheriff and tore a chunk of bread from the loaf. He sat back in the armchair opposite the one his father used and relaxed into it with his leg cocked over the arm.

The Sheriff sat back down and asked, "How did you escape?"

"I didn't," Alaric said between mouthfuls of food. He reached for the block of cheese and bit a large chunk from the corner. As he swallowed, he confirmed, "They let me go. They're not that bad when you get to know them."

The Sheriff's anger was rising, which was evident from the dark shade of red that his face was swiftly turning, "Not that bad!" He bellowed.

Alaric stopped chewing and placed the cheese back down. "Ok, I mean they are bad for kidnapping me and stealing your gold, but hear me out, they've got a point. Some things could do with changing."

The Sheriff couldn't believe what he was hearing from his only son. He figured they had brainwashed him, or somehow replaced him. He stood up and lingered over Alaric before slapping him around the face. "Don't talk to me about change. We do not take advice from bandits, we squish them like a nest of ants."

CHAPTER 16

With the image of the white peacock in her mind, Scarlett knew where she needed to go. She set off running as fast as she could through the forest to Ledecestre, hoping that the witch was still there.

By late morning she had made it to the outskirts of the town. She had set off at full speed but it had taken her longer than she had hoped. She hunted two pheasants and bartered them at the local market for some bread and cheese. She enquired about the oddities and was thankful to hear they were still in town.

She recognised the witch's wagon and marched up to it confidently. She knocked on the door and waited. She thought she heard movement inside but no one came to the door. Adamant that she had not travelled all this way for nothing, she wrapped her knuckles on the door again and waited.

This time, she definitely heard movement and moments later, the top half of the door cracked open a sliver. The witch's face appeared in the gap. Her hair was wild and her lips swollen. Scarlett could see the bare flesh of her shoulders and she clutched a fabric blanket around herself.

Scarlett should have been embarrassed, but after her recent brush with naturism and her focus on her mission, the emotion didn't register.

The witch recognised her instantly and smirked. "You're aura is different. You broke the curse, but why do you seek me out again?"

"I need your help," Scarlett paused, assessing the witch's interest, "How do I kill the witch who cursed me?"

"You can't kill a witch that powerful, she will see you coming." The witch went to close the door, but Scarlett raced forward and pushed back with her forearm.

"She was watching me through a black raven but I shot it out of the sky."

The witch's left eyebrow rose as if impressed. She stopped trying to close the door and instead gazed upon Scarlett.

Scarlett felt like the witch was searching through her soul as she stared at her without speaking. Finally, she said, "The devil can kill a witch, but are you willing to pay the price?"

Scarlett gulped and the witch continued, "A life for a life. The devil only trades in souls."

Scarlett shook her head, "I'm not trading my soul. I feel like I only just got my life back. I'll just have to do it the old-fashioned way, without any magical help."

The witch nodded, "A knife to the heart, strong and true."

Scarlett turned to leave, exasperated with the conversation and the time she had wasted. She hoped she still had the element of surprise and Alaric had not revealed her intentions.

The witch shouted, "Wait," and Scarlett froze. She glanced over her shoulder and the witch plucked the peacock feather from her hair. Then she disappeared into the wagon and returned momentarily with a slim vial. Scarlett turned around fully, intrigued.

"This potion is powerful," remarked the witch, "It will induce a hallucination moments after being drunk. It will buy you an opportunity, but in return I want the witch's tarot cards."

Scarlett couldn't help but smile. She reached for the vial as she agreed, "Deal." As the words escaped her mouth, a feeling of dread writhed in her gut. Had she just made a deal with the devil? She shook the thought from her mind and headed back towards Nottingham.

The Sheriff wasted no time in summoning Morgana to his quarters. As Alaric heard the tapping of her cane on the flagstone steps, he steeled himself for the fortress he would need to put up to protect his thoughts. He was worried in case they gave away his involvement in plotting against her and the death of her raven.

Morgana's eyes grew wide when she saw him. Not one to miss an opportunity to inflate her own predictions, she slyly remarked, "Did I not tell you all was in hand, the boy has returned."

The Sheriff rolled his eyes, but not so Morgana could see. "Morgana, I want you to check him over. He's returned speaking nonsense."

Alaric had unfortunately just taken a swig of ale and sprayed it all over himself at his father's words. "Whoa," Alaric said standing and raising his hands, "I'm perfectly fine. I do not need to be examined."

"What do you expect boy, when you return after you have allowed them to hold you prisoner, spouting nonsense. Next, you will be telling me we need to lower taxes. Do you think I can give my protection to the people for free?"

This was the first time he had ever questioned his father on policy, but Scarlett had opened his eyes further than he had cared to admit. A fire had been lit inside of him, to do the best for ordinary hard-working people, and it burned bright in their defence.

"But what are we protecting them from? As far as I can see, we are adding to the misfortune they are suffering. Have you seen how the working man lives?"

The Sheriff gesticulated to Morgana. "See, this is how he has returned." Turning back to Alaric with anger in his eyes, he continued, "Infrastructure costs money and I am building a better future, this is what outlaws cannot comprehend, the bigger picture."

Alaric had no comeback to that. He too couldn't fathom the bigger picture when his father had not chosen to share it. Morgana started to approach him and he tried to act natural as he stepped back, keeping the distance between them. He needed a reason to leave without being scrutinised. Thinking on his feet, he replied, "Father, you are correct. The bigger picture I cannot see, which is why you are the Sheriff and I am head of the guards. I will go back to doing my duty. Excuse me." He nodded to them both and marched quickly to the door.

Morgana was still eyeing him up and before he could turn the handle, she asked, "Boy, could you show the guards where to find the outlaws?"

Alaric found the distance across the room made him feel more confident to lie. Whilst he didn't know the exact way, if he could get to the lake, he was confident from there. Knowing what his father's intentions would entail, he felt a need to protect the group. They were mostly harmless, definitely only violent when provoked. As harsh as they had been to him, they had taken care of him, sharing what little food they had. They lived a simple, basic life and he didn't feel they should die for the idealistic values they had.

"No," he lied, "They kept me blindfolded." He hadn't dared to make eye contact with Morgana and he didn't wait for her to ask him further questions. He opened the door and stalked through it.

Morgana mused over the exchange and Alaric's behaviour. She knew he was lying but the intriguing point was why. She stayed around to discuss plans with the Sheriff. The afternoon passed into nightfall, but Alaric remained away.

Just as Morgana was intending to retire to her bed, a guard walked in unannounced. He addressed the Sheriff, who stared at him blankly, not recognising him. "Sire, you asked me to follow the young lad that the child ran to."

It suddenly dawned on the Sheriff who this guard was and the mission he had set him. The Sheriff nodded, making casual hand gestures for him to continue.

"I followed him. I found the outlaw's settlement. It's deep in the forest."

The Sheriff's eyes lit up, greedy for revenge. With excitement evident in his voice, the Sheriff asked, "Could you find your way back again?"

Eager to please, the guard replied, "Aye, I left marks on tree barks to find my way back."

Morgana placed her cold, ageing hand over the Sheriff's and he jerked back at her touch. Ignoring his reaction, she continued, "See my lord. Everything is falling into place as I said it would."

Scarlett was shattered when she finally made it back to the outskirts of Nottingham. It was late and she had been travelling all day with no sleep. On the journey, she had caught two rabbits. She made quick work of skinning them and made a small fire to roast them on. Once her hunger was sated, she climbed a large tree and found a safe branch to rest for the night.

She woke to the sound of a bird cry and her eyes flew open, thinking it was the raven back from the dead. She scanned the branches of the tree and found the culprit. It wasn't a raven and relief washed over her, enabling her to take a deep breath.

Scarlett climbed down from the tree and set about putting phase one of her plan into action. She nocked an arrow on her bow and started her hunt. After a few successful hours of hunting, she had a healthy catch to trade.

With the hood of her travelling cape up, she managed to hide behind a wagon and enter the walls surrounding Nottingham Castle. She continued to the rear entrance of the largest brothel in town and knocked loudly. The madam who ran the establishment answered and recognised Scarlett from their recent dealings. Her hair was loose, curls fell around her face and onto her chest provocatively. She raised her eyebrows but stood back and gestured for Scarlett to enter.

"Back again? Have you decided your talents could be

better spent working for me, than living with a group of unwashed outlaws?"

"Not exactly. I've come to make a trade," Scarlett lifted the catch-up to signal what she intended to offer.

"Go on," instructed the madam, intrigued, whilst subconsciously licking her lips.

"I need to impersonate one of your ladies and for that, I need to borrow a dress."

The Madam's eyes showed wariness, but the greed prevailed. Meat was expensive and she had a lot of ladies working for her that needed to be fed, but she couldn't afford to cause any contention. She asked, "What will you do when you impersonate one of my ladies?"

Scarlett knew that she held a strong hand, meat was a difficult thing to refuse, so she stood her ground. "That's my business, but know nothing will be linked back to you."

After a moment of contemplation, with the madam scrutinising Scarlett's face, she nodded and confirmed, "Deal. Follow me."

Scarlett handed over the catch and the madam led her through the establishment, past several ladies waiting for clients.

"Has anyone seen Matilda?" The madam asked. Several ladies pointed in the direction they were heading. They came across a young girl who looked up when she heard the name and Scarlett assumed they had found the woman they were looking for.

Scarlett watched her as she sat on the floor chopping vegetables. She was throwing them into a large stewing pot. "Ah, there you are. I'm giving you a night off and promoting you to head chef. You like cooking, do you know what to do with these?" The madam handed over the rabbits and pheasants Scarlett had traded. The young girl's eyes lit up and her smile reached from ear to ear. She nodded vigorously in confirmation.

"Then swap clothes with," she paused, realising she didn't know her name, "Our patron here. She is in need of your dress and you look the same size." Even though they'd had dealings before, Scarlett had been careful not to share too much and was not on a first name basis.

The young girl stood immediately and started to undress. Scarlett paused and looked around the room they were in. It was just them and this seemed like a room men didn't visit. Scarlett followed suit and they swapped outfits.

Scarlett adjusted her bosom in the dress, ensuring that her cleavage was amply displayed. This outfit showed far more of her body off than the beautiful dress she had borrowed from Beth. There was split in the skirt that went all the way up to her waist. The cut around her breasts was low and Scarlett felt exposed and rather cold. It was unsettling to have so much of her shoulders and chest on show, exposed to the air.

The madam stood back and looked her up and down. "Unbraid your hair, wear it half up and half down, and then you will pass for one of my ladies."

Scarlett did as instructed and before she knew it she was walking towards the guarded side entrance. She kept looking ahead, trying to conceal her nerves. Bile was rising in her throat from the memory of being taken prisoner and the pain she had endured in the dungeons. If she came across the guard who whipped her, would she really be able to contain her anger and would he really not recognise her? She looked up as she approached the guards and felt a wash of relief as she didn't recognise either of them.

She gave the same handkerchief signal as before and a guard opened the door. One of them followed her inside. "So, who's the lucky guy?" He asked whilst ogling her body.

With more confidence than she felt, Scarlett replied clearly, "The Sheriff's son, Alaric."

The guard smirked and instructed, "Follow me." As she followed the guard to Alaric's chambers, she congratulated herself on a well-thought-out plan. So far, so good. The shawl she had borrowed from the mistress hid the colour of her hair and the outfit she had on left no assumptions as to her profession. Therefore, all eyes were on her womanly assets and not her face, exactly as planned.

The guard stopped in front of two guards manning a heavy wooden door and nodded toward her. He grunted, "Alaric ordered company."

Scarlett tried to keep her gaze low, but she looked up through her lashes and saw the two guards look at each other. Then one replied, "He isn't here."

"Well, what does that matter? Show her to his bed and then she will be there waiting when he returns. The man's been deprived for too long, stuck in that forest. Do you want to tell him you sent his afternoon of fun away?"

Scarlett heard the door creak open and another guard stated, "Follow me."

Scarlett was led into a large room with three doors off it. The guard showed her to the furthest one and let her inside what was obviously Alaric's bed chamber. He remained outside and as he went to grab the handle he stated, "Wait here, he won't be long." As he pulled the door closed, Scarlett saw him freeze as if he was contemplating saying something else. Then he looked her up and down and licked his lips. "If you're interested in earning a little extra after, come find me."

Scarlett fought hard to keep the disdain from her face and all she could do was nod in response. The door closed and she was left alone.

She stood in the centre of the room and took in her surroundings. It was sparse. There were few personal effects. Tapestries' hung on the wall but she knew that they weren't Alaric's style.

She took a step closer to the four-poster bed and placed her hand on the fabric that adorned the frame. It reminded her of her bed as a child, an indulgence she hadn't even realised was a luxury at the time. The deep red fabric felt soft and expensive beneath her fingertips.

Scarlett allowed her mind to drift to spending a night in

this luxurious bed. The urge to lie down was too strong and she climbed onto the bed. She lay down on her back with her eyes closed. She was in a state of flux, where she could easily fall asleep for the next ten hours, but her mind was conscious enough to force her to snap out of it. Her mission was too important for her physical needs to get in the way.

Scarlett forced herself to open her eyes and as she did, she saw the personal touch that had been missing. She scrambled to her feet and stared at the embroidery hanging from the top of the canopy. She ran her fingers over the rough stitching holding it in place. This was definitely not done by the artist, whose stitching was exquisite.

She ran her fingers across the embroidery. Scarlett would know these flowers anywhere. The scene portrayed the fields of poppies that grew on her father's lands. Alaric's mother must have done this embroidery for him. The touch of personalisation made Scarlett suddenly very aware she was alone in Alaric's bed chamber. This was where he slept, where he must have slept yesterday when he got home.

Images of him flashed through her mind. An image of him naked from the waist up, was replaced by him smirking at her as she exited the lake. Her mind transported her back as if her brain was tricking her. She could feel the way he wrapped his arms around her to stop her from entering the water fully clothed.

Then she reflected on the way his body felt pressed against hers when he pinned her in place. She could feel every taught muscle and his hardened cock pressing into her back, as if it was happening right now. Her mouth dropped open and she allowed herself to revel in the ecstasy of her mind replaying the most erotic moment of her life.

She had cut him off and made snarky remarks at the time, but they were only to hide her true feelings. They were sworn enemies and had nothing in common, but she missed the verbal sparring that came so easily. It took the sound of a door opening in the distance to snap her out of her fantasy and back to reality. She withdrew her dagger from her boot and marched towards the door.

Scarlett pressed her ear against it but heard nothing. She tentatively turned the handle and came face to face with Alaric.

Alaric spat the bite of his apple out that he had just bitten off. "What the hell are you doing here?" He proclaimed bluntly.

Scarlett exhaled and nonchalantly remarked, "Forget you saw me."

"I can't forget!" He insisted adamantly as he blocked the doorway, pushing her further into the room.

"Then help me," she asked.

"No chance. Are you here for the witch?"

Ignoring his question, Scarlett insisted, "Then get out of my way." She took a step closer to see how he would respond.

He watched her intensely, his eyes darkening. "I told you if we met again, we would be enemies."

Scarlett gulped and raised her dagger, poised for an attack as she replied, "So you did."

He smirked in response and Scarlett had to admonish herself for the indecent thoughts she had been having moments before.

"You think that would stop me?" He laughed as he took a large step forward. He was close now, close enough to touch. The heat from his body and the feeling of his imposing presence in her personal space were alarming. Her core started to spark with feelings she couldn't describe. She licked her lips in anticipation of his next move. He was threatening violence, but his actions weren't menacing.

She spotted the open door out of the corner of her eye. She knew she needed to take control before this heady feeling took over her mind and body. She refocused and thought quickly about how to get back on track to the task at hand. She thought about any similar situations she had found herself cornered with a man and how best to subdue them without weaponry. She recalled an event that gave her an idea and she closed the remaining gap between them.

Alaric touched her face and tilted her head upwards. His

gaze was pure desire. She could have lost herself in the darkness of his eyes for hours, but she had a job to do. The people she loved were counting on her. She allowed him to touch her. She felt his body lower to meet hers and then she swiftly kneed him in the groin and fled the room, taking the key with her.

She locked him inside and then began her search for the hidden staircase he had told her about, that led to Morgana's quarters.

CHAPTER 17

Scarlett looked around the room for any sign of a hidden door. The walls were adorned with paintings and tapestries, in stark contrast to the sparseness of Alaric's room.

She noticed a heavy curtain in the corner that appeared to cover a window. She scurried across the room and disappeared behind the curtain. There was a concealed corridor and she followed it. It led to a dark spiral staircase and she stealthily descended the steps, straining her ears for any sound to indicate that she wasn't alone.

Her heart was pounding faster with every step. Her dagger was raised, ready to be used. At the bottom of the stairs was a similar plush curtain strung across the path. She held her breath and listened tentatively. She heard nothing, so she dared to peek behind the curtain for a look. She scanned the room, but saw no one.

Scarlett took a deep breath and stepped out from behind the safety of the curtain. On a large table that looked like a church altar, she saw a jug. She peered inside it. It was half full and she swilled the liquid inside, trying to decipher if it was water. It was hard to tell and Scarlett decided to dip her finger in. She licked the droplet off her finger and was filled with relief when she tasted water.

Scarlet retrieved the potion vial and poured the deep purple liquid into the jug. She swilled the jug around to try and dissolve it. She wished she had asked if the concoction had a strong taste and whether it should only be mixed with something pungent like wine. She surveyed the rest of the table and saw a stack of cards like the travelling witch had. She pocketed them just as she heard the creak of a door opening nearby.

Panic set in and her eyes darted back to the hidden staircase. She wouldn't have time to get back there to hide, so she ducked down and crept behind the altar. The top of the table was large, with a central plinth and a fabric cloth that draped on the floor. Carefully so as not to draw attention or make a sound, Scarlett slipped underneath the cloth.

Scarlett tried to calm herself and slow her heart rate, fearing the heavy breathing would give her away. She could hear odd footsteps and possibly a cane hitting the flagstones. The footsteps neared, until they stopped.

Scarlett heard a gruff voice cough several times and then she heard the clunk of what she believed was the water jug on a cup. She held her breath and strained to listen to what was happening. She heard the sound of water being poured. It was followed by silence and then a loud belch as something landed back on the tabletop.

Scarlett took a breath and poised herself ready to attack. She waited, but there was silence.

Alaric crumpled to the floor in agony from the pain in his manhood. Anger pulsed through his veins. Scarlett was just a tease and that's all she would ever be. She had been in his bedroom and dressed like a harlot. The only explanation was that she had used him to get to the witch. He chastised himself for being so foolish to think that she had been there for him. All he had ever shown her was kindness and his anger twisted into self-deprivation at how foolish he was to think she felt anything for him.

The pain in his groin subsided and he dragged himself up from the floor to standing. He tried the door handle, knowing that she had likely taken the key. It wouldn't budge. He banged his fists on the door and hollered, but no one came.

He had had the same room since infancy and his father had locked him in many times to teach him a lesson. He looked to the window and wondered if he would still fit through it. If he could, he would be able to climb down and re-enter the castle. He pushed his desk over to the window and climbed on top of it.

The window was narrow, but there was a good chance he would still fit. He stuck one leg through and straddled the ledge. Then he ducked his head to ensure he cleared the arch. Vines grew up the side of the castle and he gave them a tug to ensure that they would hold his weight. He wasn't certain they would and he glanced down. The drop was substantial and he didn't fancy becoming a cripple.

He gave the vines a strong pull and they held, so he made an impulsive decision to just go for it. He launched himself out of the window and onto the vines. His footing slipped but the vines held. Using his upper body strength, he started to climb down the castle walls when he remembered his father's window.

He glanced upwards and saw the same vines trailing past the opening. The window was the same size and shape as his, so he took a gamble he would fit through. He reached upwards and heaved himself across to the nearby opening.

If anyone was watching from the ground they would think him a madman, or an intruder and shoot him. He hoped no one was that observant.

Alaric breathed a sigh of relief when his feet landed on solid flooring again. He wiped the sweat from his brow, before marching across his father's bed chamber towards the living area. Scarlett was nowhere to be seen. He guessed she must have found the concealed entrance to the staircase. He quickly descended the stairs, not caring if he made his presence known.

Scarlett felt a slap on the tabletop above her and a cup smashed onto the ground. A cane rattled on the floor as the witch lost her grip on it. Scarlett darted out from under the table;

it was now or never.

The moment she came face to face with the witch, her lungs felt like they were void of oxygen. She froze for a split second and she watched the realisation cross the witch's face. The witch let out an eardrum-piercing scream and flung her hands to her head, as if her own wails were hurting her brain. Scarlett watched Morgana stumble and then fall backwards. The witch raised her hands again in self-defence.

Panicked and lost in her own hallucinations, Morgana shouted, "You wouldn't eat a weak old woman in her own bed chamber. Please, why did the Devil send you? I have done all his bidding. I can get you virgins to feast upon. Name your preference, boy or girl."

Scarlett heard faint footsteps to her right and she tore her focus away from the witch to see who was approaching. Alaric's face appeared from behind the curtain. He had clearly been running, sweat was pouring from him and he was breathing heavily.

Alaric shifted his gaze to Morgana and Scarlett thought she could see a mixture of disgust and shock weave across his face. Scarlett interpreted Alaric's lack of action to mean he would not stand in her way. She had no idea how long the effects of the potion would last, so she stepped forward towards the witch with her dagger raised.

Morgana was wailing on the floor, shouting over and over, "No, not me! Don't take me, I'm too young to die, I'm only a child."

Her words disturbed Scarlett and she had a moment of hesitation as she stood over the witch. Her irises had turned purple and she looked truly horrifying.

Suddenly, Morgana grabbed Scarlett's leg and pulled her over with a force Scarlett didn't realise an old woman would possess. In an instant, the witch had climbed on top of her and grabbed a fistful of Scarlett's hair. She was pulling so hard that Scarlett thought she would go bald and the pain was blinding. Morgana's other hand applied pressure to Scarlett's neck, pushing the full force of her weight down.

Scarlett was gasping for air and dizziness was taking over. She had dropped her dagger as she fell backwards and she waved her arm about trying to feel for it. Her other hand was wrapped around Morgana's wrist, trying to remove the pressure on her throat. Scarlett's vision was blurring and it felt like her actions were in slow motion, when suddenly the pressure was gone.

Scarlett sucked air in her lungs greedily and blinked profusely to see what had happened. Alaric's form came into her vision and she pushed up from the ground to see that Alaric was holding the wailing witch in a headlock as she thrashed about.

"Do it now!" Ordered Alaric. Scarlett looked around for her dagger. She scooted back on the floor not having the strength to stand yet and reached for it. Scarlett crawled forward and then sat back on her ankles with the dagger poised for the attack. She took a deep breath, the words of the travelling witch ringing through her ears, 'A knife to the heart, strong and true'.

Her eyes connected with Morgana's and she saw them change colour, as if the potion was working its way out of her system. Scarlett lunged forward and pierced the witch's heart with her dagger. Morgana went limp in Alaric's gasp, but he held her upright and Scarlett forced the dagger in further. A blood-curdling scream filled the room and a black ghostly force billowed out of Morgana's mouth.

Alaric dropped the witch to the ground in shock and Scarlett stumbled backwards, trying to get as far from the evil force as possible. Alaric drew his sword even though the idea of defending himself against a ghost was illogical.

The ghostly force hovered in mid-air for a second and then drifted towards the end of the room with the arrowslit windows. It disappeared through the gap and Alaric snapped into action. He stepped over Morgana's dead body and extended his hand to Scarlett.

Scarlett was panting, adrenaline coursing through her body. She couldn't put into words what she had just witnessed. She stared up at Alaric, who was offering his hand.

She couldn't understand how he was so calm and why he had helped her. Without him, the witch would surely have killed her. She owed him her life and more than that, she owed him Robin and Susanna's lives too. He wasn't completely altruistic, or blameless. He had been the one to curse her, but he'd had every opportunity to let the curse play out and he prevented the worst from happening every time. He even helped her be rid of the curse when he could have left her for dead, and now this. She was indebted to him for life.

She took his hand and rose from the ground. Words failed her as she stared into his eyes, searching for the reason behind his kindness. Thinking she was in shock, Alaric grabbed both her upper arms and shook her.

"You need to get out of here before you're discovered. Follow me." Alaric picked up her shawl that had been discarded during the struggle. He carefully placed it over her head and wrapped it around her neck. Then he slipped his hand in hers and led her from the room.

The passageway to Morgana's chamber was dark and dank, and thankfully vacant. Alaric took charge and Scarlett stealthily climbed the stairs behind him. Alaric checked that the coast was clear and headed for the door to the walled garden. He lifted the drawbar and they made their escape into the garden. Alaric confidently marched to the other side. He wasn't used to Scarlett being so quiet or obedient, but right now it worked to his advantage. He needed to get Scarlett clear of the castle and then back upstairs to stage his alibi. He knew his father wasn't going to take this well.

This garden had been his mother's favourite refuge and she had allowed the cook to grow herbs in it because they smelled so wonderful. The cook often left the door unlocked so the maids could fetch the herbs and he was hoping it was open now. He tested the door handle and it moved. He peered through the gap and saw the corridor was clear.

He led Scarlett through several passageways that went deep into the servants' quarters. He knew it would be hard to explain why he was there if he was caught, but then he didn't have to answer to a servant. His rank in the guards alone justified his access to anywhere without the fact that he was the Sheriff's son, but he would rather not be recognised. Just when he thought they would escape without being seen, he heard footsteps.

He turned to Scarlett as an idea formed in his mind. In earnest, he asked, "Do you trust me?"

Scarlett replied instantaneously with a quizzical, "Yes."

"Then follow my lead," he instructed as he pushed her against the wall. He grabbed her thigh through the slit in her dress and held it to his side, positioning himself between her legs. The material of her skirt fell away, exposing her flesh. He leaned in close so that their faces were touching and she could feel his breath on her lips. Her body tingled all over from the pressure of his body touching hers. He raised his free hand and covered half her face with his large palm. He grabbed tightly at her thigh and started rocking into her gently.

Scarlett was embarrassed by the feeling his touch was having on her body. She was growing wet and the thought of her soaking through his breeches was mortifying.

The footsteps stopped abruptly. Scarlett heard a grunt, followed by an elderly man's voice disapproving mumble as he walked past them. "You shouldn't be doing that in here," then more to himself than to them, he grumbled, "In the middle of the day, oh to be young again."

Once Alaric was certain the old man had passed, he stopped gyrating against her, but continued to hold her in position. She was staring up at him through her lashes with her big brown eyes and his breath caught. He almost dipped his head to make contact with her lips for real. Then his brain kicked in. She had already spurned him once today. His cock and balls were likely to be black and blue, even though he was acutely aware that his traitorous cock had grown hard due to the proximity of her body. He released his hold on her thigh and forced himself to look away from her bewitching eyes.

He took her hand firmly and rounded the corner. They made it through several more servant passageways without being caught and came to a servant's entrance. He lifted the drawbar and as he opened the door, he smirked as he mockingly stated, "Freedom awaits my lady."

Alaric wasn't sure if it was his smirk or the jest at calling her 'my lady' but it had the desired effect. Scarlett scowled at him and their comfortable repartee was back. "Do you think you can find your way back to the forest from here?" He gibed.

Scarlett shook her head and replied, "Do you take anything seriously?"

"I seem to be serious about saving your life. How many times is that now, three or four, I'm losing count. Try not to die whilst I'm clearing up this mess."

Scarlett couldn't scowl at him for that. Something changed at that moment as realisation hit her square in the face. He had helped her in every twisted act of fate and he had never asked for anything in return. Before she stepped through the door, she leaned up and kissed him softly on the cheek. Stepping back, she humbly said, "Thank you." Then she disappeared through the doorway.

Her gestured had surprised him. His mind briefly questioned what the kiss had meant, but then he shook the thought from his mind. He had more important things to do right now.

He hurried back through the corridors the way they had come. When he reached the door he left the drawbar off so it would serve as the escape route for the phantom murderer. He stealthily crept down to Morgana's chambers, listening out for anyone who may have found the body.

He took a deep breath and entered the room. Everything was as they had left it, including Morgana's body. He debated removing the blade, but then he remembered Scarlett's words about the raven. The black ghostly figure was spooky enough, that he hoped he never witnessed magic again. He walked past the body and quietly made his way up the staircase.

He hovered at the top of the stairs to make sure he was alone and then he locked himself in his room. Alone with his thoughts, his mind wandered to Scarlett. The moment they had shared felt like something had changed between them. Enemies didn't kiss like that.

By dinner time, he was dressed and ready to put on a merry performance of someone who had been sowing his wild oats all afternoon. He timed his exit just when the guards changed shifts, so no one would question when his guest had departed. As he marched towards the banquet hall to have dinner with his father, Aengus stopped him at the door and jeered, "I've been hearing about you enjoying yourself, lounging around in bed all bloody day. Are you a lord now and not a soldier?"

Alaric loudly burst into laughter, grateful for the opportunity to elaborate his alibi. "What can I say, I'm making up for lost time." He patted his friend on the shoulder in a private thank you and entered the hall. He had no doubt his father heard the exchange, given the expression he was displaying.

"What have you been doing all day?" He asked as he ordered a servant to refill his glass.

"Did you not hear?" Alaric purposefully exaggerated, "I treated myself to a whore and spent a glorious day in bed."

His father scoffed, "You're young and you were a good-looking boy before that scar, why pay for it when you could get it for free? Your cock clearly works if you could go at it all day."

Alaric shrugged off the comment, not knowing if it was more of an insult than a compliment. He nodded to the server to fill up his glass and then sat back in his chair, acting the part of a man without a care in the world.

He was clearly doing a good job of playing his part as his father looked at him as if he was assessing him. "You need a wife boy, you're old enough."

Alaric coughed and sprayed out the contents of his mouth.

"Why are you so surprised? Did you think you could be single forever?"

Alaric wiped the spray from his face and replied, "I hadn't given it much thought, to be honest. I'm surprised you never arranged a betrothal for me."

The Sheriff laughed and took another long slurp of his wine. "Of course I did. It's laughable now. She's definitely not suitable anymore, unless you want a common whore for your wife and to sleep with one eye open."

Alaric stared at his father, completely bewildered. "What do you mean? Who am I betrothed to?"

The Sheriff chortled and pointed to Alaric's face. "To the bitch who gave you that scar. It was your mother's wish. As soon as Lady Loxley had a girl. Those women were thick as thieves plotting your betrothal."

Alaric sat back in his chair shell-shocked. It had been his mother's wish for him to marry the woman he couldn't get out of his head. He wondered if this was his mother's doing from heaven, ensuring her plan came to fruition. His thoughts were interrupted when the Sheriff banged his fist on the large wooden table and demanded to know where the food was.

Nervously, a young servant girl stepped forward saying, "Cook was waiting for me to say everyone had arrived. You said Lady Morgana was joining you."

"Ah yes," grumbled the Sheriff, "Well, send someone to fetch her and tell the cook I do not wish to wait any longer." Then he turned to Alaric and complained, "I seem to spend my entire life waiting around for people."

Alaric nodded and kept up his smile even though he was dreading what was about to happen. He swallowed his doubts, ready to put on the performance of a lifetime.

He tried not to watch the doorway but as time ticked by, he couldn't help glancing. When the food arrived, it served as a welcome distraction and he loaded his plate up. Just as he was tucking into a forkful of lamb, Aengus appeared in the room looking nervous.

The Sheriff hadn't noticed him, so Alaric addressed him. "Aengus, did you want to join us?"

The invitation caught the Sheriff's attention and he started to choke on his food. He gave Alaric a stern look, as if to silently convey he was not to invite people to dine with them. Then he addressed Aengus curtly, "What do you want?"

Aengus looked like he wanted the ground to swallow him whole as he replied, "Sire, I have grave news to impart."

The Sheriff put down his fork and looked up, paying more attention. Whilst still chewing his food, he ordered, "Go on then, I don't have all evening."

"It is Lady Morgana. She's dead."

It took a second for the realisation to hit the Sheriff and Alaric tried to feign a shocked expression.

The Sheriff snapped, "Natural or foul play?"

Beads of sweat were forming on Aengus' forehead as he replied, "It would appear she was murdered."

Alaric focused his attention on his father, waiting for his reaction. The Sheriff slammed his fists on the table and stood up. "Take me to her," he ordered sternly.

CHAPTER 18

Scarlett kept her eyes forward and her feet moving as she strolled through the market. She saw a group of guards walking her way and she diverted to the baker's stall. She began perusing the loaves. The guards passed by her without a second glance.

She set off again on her walk to the whore house. The madam greeted her with a nod and she entered the establishment. For all intents and purposes, she was just a returning whore, but Scarlett knew it would not look like that when she left in her own clothes. The town was busy now, being midday. She needed to think of a way to escape without being detected. If Morgana's body had been discovered already, the guards would be on high alert.

Scarlett made her way through the corridors to the kitchen setup and found the maid with whom she had swapped clothes. She looked up when Scarlett entered the room; her disappointment was clear.

"You're back already. I thought I might be spared a day's work," she grumbled.

"Sorry," Scarlett offered before asking, "How so?"

The girl stood and looked down at her attire and then back at Scarlett. "Well, no punters going to want me in these clothes, they're boys."

Scarlett stared at her blankly and embarrassed, she apologised again.

They exchanged clothes in silence, but just as Scarlett was about to leave, Matilda tentatively stuttered, "Wait." Scarlett turned and she continued, "Where you live, do they pass you around?"

Scarlett frowned, not fully understanding the question. "What do you mean?"

Matilda's cheeks flushed as she reiterated her question, "Do they force you to do things with them, to please them?"

Scarlett caught on and quickly responded, "No, no one forces me to do anything. They're good, honest men, usually too merry and a little lazy, but good Christian men."

"Can I come with you?" She asked eagerly, her eyes darting warily around to ensure that she wasn't overheard.

Scarlett saw the hope in the young girl's eyes and didn't know how to respond. It was a harsh life living as an outlaw, but then she supposed it was no picnic living here either.

"Won't you be missed?"

"I will, but I'm my own person. Why shouldn't I live the life I want to live?"

Matilda's eyes had more than a twinkle of hope in them now and Scarlett didn't have the heart to extinguish that light. "If you want to follow me, I can't stop you. You're your own person like you just said, but don't expect me to make exceptions for you. I have business in Ledecestre to attend to before going to camp. It's a long walk."

The girl's face beamed, "I like walking. I won't be any trouble. I'm a good cook."

"Ok then, grab your belongings. I need to find a way out of Nottingham town without being seen."

Matilda shrugged her shoulders, "I haven't got anything worth carrying all the way to Ledecestre and I can help you get out unseen."

"What's your idea?"

Matilda pointed to the door opposite, where some loud grunts were echoing through the hallway. "Dave the rag and bone man is in there. He comes in here every week like clockwork. He has a wagon. He'll be finished in a minute. He doesn't last long."

"Will he take us?"

"He will if I ask him nicely. I might have to give him a freebie, but if that's the last man I have to pleasure to escape, I'll happily service him."

Just as Matilda had predicted, the door opened and a young girl exited. "Got any warm water, Matilda?" She asked as she hoisted her skirts up around her waist, exposing her bare womanhood.

"Aye," Matilda confirmed and held a jug of water to the girl. The girl cupped her hands as Matilda poured the lukewarm water into them. Then she washed her lady parts before lowering her skirts and leaving the room.

The door opened again and a balding, portly man exited. Matilda raced over to him and placed her arm in the crook of his. Flattering him, she said, "Dave, you haven't asked for me recently, I've missed you."

The man's face lit up into a tar-stained smile as he patted her arm. "I'll be back next week, young lass. I'll be sure to ask for you then."

Matilda reached up to whisper into his ear, but Scarlett couldn't hear what she said. The man looked at Scarlett and then back at Matilda. He licked his lips and then nodded his head. "Meet me at my wagon. Don't tell no one. I don't want to be blacklisted from the best brothel in Nottinghamshire."

Matilda's face beamed as she clasped her hands and she turned her attention back to Scarlett. She grabbed her hand and led the way out through the back of the building.

Ten minutes later, Scarlett found herself hidden away under a blanket in the back of Dave's scrap wagon. Once they were out of sight of the guards, she lifted the cloth and breathed in the fresh air of victory. She had accomplished what she intended. She had broken the curse that haunted her, killed the witch from enacting another curse on her family, and wounded the Sheriff by removing his greatest ally.

As Scarlett relaxed into a feeling of relief, her mind drifted back to Alaric. He had risked everything to get her to safety and she couldn't stop thinking about when he held her against the wall. The feel if his body pressed against her.

The wagon ground to a stop. Scarlett tried to place where they were on the road and what direction Ledecestre was. She had lost concentration after she began to think about Alaric.

Dave's face appeared at the side of the wagon. "You didn't say where you wanted to be dropped off, but I assumed it was clear of the town."

Scarlett mumbled, "Thank you."

Matilda enthusiastically asked, "Where are you going now, Dave? We need to get to Ledecestre, you wouldn't happen to be going that way would you?"

Dave smiled his toothless, tar-stained smile again as he replied, "For you miss, I can be. Why don't you hop upfront with me and keep me company."

Matilda stood up and Dave lifted her from the wagon by her waist. Matilda winked at Scarlett, "Well it's better than walking."

Scarlett smiled and mouthed, 'Thank you'.

They reached Ledecestre much faster in the wagon than they would have done walking. Scarlett recognised the signpost on the main road when they reached the outskirts. The wagon slowed again and Matilda leaned over the back of the wagon. "I just need to thank Dave for his kindness and then we can walk the rest of the way. You will wait for me won't you?"

The light in her eyes was now shining brightly with the hope of freedom, but there was a nervousness in them. Her voice trembled slightly like she was pleading for her life.

"Of course. I'll be right here when you get back," Scarlett confirmed.

True to Matilda's predictions, she was back in no time. Dave looked pleased as he left them on the main road. Matilda wiped her mouth with her sleeve and spat on the ground several times.

"I could do with something to drink to take the taste away. Do you have any money?" Matilda asked.

Scarlett shook her head. "But there's a pub just up here if you do."

Matilda linked arms with Scarlett and marched off in the direction Scarlett had pointed. "Come on then."

They made it to the pub in no time and as Matilda opened the door, the sound of joyful men billowed out. Scarlett freed herself from Matilda's arm and said, "I'll meet you back here. I just need to deliver something."

With complete trust in her, Matilda nodded and entered the tavern.

Scarlett headed for the travelling party to deliver the tarot cards as promised. As she walked up to the witch's wagon, the witch was sitting on the steps. She looked up when she heard someone approaching and smirked at the sight of Scarlett.

"You've got more lives than a tomcat," she taunted, as she addressed Scarlett.

Scarlett smiled and produced the tarot cards in payment for the potion. The witch took them and started to shuffle them. "Let me do you another reading, free of charge."

"I don't think so," Scarlett replied, "I've had enough of witchcraft."

"The cards are not magic. All the cards enable me to do is interpret your fate. Your fate is already written. Let me read them for you. See if your luck really has changed."

Scarlett hesitated but her curiosity got the better of her. If the witch could see her future now, at least that was a start. The last time she had said she had no future. Scarlett's mind drifted to Alaric and she wondered if there was any possibility of a future where they were allies rather than enemies. She followed the witch into her wagon and sat on the stool opposite the witch.

The table was set out exactly as before and the witch fanned out the new deck of cards in a line on the table. "Just like before, you need to pick three," she instructed.

This time, Scarlett felt a pull towards the first two cards she selected, but a third card wasn't speaking to her. She looked up at the witch, who took her hand and hovered it over the cards an inch above them. She let go and Scarlett trailed her hands over the full deck until she felt her hand lower on the last card. The feeling shocked her and she looked up at the witch, who was smirking. "I think the card chose you," the witch stated.

She took the last card and added it to the deck of three in her hand. The witch flipped the first card over that Scarlett had selected. Scarlett looked at the card, it was an upside castle tower from her angle. She couldn't read the words on the card from this angle but she wasn't sure it was in a language she could read anyway from the letters.

"The upright tower," said the witch, "Disruption to your current way of life is coming. I could feel it in your aura when you approached me."

She flipped the next card and Scarlett could see the image more clearly. It was the correct way up for her but upside down from the witch's point of view. The witch made a tsk sound before saying, "Upside down lovers. There will be suffering in your future."

Scarlett gulped, trying to remain stoic as the witch flipped the final card over. She glanced at the card and then at the witch's face to watch for a reaction. The witch smiled. "The pain will be worth it. It brings about liberation and redemption."

Scarlett screwed up her face, trying to work out whether she believed anything that had been said. "So to summarise," she started, "I will suffer and my life will change, but then I'll be liberated and happy about it."

The witch could tell from the tone of Scarlett's voice that she didn't believe her. "Have I ever told you a lie? What motive do I have to lie to you?"

Scarlett went to reply but words failed her. This witch had no reason to lie to her. "Lie is too harsh a term, but maybe you believe what you say even though there is no basis for it."

The witch nodded and then gazed into her crystal globe on the table. She closed her eyes and when she opened them again, her eyeballs were completely white. Scarlett fell back off the stool in shock and scrambled to her feet. The witch remained staring at the ball in front of her for several minutes. The witch closed her eyes again and when she opened them, her bright emerald eyes had returned.

Scarlett lowered herself back onto the stool. "Your eyes disappeared," she mumbled.

"That sometimes happens, apologies, I should have warned you. The fate the cards have shown today is not your distant future. It is showing you the future you have set in motion by your actions earlier today. Disruption to your way of life is coming sooner than you think. My party is leaving within the hour. We are heading to Nottingham. We can take you back if you will accept a lift."

Scarlett went to decline, but she thought about the sacrifices Matilda had made to get her here and if the witch was to be believed, she needed to get back to camp as soon as possible, to warn everyone to be on their guard.

"I have a companion; can you accommodate her as well?"

The witch nodded, "Be back here within the hour, we will not wait."

Scarlett nodded and headed back to the tavern to collect Matilda.

As Scarlett entered the pub, she scoured the room and found Matilda drinking ale with a group of men. One of the men had his arm around her and Matilda was smiling as she bit off a chunk of bread from the plate in front of her. Scarlett sank into the available seat next to her and Matilda smiled. She pushed a bowl of lamb stew and a noggin of bread over to Scarlett. Scarlett's greedy eyes devoured the meal quicker than she could eat it and she started tearing off chunks of bread with her teeth as she spooned in the stew between chews. Matilda handed her a tankard of ale and then grabbed her own. She raised it in a cheer to Scarlett.

"How did you get all this?" Scarlett enquired.

"You always have currency as a woman. Suppose I can thank the brothel for teaching me that."

Scarlett smiled in gratitude. However, she didn't like that

Matilda used her body like currency. Maybe being away from her old life would teach her that she was worth more. "We need to finish this and leave. I have us a ride back to Nottingham."

Matilda's smile grew so that it fully reached her eyes, "Marvellous," she exclaimed.

Within half an hour, both women were sitting in the back of a wagon en route to Nottingham. Matilda was curled up next to Scarlett, asleep on her shoulder, but Scarlett remained vigilant. When she recognised the main road that led to Nottingham, she woke Matilda up and quietly signalled for them to jump down from the wagon.

Matilda appeared to land on her ankle funny as she landed and she limped behind Scarlett, who had sneaked into the bushes.

"Are you ok?" whispered Scarlett.

"Why are we whispering?" She replied as she rubbed her ankle.

"I don't exactly trust our travelling companions and I don't want anyone to follow us."

Matilda nodded in understanding and then yawned. "How much further is it? Without any candles and the moon hidden by the trees, it's pitch black in the forest, it must be gone midnight by now."

"It's a few hours still," Scarlett replied. She saw the disheartened look on Matilda's face before she yawned again. This time, it started a chain reaction and Scarlett couldn't help but yawn as well. "I know a place, it's not far from here, we can camp there for the night, but we need to be on our way at first light." Matilda smiled and followed Scarlett into the thicket.

Alaric marched behind the Sheriff in silence, matching his strides. He knew where they were going, but he kept the distance between them as if to maintain he didn't. When the Sheriff stopped abruptly at the doorway to her chamber, Alaric held back. His father stepped into the room and loomed over the body.

It gave Alaric the line of sight to the body now. She had been moved. She was lying on her back with the dagger protruding from her heart. The anger in his father's glare was unmistakable.

"Alaric, come closer," the Sheriff ordered.

Alaric entered the room and took the opposing side of her corpse. Her eyes were open wide with the hue of purple still visible. She looked like she had been petrified to death. Her features seemed softer in death. She looked strangely younger, like death suited her. Oddly, Alaric felt nothing for her as he stared down at her lifeless body. He had plenty of thoughts swirling around in his mind, but none were based in sorrow. She had been around him for the whole of his life. For all intents and purposes, she was a third wheel in his parents' marriage.

Yet, as he gazed upon her, he wondered what he really knew about her. He certainly didn't have any warm and fuzzy memories of her, she had always given him the creeps. The irony was not lost on him. She actually looked less creepy in death than she did alive.

The Sheriff continued, "What do you see? Talk me through her murder."

Alaric bent down to touch her skin, choosing to take her hand. He flipped it over in his and back again. He replied, "Her body has gone stiff but," he paused whilst he got closer to the body and sniffed up her scent, "She doesn't smell any worse than normal, so I'd say she's been dead more than a couple of hours, less than a full day."

Alaric watched as the Sheriff's eyes darted to the door and then to the heavy curtain that only he and his father knew about.

Addressing Aegnus, the Sheriff barked, "How was the door when you found it, open or closed?"

"Wide open, my lord," he replied swiftly.

The Sheriff pulled a face and looked around the room.

"What are you thinking?" Alaric asked.

"It's highly unusual for Morgana to not have the drawbar in place, so she must have let them in. I see nothing missing, so it wasn't theft. Every crime has a motive, but I don't see one."

"Perhaps they requested aid and she refused?" Alaric proposed.

The Sheriff waved his comment aside, "Morgana would do anything if the price was right. It doesn't fit." The Sheriff scanned the room a second time. "There doesn't appear to be a struggle. Morgana would fight."

From where Aengus stood, he could see a slightly different angle and he pointed to the altar as he exclaimed, "There Sire, a smashed cup on the ground by that table."

All eyes turned to the altar. Alaric felt a sinking feeling of dread. He knew Scarlett had hidden there, and he hadn't checked that she didn't leave anything incriminating behind. Trying to defuse the attention, Alaric hastily offered up a reason. "Could it be a potion gone wrong?"

The Sheriff turned and eyed him with contempt. "And how do you explain the dagger?" Mockingly, he added, "Did she miraculously fall on it in the exact place that would pierce her heart? Speak sense boy, or not at all."

The Sheriff shifted his attention back to Morgana's body. "Pass me the weapon," he ordered. As Aengus bent down to retrieve it, Alaric took a deep breath. Aengus passed the weapon to the Sheriff without cleaning it. The Sheriff gave him a look of disgust and ordered, "Hold your arm out."

Aengus did as instructed and the Sheriff wiped the blood off the blade on Aengus's sleeve. Alaric held his breath as his father inspected the dagger.

The Sheriff scoffed loudly as he recited the motto, now clearly visible on the blade, "Quod justum, non quod utile," The Sheriff shot Alaric a knowing look. "Do you know whose motto that is?"

Alaric gulped and nodded his head. There was no use hiding the fact, he knew his father knew the answer. "House

Loxley," he stated. Inwardly, Alaric was cursing himself for not removing the dagger when he had the chance. Scarlett had left a calling card telling the Sheriff who exactly had murdered his ally.

"Self-righteous prick used to put it on everything and now I have proof of who killed Morgana. The punishment for murder in England is death. Now even the Lord our God is on my side against those outlaws. Robin of Loxley will pay this debt he owes me with his life." Pointing his finger into Alaric's chest, the Sheriff squared up to his son.

"I don't care that you knew him as a boy. Order the warrant for his arrest. Bring him to me dead or alive, I don't care, but I want to see his body this time. And while you're at it, find out which one of your guards is to blame for allowing Robin to roam these corridors. That body could easily be you or me. Robin has an axe to grind and if I were him, I would be feeling pretty invincible right about now. He might intend on striking again."

With his father looming over him and the shame he felt from leaving the dagger in plain sight, Alaric felt like a little boy being scolded. The only consolation was that his father had automatically jumped to the assumption that the culprit was Robin and not his sister. The guards would be looking for a man and not a woman. He knew that somehow he needed to warn Robin and Scarlett, but he didn't know how.

His father stomped out of the room and Alaric knew he was now in charge of sorting out this mess. He ordered Aengus to take care of the body disposal; he wanted it burned. He had seen the darkness within and he didn't want to leave anything to chance. He then set off to issue the warrant personally.

It was late into the evening by the time Alaric walked back into his chambers. He had stayed away on the pretence of conducting the investigation, when really he was just hoping to avoid his father. As soon as he entered the living quarters, he realised he wasn't in luck. His father was brooding by the fireplace, staring into the flames. He didn't respond to Alaric's obvious arrival and Alaric wondered whether he could slink off to his room without having to converse. Again, no such luck. Slurring his words the Sheriff asked, "What did you find out?"

The Sheriff turned to face him and Alaric tried to stay in the shadows to hide his face in case his expression gave away the truth. "Nothing yet, no one is owning up to letting Robin inside."

The Sheriff scoffed and took another long sip of his drink. "Maybe when you let him play guard, he found a way in that is unmanned, or maybe more of his outlaw friends are within our ranks."

Jumping to his men's defence, Alaric insisted, "I trust my men father." However, Alaric had seriously misjudged his father's mood and the Sheriff rose from his seat and threw his cup at Alaric. Alaric shielded himself with his hands just in time.

The Sheriff bellowed at him, "You trust your men! Trust! Did I raise you to be a fool? Morgana is dead! There'll be after us next. I was giving you a day to rest, but tomorrow be ready. Tomorrow we go to war'"

"War?" Alaric repeated, hoping to be given some answers, but his father just turned around and returned to his melancholy by the fireplace.

CHAPTER 19

The next morning, Alaric woke, startled by the banging of fists on his bed chamber door. He could tell it was early by the dim light filtering through his windows. "Bugger off and come back when its morning," he shouted loudly. Aengus' voice replied far too jovially, "Come on, get up, or you'll miss all the fun. We've got outlaws to kill."

Alaric leapt out of bed and unlocked the door. Aengus laughed at the sight of him, "Well, I thought you would be excited but not that excited. You've got time to get clothes on."

Alaric looked down and realised his error. He rushed back into his chamber and dressed quickly, tucking his shirt in as he marched out of the room. "How do we know where to go?"

"Your father had a spy follow one of the men back to their camp. Deep in Sherwood Forest it is. He left marks on the trees so he could lead us back there."

Alaric grumbled, "Clever," as he marched through the corridors to the stables.

By the time he was in his saddle, a squad of twenty guards were assembled, along with Alaric's best men on horseback. The Sheriff was just finishing off a speech to incite them to victory. Alaric heard the words, "And now we march forth to do God's work." The guards erupted into a cheer and started to march.

The squad moved as one, just like he had taught them and a guard Alaric didn't know well led the way on horseback. Alaric cantered up to the front to find out if he truly knew the location of the outlaw's camp.

The guard looked like the cat that got the cream, so Alaric decided flattery was the best route to take. "I hear you're the one to thank for finding out the location of the outlaw's camp."

The guard clearly recognised Alaric and smiled smugly. "I am, Commander. I followed one back to their camp."

"And you're certain this camp is the one we are looking for, with Robin of Loxley?"

Alaric watched the guard twitch uncomfortably, a sure sign he wasn't sure, no matter how much he attested he was.

"I am," the man insisted.

"As you know, I recently spent time with these outlaws. Did you catch the name of the one you followed?"

"Aye, his name was Thom."

Alaric struggled to hide his annoyance. It wasn't an unusual name, but he didn't believe in coincidences. He had no doubt they were heading in the right direction. With this many men, the outlaws didn't stand a chance. He needed to find a way to warn them, and his mind went into overdrive trying to come up with an idea.

It had been a wet night, but luckily Scarlett knew this area well and they spent the night in a small cave-like shelter. Her muscles ached when she woke early the next morning. She cracked her neck and stretched her limbs to wake them up. Scarlett glanced over at Matilda to see if she was awake. Her eyes were open but they looked glazed over. Scarlett was unnerved, so she whispered her name. On the third attempt, Scarlett projected her voice louder.

Matilda blinked profusely. Her eyes focused and she cheerily said, "Good morning. I think that was the worst sleep I've ever had, but oh well. The day can only get better." Seeing Scarlett's disturbed face, she added, "Oh sorry, I should have warned you. I sleep with my eyes open."

Scarlett smiled in relief. For a minute, she thought more witchcraft was at play. "You should really warn people about that. It's creepy."

Matilda apologised again and sheepishly added, "I never sleep around the punters, only the girls and they all know."

"Do you mind my asking how long you worked there? Is there really no one you will miss?" Scarlett asked in earnest.

"I've been there for two years. You don't need to feel sorry for me, the women weren't cruel to me. I just didn't like the work. I'd rather make my own way. I've got big dreams."

"Why don't you tell me about them whilst we walk to camp?"

Matilda was beaming and Scarlett had a soft spot for her. From her reaction, she gathered that no one had ever cared enough before to ask about her dreams. Matilda regaled all the aspirations she had for herself as they marched onwards to camp.

The small army reached the edge of Sherwood Forest quickly. Alaric recognised the point where he had exited the woods as a free man and ambled home only a few days ago. He rode ahead and shouted, "Halt." On cue, the men stopped as instructed. Purposely raising his voice, as it was the only weapon he possessed to alert the outlaws, he continued with his speech. "We do not know what traps lie ahead. Stay vigilant and proceed in a single file. Alert me to anything suspicious."

Luckily, his father had little experience leading in combat, and his right-hand men would never dare question his authority, because his advice was terrible. He was hoping to give the outlaws the biggest warning he could of their impending arrival, so they could disperse and there would be no bloodshed on either side.

He disembarked from his horse and passed the reins to a young squire. "The horses will spook in the forest and make too much noise. Leave them here." He directed his instruction to everyone with a horse, "We need to make a stealthy approach."

He didn't tell anyone about the bird signals that the

outlaws used, but he listened out, desperate to hear the sound of an owl.

Alaric positioned himself at the front of the group, but stationed his best troops at the rear. The men were talking amongst themselves and making far too much noise, but Alaric didn't chastise them. He welcomed it and started a conversation with the informant, as he searched the tree bark for his marks to lead the way.

Several times, Alaric thought he heard the warning sound of a misplaced bird cry, but he couldn't be certain. It was relatively early still, and he knew from his time in the camp that the men would likely be hung over and still asleep from a night of drinking away the bitter weather.

After over an hour of trudging through the muddy, dark forest, the merriment from the guards had subsided, and the group was far too quiet for Alaric's liking. He knew from experience that they must be nearing the camp and he was trying desperately to think of a way to alert them.

He heard the sound of a baby crying, and his heart sank. Everything happened so quickly. The guards rushed forward, brandishing their swords. Alaric heard shouting and fighting echo through the forest. He rushed forward towards the sound of Beth screaming and Susanna crying.

He found Beth on the floor, shielding a swaddled Susanna. As she tried to crawl away, a guard kicked her repeatedly. Alaric was disturbed when he observed the pleasure the guard was taking in hurting a defenceless mother.

"That's enough!" Alaric declared, rushing forward. He pulled the guard back by the scruff of his tunic, "Leave her to me."

The guard pulled a sour face and grumbled as he marched away. Alaric felt ashamed that he had always been on the side that laughed at the weak. Then he looked into Beth's fearful eyes, and he knew there was nothing weak about her. He had watched her give birth; she was a fighter, but right now, she needed his assistance, and luckily, he was in a position to give it.

He offered his hand to aid her up. She hesitated before accepting. She had blood pouring down her face from a wound on her head. The guard had likely bashed her with the hilt of his sword.

Alaric pretended to drag her forcefully into the dense shrubs. He handed her a dagger as he said, "Beth, take this and run as far away from here as you can."

Tears sprang from her eyes, and she stuttered, "Thank you."

"Clean that wound when you can," he shouted after her. Beth nodded and then disappeared into the trees.

Alaric turned and scanned the scene in front of him. He was hoping to see Scarlett's auburn hair flying through the air. He would gamble a month's wages that she could fight better than any of his infantry, but he didn't see any sign of her. His heart skipped a beat as he scanned the ground to make sure she wasn't among the fallen.

Several of his men lay wounded on the forest floor, some fatally, others just injured. The rest were fighting, but he grew curious when he could not see Aengus, or any of his other elite soldiers.

He doubled back on the angle they had approached the camp from. He saw Aengus and the rest of his men, but before he could challenge them, he saw his father instructing them. Aengus was lighting a rag attached to an arrow, and before Alaric could stop him, the arrow was fired.

Alaric followed its trajectory and it hit its target, setting one of the tree houses ablaze. Several more followed until the whole area was ablaze. By the time he made it into the centre of the camp, the heat from the fire was overpowering. Thick, black smoke was billowing from the trees. A crash sounded as one hut collapsed to the ground and took out an unsuspecting guard.

Alaric was spluttering and coughing as he searched for Scarlett. He had an intense feeling that he had to find her and get her to safety. A force pushed him to the ground as wood from a tree house collapsed mere feet away from him. He felt a slap across the face, and his eyes shot open to see the attacker. He recognised the hazel brown eyes with flecks of amber instantly, as they bored into him. Scarlett was straddled on top of him with a look of disbelief.

"Did you lead them here?" She shouted angrily, as tears rolled down her cheeks.

Alaric couldn't bear to see the betrayal on her face. He hoped to convey his sincerity when he answered, "How could I? I never knew the way." He forced his body upright, and Scarlett slid into his lap. "My father had a guard follow Thom here. You need to get away."

"Have you seen my brothers or Beth?" She asked desperately. In that moment, Alaric knew the only opportunity he had to save her was to lie. Her safety meant more to him, than what she would think of him when she found out he had lied.

He grabbed her head in his hands, forcing her focus on him. "Yes, I saw them running away towards the lake. Now go!"

Scarlett scrambled to her feet, and so did Alaric. He thought he had won, and she had seen sense when she wiped her tears on the back of her sleeve. But rather than running, she started frantically searching around.

"What are you looking for?" Alaric shouted.

"A girl."

Alaric could only see men fighting, fire, and smoke. The visibility due to the smoke was becoming treacherous. He had to get Scarlett away, and if she wasn't going to go willingly, he was going to have to force her. He grabbed her by the waist and threw her over his shoulder, clamping her legs tightly together. She thumped her fists on his back and tried to kick as he hurried towards the trees.

Her shouting drew the attention of a guard who approached him with his sword drawn. Alaric had his hand on his sword, ready to fight, but luckily the guard recognised him and hesitated.

"Mind your own business, this spoils mine," he shouted, and the guard smirked as he backed away.

Scarlett heard the exchange and stopped resisting. When they were out of ear shot Alaric whispered, "Calm it down or you'll get us both caught."

When Alaric was satisfied the thicket could keep them hidden, he released her. He guided her down by the waist. Her body was flush with his as she slid down and he felt every aspect of her body. His body responded on instinct. Her face was mere centimetres away, her breath hot on his face. He raised his hand to her cheek and his thumb circled her soft skin. There was intensity in Scarlett's eyes that he hadn't seen before, and then a movement in a tree above broke their gaze. A squirrel scurried away across a branch and the moment was gone.

"I have to go back," she said adamantly.

Alaric was caught in the previous moment and it took him a minute to respond. He was desperate for her to see sense. His father blamed Robin for Morgana's death, but Scarlett didn't know that. "If you go back there, you'll die. They won't take you prisoner for a trial. Not after what you've done. This girl you're searching for, if she's alive, I'll find her and release her. Now go!"

Scarlett hesitated as if she was about to say something, but thought better of it. She disappeared into the undergrowth, and Alaric ran back to his men.

Upon his return, he saw several bodies from both sides on the ground, and he shook his head in anger at the situation. He didn't want either side to have fatalities. Both sides had good, honest men, and this fight wasn't theirs to die for. His rage was building, and turmoil was pulling at his insides. He knew he should have made his father listen to him and see sense. His father had just wanted revenge, no matter the cost.

As if God had read his mind, the rain that had been threatening to fall all morning did. The heavens opened, and a torrent of rain fell, extinguishing the worst of the fires.

In front of everyone, Alaric marched up to his father and exploded. "We didn't need to do this. You could have set the whole forest on fire. How many men have we lost?"

The Sheriff squared up to his son, and he spat back,

"You need to watch your place, boy." The Sheriff smirked as he announced, "I got what I came for."

Panic struck Alaric. He searched around for Robin, hoping that he was captive and not dead. He couldn't see him, so he asked, "You have Robin?"

His father's smirk turned into a sneer, "I have leverage."

Aengus pushed a prisoner with a sack over his head forward, then kicked him in the back of his knee. The prisoner went down, and Aengus removed the sack. He pulled the man's head back by his auburn hair, and Alaric came face to face with a gagged Billy.

Alaric's heart sank. He knew his father would use him to bring Robin out of hiding. But regardless of whether Robin turned himself in or not, there was no way his father would let either brother live.

Scarlett raced to the lake in the hope that she would find the random bunch of outlaws she called family. She knew in her gut that not everyone would have made it out alive from the ambush. She was angry at herself that she had not been there to defend them.

Scarlett knew she couldn't risk shouting any names, so instead, she headed for the hidden stepping stones to cross the lake towards the thicker bushes on the other side. The torrential rain made it harder to see anything, but once she made it across the lake, Beth raced towards her with her arms stretched wide. She was followed by her father, who was limping. He had a bloody wound visible on his leg. Scarlett rushed to his side and allowed him to lean his weight on her.

"No one followed me. We need to clean up this wound. Come to the water's edge."

John allowed her to lead him to the water, and she went to reach for her dagger, but it was missing. She thought back to when she last had it and realised where she had left it. She cursed under her breath. It had been a gift from her father, and now it was lost forever. She pushed stray, dripping wet hair from her face and asked, "John, do you have a dagger? I've lost mine. We need to rip this cloth away to clean the wound."

Beth held out a weapon before he could respond, "Here, have this."

Scarlett took the blade and was about to slice the fabric when she brought it closer for inspection. It was her dagger, without a doubt. The inscription was personalised with her family motto.

"Beth, where did you get this?" She immediately asked.

"Alaric saved me. He gave it to me to protect myself. Is something the matter?" Beth asked nervously.

"No, nothing's the matter. It's my dagger. It was a gift from my father."

"I'm sure Alaric was planning on giving it back to you if it meant that much to you," Beth offered reassuringly, although Scarlett couldn't help but notice her focus wasn't on her injured father. Scarlett couldn't help but smile as she thought about Alaric. Once again, his actions had surprised her. Not only had he saved her, but he had saved Beth. He really was becoming a knight in shining armour.

Scarlett allowed her mind to wander as she washed John's wound. She pondered whether damsels in distress were his thing, or whether he might feel something for her, like she did for him. She couldn't deny it any longer. When she saw him in camp during the fighting, her heart had nearly broken, imagining he had betrayed her and led an army to kill everyone she loved. But she believed him when he said it wasn't him and now Beth's words proved it.

Now that the wound was clean, it was obvious the gash on John's leg was deep, and Scarlett was worried about infection. Her eyes met John's, and she could see the realisation sink in as she said, "John, we need to cauterise this." He nodded in acknowledgement. "As soon as the rain stops, we need to find dry kindling to heat a blade."

Scarlett helped John up, and both women aided him

back into hiding behind some thick bushes. Scarlett drew her attention to the group of men that had made it out alive. Robin was coughing, and his face was black with ash as he finished stitching a cut on his forearm.

It suddenly hit her, Billy wasn't here.

CHAPTER 20

"Has anyone seen Billy?" Scarlett asked in panic. Tears fell from Beth's eyes, and she shook her head.

"I haven't seen him," Robin stated firmly, "But that doesn't mean he didn't get away. We should lie low here for a bit and then go searching for anyone who's missing. You've been missing for days. Where have you been?"

Scarlett bit the inside of her cheek. "It's a long story."

"Well, we've got time, so spill. Does it have anything to do with why Alaric is leading the Sheriff's men into camp and attacking us?"

Scarlett jumped to Alaric's defence. "It wasn't him. He saved Beth and me."

Robin frowned, but Beth supported her story. "It's true, he saved me and Susanna."

"Then how did the Sheriff's men just happen to stumble on the camp?"

Scarlett's eyes sought out Thom. "Alaric said that one of the Sheriff's men followed Thom." All eyes spun around to Thom, who looked aghast.

"He was lying! It can't be," Thom said desperately.

John clouted him around the head. "You fool! Going on a two-day drinking bender and stumbling back here before you were even sober. You led them right to us."

Nursing his head, Thom ran off into the forest.

Aengus led the troops back through the forest to Nottingham Castle. Alaric hung back to make sure that the prisoners weren't being treated unduly. He could feel Billy's glare on him, and as he tried to convey with his eyes that this wasn't his plan. Billy just stared at him with a look of utter repugnance, and as Alaric approached him, Billy spat in his direction. Alaric hung his head in shame and held back to watch from the rear.

Alaric intended to follow the prisoners to the dungeon, but the Sheriff shouted to him. Begrudgingly, he left the prisoners under Aengus' charge and stood before his father. "Time to celebrate; will you join me in a drink?"

Alaric looked up at his father and struggled to hide his abhorrence. "I don't feel like celebrating. We lost men, and we just left them to rot."

Lowering his voice so that not everyone in the courtyard could hear, the Sheriff stated, "You need to learn that some people matter more than others. Stop your sulking and help me plan for phase two of my master plan."

Alaric's ears pricked up. He needed to find out the rest of his father's plan if he was to free Billy. Begrudgingly, he agreed and followed his father to their chambers.

A young serving boy swiftly laid a jug of ale on the table and scurried away without pouring. The Sheriff rolled his eyes and gestured with his head for Alaric to pour it. Alaric assumed the role of server and then slumped into a chair by the fireplace, opposite his father. Eager to learn more about his father's plans, he asked, "What do you plan to do with the prisoners?"

The Sheriff eyed him up suspiciously, and Alaric cursed himself for being too eager. The Sheriff took a long swig from his tankard and cleverly set about laying his trap.

Alaric's behaviour had been off since he had returned from captivity. He had defended the outlaws rather than demanding their heads. Then he had conveniently spent all day in bed with a whore and boosted about it, whilst Robin had been let into the castle to murder Morgana. That was out of character for his son. If he did have a thing for whores, he had never boosted about his activities before.

There was only one thing that he knew could shake the very beliefs of a man, causing them to turn their backs on everything they stood for. Love. Since Alaric had come of age, he had thought him indifferent to women at best. Alaric's behaviour during the ambush had further fuelled the Sheriff's suspicions. He had no blood on him and claimed no victories. His attitude and outburst had seemed against the attack.

The Sheriff had spent the journey back to the castle seething and calculating a way to test his son's loyalty. Capturing master Loxley had been a fortunate opportunity. The Sheriff remembered that as boys, they were friends, spending all summer together because of their mother's friendship and his mother's request to get out of the city during the stench of summer.

He had secretly ordered Aengus to keep the guards light around the prisoners' holding cell. Then he had purposely tasked Aengus with shadowing his son and reporting back. Aengus was a cut above the usual intelligence of the guards. He clearly had the same suspicions about Alaric, and he had queried at what point his shadowing should result in action.

The Sheriff had taken stock of him and recognised the greed for power in his eyes. He first flattered him and then incentivised him, knowing this approach was guaranteed to win his loyalty. "You are a clever man, and I am in need of a captain of the guard I can trust implicitly. If you feel Alaric is a danger to himself, you have the approval to intervene. Should you come across Robin of Loxley, you are to enforce justice for Morgana's murder. You will be rewarded in this life and the next." Aengus had agreed, and so it was now down to him to lay the trap to test Alaric.

"We will plan a grand trial that will end with their beheading. It will serve as a warning to all rebels, and it will bring Robin out of hiding. Then I will have two brothers' heads to mount on my walls. You can do as you wish with the sister." He laughed cruelly before adding, "Have your fun with her. Wed her, bed her, or behead her, it doesn't matter to me."

Alaric gripped the side of the chair tightly to prevent himself from lunging at his father. The Sheriff's ignorance shone through in how quickly he cast Scarlett aside as non-threatening, when she was the one who led the rebels against him and killed his precious sorceress. His arrogance would be his downfall.

The more he sat and listened to his father, the more he realised how unlike him he was. He had believed whilst serving in the guard, that he was providing much-needed justice to the people of Nottingham, not the slaughter of people who didn't conform. Neither side was blameless in the war that raged between them, but Alaric had seen firsthand how everyday people were starving. His father was hoarding riches and paying off Barons, but Alaric had never questioned why. Now he was desperate to know the reason.

Alaric kept his true feelings guarded when he replied ambiguously, "Don't think I haven't been trying. She's very elusive." He sighed and reached for his drink, taking a long swig. The Sheriff seemed appeased for now, and Alaric ensured his cup was never empty. He soon fell into his usual drinking stupor, and Alaric probed him for more information on his master plan.

"I know I have never taken a keen interest in the running of a city, but I feel I must start to learn. Taxes, for example. Other than to pay guards to protect and serve, what are they used for?"

The Sheriff hiccupped, followed by a laugh. "You have a lot to learn, boy." He hiccupped again, before continuing. "Taxes are vital to keep the poor where they belong. If they are focused on putting food on the table to survive, they have less time to think about how life is so unfair."

Alaric forced himself to smirk, mirroring the Sheriff's expression. Eager to understand, he continued, "But that doesn't explain how we spend the money taxes generate?"

The Sheriff raised his cup but missed his mouth and ale

dribbled down his chin onto his clothes. "What money do you think you were taking to the perfidious Baron of Loidis?"

"I hadn't given it much thought until tonight," Alaric confessed as his father scoffed. Alaric was in no mood to back down, and he was hopeful his father was sufficiently drunk enough now to give him some answers. He continued to challenge the Sheriff, asking, "How does sending our city's money to the Baron of Loidis help the people of Nottingham?"

The Sheriff hiccupped again, and he gestured for Alaric to fill up his tankard. Alaric did so through gritted teeth, just so he could continue to pry.

"It doesn't directly, but when I am King, the people of Nottingham will rejoice. Morgana foresaw it all. I will be King!"

Alaric sat bolt upright and stared into his father's eyes as he spoke. "That's treason!"

The Sheriff hiccupped again before answering. "It's only treason if you get caught plotting. Do you think being born into the right family gives you the right to be King? How do you think the current royal family came to be in power in the first place? Men earn the title of King by usurping the previous one. I'm just paying the Baron's to stay out of the way and do nothing. Then support me when I stake my claim." He frowned at Alaric's shocked reaction and added, "Do you not want to be a prince, boy? Unless you toughen up, someone will usurp you before you replace me." He laughed at his own insult, and then his eyelids grew heavy. His head lolled on the headrest of the chair, and then Alaric heard loud snores.

Astounded at his father's ambition, he sat in silence, deep in thought. He chastised himself for never realising the true motives behind the instructions he blindly followed. He questioned whether Morgana had really seen his father becoming King. To make an enemy of the Sheriff of Nottingham was one thing, but to make the King of England an enemy was very foolish indeed. Then he rationalised that Morgana clearly couldn't see everything. She hadn't foreseen her own demise. Surely she would have prevented it if she had.

Mulling over his thoughts, the one constant path he had always followed was to do what he believed was right. Billy shouldn't have to pay for a crime he didn't commit. Beth and Susanna would be the real victims. Alaric had felt the loss of a parent and didn't wish it on anyone, let alone a baby who would never even have memories to comfort her.

If he could free Billy and he lead him to Scarlett, he could warn her about the trap. They could come up with a plan together, to save the rest of the outlaws from certain death. The desire to be near her had ignited in his chest. The burning hate he had once had for her had burned so hot that the molten rage had formed into something else. An almost tangible feeling. He didn't know how he could feel this strongly and she just be indifferent. He had seen glimpses of longing in her eyes and her actions, enough to hope. He yearned to find out once and for all if she felt the same way.

With a final glance at his father, he made the decision to go against him and follow his heart. Maybe his father would see sense in time, or maybe his ambition would get the better of him. Tonight, he needed to make a stand for what he believed was right.

The outlaws waited around the lake until sunset. They hoped that the Sheriff's men would be long gone, spooked by the forest at night. Scarlett led the group of able-bodied men back to camp. It was a haunting sight, more like a battlefield than the home it once was. Bloodied bodies littered the ground, and even the trees looked dead. Their trunks black and charred, their branches bare.

Scarlett carefully rolled over the first body she came across, and tears sprang to her eyes when she recognised who it was. Robin was crouched by the side of another body. He looked towards Scarlett and concern flooded his face at the sight of her. He shouted over, "Is it Billy?"

Scarlett shook her head as she wiped her eyes on her

sleeve. "No, It's Aimery." She closed his eyes as a mark of respect and held his hand as she whispered a prayer.

Robin had moved onto another body, and it was obvious from his lack of emotion that it was another guard. He caught Scarlett's eye and shouted, "They've even stripped the bodies. There's no weapons on any of them."

Scarlett shook her head in disgust. "They didn't even bury their own." Scarlett moved on to the next body and felt relief when it wasn't one of their men. Her relief quickly turned to guilt. She made a silent prayer for all the fallen, but it was cut short when Robin started shouting for assistance.

Scarlett and Eddie both ran to help him as he tried to move a pile of wood from a fallen tree house. "There's someone under it," he explained. The three of them worked together to remove the debris, and Scarlett's heart sank when she recognised Benedict's young, sweet face. Even Eddie looked like he was going to shed a tear at the sight of him.

Scarlett said a silent prayer, and then her eye caught on an exposed bare leg half buried under a fallen branch. She raced over to the body and screamed, "Help me!"

Robin and Eddie ran over to help her, and together the three of them removed the large, heavy branch. Scarlett gasped at the sight of Matilda lying lifeless on the ground. Scarlett collapsed onto the ground, and grief overtook her.

Robin and Eddie exchanged glances as Scarlett grieved for someone they had never met before. Robin put his arm around her, and she wept into his chest. The emotion of the day overwhelmed her, and she couldn't hold back the tears. Matilda had only been here because she had brought her. This wasn't her fight, she didn't even own a weapon.

Guilt crushed Scarlett from the inside, weighing heavily on her heart. She couldn't shake the feeling that this was all her fault. This was revenge for the murder of his witch. She had been free of the curse; if she had not sought her own revenge then everyone would still be alive.

As she wallowed in her grief her thoughts drifted to

Alaric and she replayed everything he had said. Thom had been followed, meaning the Sheriff was planning this before she even killed the witch. A shred of relief washed over her. This wasn't all her fault.

The Sheriff had had it in for her family since he killed her father. He clearly intended to wipe out the whole Loxley line. Her thoughts shifted to Billy again. She watched Eddie as he continued to search for any other bodies. He paced around the outskirts of camp before declaring, "That's it. There are no more bodies."

Robin cocked his head up and scanned the area to make sure. "So who's missing apart from Billy?"

Eddie scratched his head and confirmed, "Aldo and Edmund."

Robin leant away from Scarlett and placed his hands on her shoulder. "So the good news is, Billy, Aldo, and Edmund aren't dead."

Hope surfaced in Scarlett's eyes until Eddie asked, "So where are they?"

Realisation sunk in. Even if the other two had run, there's no way Billy would have left Beth and Susanna. It was more likely that all three of them had been taken. The fact that they hadn't been killed meant the Sheriff had a plan, and it more than likely meant they wouldn't be alive for long.

Alaric packed a bag with every weapon he had in his room, a spare uniform, and his helmet. Then, using his curtain tieback, he lowered the bag out of his bed chamber window. He quietly descended the hidden staircase to Morgana's quarters. From her chamber in the basement, he took a secluded route to the dungeons. Years of wandering the hallways with no friends paid off tonight. He knew at this late hour the guards would be minimal, but it would still be challenging to sneak in and out without raising suspicion.

When he reached the final corridor, he held back in the

shadows. He listened to the guards talking. He recognised them from their voices alone. He knew Jarvis regularly cheated on his wife, and Blaine was a drunkard. He wasn't a big fan of either of them. He rotated his shoulders back and stood tall as he strode down the corridor towards them.

"It's about to be your lucky night. The Sheriff has decided that as a reward for our successful triumph against the outlaws, that all guards will have shorter shifts. Me and Aengus are taking over from you, but the idiot is late. I hear Marion is working in the tavern tonight. She's a favourite of yours, isn't she?"

"Aye," Jarvis replied, "You don't need to tell me twice. I'm out of here." Blaine concurred, and they left Alaric alone. When he was sure the corridor was clear, he took the keys from the hook and unlocked the first gate. He held a lantern up high to peer in each cell. The smell was atrocious, and he had to breathe in through his mouth to stop himself from gagging.

Tucked away in the corner, Alaric found him. Billy was hugging his knees, rocking in the dark on the floor. He held the light close to his face as he gestured to keep quiet. Hatred burned through Billy's eyes until he saw that Alaric was opening the cell. His head cocked to the side, unsure of what was happening. Alaric beckoned him with his finger, and Billy scrambled up off the floor. Alaric swung the cell door open, careful not to make a sound, and Billy followed him. Alaric locked the gate back up, then placed the lantern and keys back where they belonged. Only now did he speak, but he kept it to a whisper. "We need to leave, and I want you to take me to Scarlett."

Billy's voice was hoarse when he responded. "Why should I trust you?"

"Because Beth and Susanna are alive because of me. Because I've saved Scarlett's life, I can't remember how many times, and I am freeing you right now."

Billy chewed the inside of his lip as if he were thinking. "How do I know this isn't a trap?"

Exasperated, Alaric pleaded with him. "You don't, but you

and I were friends. The best of friends, and I was raised more by your father than my own, to do what was right-" They finished the Loxley family motto together in unison, "Not what is easy."

"Nothing about this is easy for me. I'm betraying my own father, going against the law I help enforce and against the men I trained. Men who would be forced to fight me if we get caught. But still, I'm saving you because it's the right thing to do. My father is not doing what's right for Nottingham, and he's setting a trap. I need to warn Scarlett."

Billy nodded, and Alaric turned to flee when Billy pulled him by the arm. "We need to save the rest of the outlaws." Alaric's initial thought was to refuse, but he paused and instead moved towards the keys. When suddenly, they heard a whistling echo through the corridor.

Alaric whispered, "We don't have time. Follow me."

Alaric led the way through another windowless passageway, perfectly navigating the warren of tunnels until they came to Morgana's chamber. Alaric led the way up the stairs to the heavy wooden door that led to the walled garden. Together, they lifted the crawbar. Alaric went through first and checked that the garden was empty. Then, following the same path he had led Scarlett to freedom through they arrived in the courtyard.

"Stay here," instructed Alaric as he paced around the castle to collect his bag from beneath his window. He figured if no one had seen him abseiling out of his window, then no one would be observant enough to notice a bag, and he was right. He knocked sharply on the wooden door, and Billy opened it. Once inside, Alaric shared out the uniform and made Billy put on the helmet to hide his appearance.

Alaric toyed with chancing a trip to the stables, but it was on the other side of the castle, and time was of the essence. He decided they would be less conspicuous on foot.

"Do you have a plan?" Billy asked.

"No, I'm thinking on my feet," Alaric responded, "I guess we should just walk right out the front gate."

"Will that not look odd?"

With more confidence than he felt, Alaric affirmed, "Not if you hold it together. I'm the Sheriff's son and Commander of the guards. I can do what I like."

Billy raised his eyebrow but nodded. Together, the two of them walked right up to the gate. One guard was asleep, but the other frowned at them. He went to speak, but clearly recognised Alaric and just nodded. When they were out of earshot, Alaric smirked, "See, I told you so."

Neither man saw that they were being followed.

CHAPTER 21

Billy led the way, desperate to get back to his family, to let them know he was alive. "How will we save the others?" He asked Alaric.

"That I don't fully know. I'm hoping your sister will have a good idea."

Billy eyed his old friend suspiciously, but he said nothing. As they reached the edge of the forest, it was so dark they could barely see each other. The moon was just a sliver, and the cloudy sky was obscuring any light.

"Do you know where they'll be?" Alaric asked.

Reassuringly, Billy replied, "Yes, stay close, I'm not wasting time finding you if you get lost."

Alaric followed closely behind. In the dark, the sounds of the forest seemed heightened. He heard noises all around him and he didn't want to admit that they bothered him. The forest was eery in complete darkness and tonight it just felt different. He was still running on adrenaline, but in this heightened state, he knew he was draining his energy levels. He pushed onwards, keeping close to Billy. The only hope he had of explaining himself fully to Scarlett and winning back her trust was if he delivered Billy safely.

By the time they reached the lake, the clouds had shifted and the moon was visible again. Its silver glow reflected off the surface of the water and sounds of human voices whistled through the trees. Billy almost ran down the bank towards the water and his heavy footsteps alerted the campers to his presence.

Two figures emerged from the bushes, and Alaric heard a female gasp. He caught up with Billy just in time to see Scarlett running across the hidden stones in the water. She flew across the water's surface as if she were floating and flung her arms out wide to greet Billy.

Her head twisted to the side, and she saw Alaric. Her smile changed from utter joy to something else. Their gazes lingered on one another.

Alaric couldn't decipher her expression, but he also couldn't take his eyes off her. She let go of Billy slowly as Robin approached. Then, without warning, she flung herself toward Alaric. Her arms landed around his neck and her body pressed against his.

Alaric was taken by surprise, but he recovered quickly, wrapping his arms around her and nestling his head into her neck. Even with the smell of smoke in her hair, the feel of her closeness was intoxicating. She let go first, but Alaric still held her close and she looked up at him. Their eyes met and conveyed a thousand words that he wanted to say, but struggled to find the words for.

They heard a deliberate cough to the side of them, and they both saw Scarlett's brothers staring at them. A knowing smirk on Billy's face and a frown on Robin's. Alaric released his hold, but slid his hand into Scarlett's, entwining their fingers.

"Should we wake the others?" Robin asked, whilst purposely looking at Scarlett for the answer.

"No, let them sleep," she replied.

The men turned to cross the lake, but Alaric squeezed her hand. Scarlett looked up at him and knew that he wanted some privacy to talk. "You go ahead. We won't be long."

Billy was eager to see Beth, so he crossed first without looking back, but Robin glanced over his shoulder and scanned Scarlett's face first to confirm she wasn't being coerced. Warmly, she responded, "I'm fine, Robin." Having Robin back in her life, watching out for her, was nice; it reminded her of her childhood.

However, it could also be a little overbearing at times, especially when she had spent so long being the one to look out for everyone else.

Once her brothers had crossed the lake, she brought her gaze back to Alaric, who was staring at her intensely. He brought his free hand up to her face and tucked a stray strand of hair behind her ear. His hand hovered for a second before he ran his thumb over her cheekbone and then down towards her lips.

In not more than a whisper, Alaric admitted, "I really want to kiss you."

Almost breathlessly, Scarlett replied, "Then kiss me."

Not waiting for him to make the first move, she lent upwards at the exact time he cupped her face with both hands. Their lips met in a passionate need to consume each other. For too long they had both denied the feelings growing between them. An all-consuming need led Scarlett to be more brazen than she ever had been before.

Alaric, too, struggled to contain his overwhelming desire as his hands drifted from her face to slide down the contours of her body.

Reaching up, he massaged her scalp before tugging on her braided hair. Her head fell back automatically, giving him full access to trial kisses down her neck and onto her collarbone. His lips trailed up back to hers. One hand still on the base of her skull and the other on her bottom, pushing her hard up against him.

Uncontrollable, soft moans emanated from her throat and encouraged Alaric on. Her moans grew louder and the ache between her legs grew.

She could feel his hard length pressing against her. The dampness at her core was beginning to pool. She was ready for him.

She trailed her hand down his hard torso and grabbed his length through the material of his clothing. It twitched at her touch, and Alaric let out a moan into her mouth. She slid her hand back and forth down his shaft as she grasped him fully. Scarlett could tell how much she was affecting him by the ferocity of his tongue in her mouth and the moans escaping from his throat.

Alaric released the hold on her arse and moved his hand to still the one she was using to pump his cock. The hand behind her head moved to her face, and his thumb traced her swollen lips. Alaric was breathing heavily, and she searched his eyes for answers. "Maybe we should talk before we go any further?"

Scarlett's emotions were conflicted as they parted. She desperately wanted to finish what they had started, but her mind was screaming that he was her enemy.

Panting, Scarlett stepped backwards, and Alaric reached for her hand. She stuttered out the words, "Do you mean to tell me we will still be enemies in the morning?"

"I'm not your enemy, I never have been. I was saving you from being my father's whore the night that you attacked me."

Shock swept across Scarlett's face, and Alaric saw a flash of regret. He continued, "You've always been mine. You and I are destined to be together."

Scarlett frowned at his choice of words. She let them settle in as she withdrew her hand from his. This was hardly the declaration of love she was hoping for. She doubted whether he felt as intensely as she did.

She turned and walked a few steps away, needing to get some space. The words *mine* and *destined* were replaying in her mind. She had had enough of people dictating and messing with her fate to last a lifetime. It made her feel out of control of her own destiny. She was no one's property.

"What do you mean?" She queried, turning to face him.

Not understanding her change in stance, Alaric answered, "We're betrothed, our mothers arranged it when you were born."

Scarlett frowned, and her temper started to soar. Instead of a simple declaration of love, Alaric had proceeded to imply that she was his property by law, through a contract made by people long since dead.

Raising her voice, her temperament clear in her tone, she responded, "So because our mothers wanted us wed, I'm supposed to fall on my back and play the dutiful wife?" Alaric was taken aback at how quickly the situation had turned. He had gone from being blissfully happy and horny as hell, to not knowing what he had done wrong in a matter of moments.

He managed to stutter out the words, "No, that's not what I was saying."

Scarlett glared at him with an incredulous expression. "So what were you saying, because I'm pretty sure my mother would have taken back her support of a betrothal when your father killed mine."

A piercing scream filled the night air. Scarlett whipped her head towards the makeshift camp on the other side of the lake. Without pause, she sprinted towards it. Alaric struggled to keep up, not having the balance she did to get over the slippery stepping stones so quickly. When he made it through the thicket, his jaw dropped open, and dread sank into his heart.

Robin was lying on the ground with an arrow through his chest. On the far side, Billy was comforting a shaking Beth. Scarlett was collapsed on the ground at his side, holding his hand.

Scarlett held her head in shame. He had been dying, whilst she was giving in to animalistic urges. She caught herself on the precipice of being consumed by grief and let her anger fuel her. Before Alaric could offer any comfort, she stood and wiped the tears on her sleeve. She threw her nearby quiver over her shoulder and picked up her bow.

Alaric watched her as her demeanour changed. She stared at the angle of the arrow for the briefest of seconds, working out the most likely trajectory, and then she bolted off into the dense forest. She reached behind her and grabbed an arrow from her quiver as she nimbly hunted her prey.

Alaric darted after her. The tree canopy was so dense that there was barely any light to see, yet Scarlett moved expertly. Alaric tried to be as quiet as possible as he raced to keep up. He fell behind but could just see her silhouette moving. He didn't see as she took aim, but he heard the cry, followed by a thud.

A gust of wind whistled through the leaves. It was just enough to shine a ray of moonlight down on a body lying face down on the ground. Scarlett nocked another arrow, eyeing the body up suspiciously. Alaric touched her on the shoulder to let her know he was with her, but she flinched at his touch. She instinctively knew who had followed her and she instructed, "Alaric, turn him over."

Alaric sighed, of course she had known it was him. She would have heard him following her, but that also meant she had flinched at his touch, knowing it was him. He felt like the moment they had just shared together was slipping away.

He bent down to the body and lifted the arm up. Then he released it, and it fell to the ground, lifeless. He rolled the body over from the torso and took a sharp intake of breath at the man lying dead before him. He knew in that moment, that any hope of holding her close while she grieved the loss of her brother was gone. He would be blamed, and the closest person he had to a friend, Aengus, was now dead. He couldn't bear to see his soulless eyes. So, Alaric closed his eyelids as a sign of respect.

Guilt flooded his conscience. He questioned whether he was to blame. Had his true feelings been so easy to read, that his father had set him up. Aengus would never have orchestrated this on his own. His father had set the trap. Aengus was loyal to a fault and a good man. If he had been honest with him, he was certain Aengus wouldn't have executed the Sheriff's orders. But now he and Robin were dead, and Alaric felt entirely to blame.

Footsteps echoed around them as several other outlaws arrived. Billy bent down beside him and pulled Aengus's head towards the moonlight filtering down through the canopy. "I recognise him," he stated.

Her voice trembling, Scarlett stared at Alaric, pointing an arrow at his heart. "Did you know him?"

Alaric didn't break her gaze as he admitted, "Yes. He's one of my men, but you have to believe me when I say that I didn't plan this."

Scarlett fought back the tears that were welling up inside

of her.

"Billy," she ordered, "Restrain him." She couldn't bear to look at Alaric as Billy led him back to the others and tied him to a tree.

In the space of an hour, she had gone from blissfully happy, to devastated and then to bloodcurdling rage. As the adrenaline from the hunt was wearing off, overwhelming grief was flooding her again. Even retribution for Robin's death didn't dull the pain. Alaric's confession only made her feel hollow. She'd lost everything in an instant.

This felt so much more devastating than the loss of her parents. When her mother passed, she was too young to really understand. When her father was murdered, she was too young to have been able to save him, but with Robin, she should have been there. She knelt on the ground next to his body and held his hand.

She had said goodbye to him once before, but in her heart, she had always known she would see him again. Now she had to say goodbye forever, and she wasn't ready. Billy had Beth and his own family, but Scarlett was alone. Dark thoughts invaded her mind, twisting the love she knew the couple both held for her. She over fixated on her recent actions and how she nearly harmed her baby niece. She questioned whether Billy would ever truly forgive her. They were her only family now, and without family, what was the point of anything?

Scarlett wondered whether her life held any purpose anymore. Had her idealistic notions gotten Robin killed? She debated what place she held in the group if she couldn't protect and provide.

Alaric could see the change in Scarlett as her adrenaline left her and realisation set in. Her shoulders dropped, defeated. He could have easily wrestled free from Billy and run, but he didn't want to. Even if she wouldn't speak to him yet, he had to talk to her and put this right. He had to make her believe him, that he had not set this up. His mind played out every possible scenario, and the words he would use to convince her of his innocence, but they never ended with them living happily ever after together. Instead, he watched her take out her anger on the earth beneath them as she dug a hole.

Scarlett was confident the shooter had been alone, but still ordered the camp to sleep in shifts. She had found a nice spot nearby to bury Robin, and she got lost in the simple, mundane task of digging a hole.

Exhaustion mixed with the whirlwind of emotions drained Alaric, so much so that he was able to fall asleep just as the sun was rising. When he woke again, his stomach was rumbling from hunger. He scanned the camp and his heart leapt when he recognised Scarlett asleep under a tree with her back to him. Her clothes and hair were matted with soil. The grave that had been dug was now filled. A simple wooden cross acted as the marker. Alaric could see that some writing was carved into it, but from this distance, he couldn't make out the words. He watched her sleep for hours.

When the sun was at its highest, Beth kindly handed Alaric a noggin of bread and spoon-fed him some fish stew. Alaric reminisced that it felt like old times, but when he saw the solemnness of Beth's face, he made no clever remarks. He kept silent and thanked Beth with his eyes.

Scarlett must have been exhausted because she didn't wake until late afternoon. Alaric could feel that the entire camp was restless and frustrated. As soon as Scarlett opened her eyes, all focus was on her for direction. Even in grief, she was formidable. Her presence inspired hope for a better life, and Alaric wasn't ashamed to admit he was enthralled with her. If she asked him to follow her and go against his father, he would. He only wished she would give him the opportunity to explain.

He called out to her but she ignored him. He knew she could hear him, so he shouted out what he had to say. "The Sheriff is planning to kill the King, and the rest of your men. He confessed it to me. He plans to lay a trap, I wanted you to know so you could evade it." Alaric saw her pause for the briefest of moments before she continued on with her task. His heart felt lighter for sharing the truth with her, but it still ached for what might have been if only they hadn't been interrupted.

Scarlett avoided Alaric all day. She found it easier to ignore him than to deal with her own feelings and what had to be done. When she had attended church as a girl, the priest would preach that the first half of the Bible taught that justice was 'An eye for an eye', but the second half preached forgiveness. Scarlett didn't understand which rule she should follow.

She couldn't deny Alaric had done a lot of good. He had saved her life more than once, along with saving Billy, Beth, and Susanna. He had even saved Robin when she was bewitched and tried to kill him. Her head was a mess. She didn't intervene when she saw Beth feeding him, and she kept herself busy hunting for food.

When night fell, Scarlett took the night shift again. She was still feeling responsible, so instead of sitting in the camp, she patrolled the area. In the early hours, Billy woke with Susanna. Scarlett heard the cries and neared the camp. Billy dismissed any concerns and offered to swap now that he was wide awake. Scarlett accepted his offer, as she still felt drained from grief.

When Billy heard soft snores coming from Scarlett's direction, he quietly approached her. He watched her chest rise and fall, making sure he was satisfied she was asleep, before he approached Alaric.

CHAPTER 22

Billy bent down low and kicked Alaric's foot. Alaric double-blinked and frowned. He'd been asleep. Alaric watched as Billy cut the rope tying him to the tree. In muffled tones, he asked, "Why are you freeing me?"

Billy turned to look at him, but continued to converse in whispers. "Because I didn't know we were being followed, so I reckon neither did you. We're both to blame for Robin's death. If I hadn't been so eager to get back," he paused as he tried to rein in his emotions. "Then Robin would still be alive."

"I swear to you I didn't plan this and I will do everything I can to put this right."

Billy nodded. "I believe you. I've seen the way you've been looking at Scarlett for weeks. You love her. You wouldn't kill Robin knowing she could never love you back if you did."

All Alaric could do was nod. Billy had seen through all the bravado and mixed messages to the truth. He was crazy in love with Scarlett and he knew she felt the same, even if she wasn't ready to admit it. If he could just prove his innocence by standing against his father, then he was certain he could win her back. In truth, only then would he be worthy of her.

"How will you explain my escape?" He asked.

"I haven't thought that far ahead, but you better get going, or I won't be able to stop her if she comes after you with an arrow." Pointing into the trees in the opposite direction to where the sun had set, Billy advised, "Head that way."

Alaric thanked Billy and then disappeared into the

undergrowth.

Alaric made it back to Nottingham Castle just after sunrise. The hustle and bustle of the town folk was just beginning. He knew his father wouldn't be awake yet, so he decided to visit the sleeping barracks of the unmarried guards. More than half of the beds were empty and he figured those men who were not finishing the night shift had found evening entertainment outside the castle.

He slammed the door with enough force to rattle the hinges and then hollered, "Get up, you lazy bastards!"

The men sprang into action. The majority jumped out of bed and stood to attention. Several were swaying from drink and one rolled out of a top bunk bed. He landed on the floor in a tangle of limbs and howled in pain. Two men closest to him lifted him up to standing. Another rolled over the side of his bed and vomited on the ground. Alaric frowned at the stench and ordered the man to clean it up immediately.

Alaric would admit he had been a bit lax lately on training everyone to the same standard. He had his elite men and he focused on training with them because he enjoyed the challenge. The majority of these men were here for the paycheque, but he would need every man to side against his father if he was to support Scarlett in her quest to end tyranny in Nottingham.

Alaric stood authoritatively with his shoulders braced back. When he spoke, he did so clearly and slowly to assert his authority. Since walking away from Scarlett, he had been planning how he could support her and weaken his father's position from the inside. He had decided to turn the guards against the Sheriff and win their loyalty for himself. He wasn't planning on telling them anything that wasn't true, but he intended to manipulate their trust to stand beside him and answer only to him.

Convincing his father he wasn't a turncoat would be harder though. He had played out different scenarios in his head, but the only one he could conceive might work was to pitch Aengus as the turncoat. When he had decided on the plan, he had sent a prayer up to the heavens to apologise. Then, to corroborate his story, he had dragged his forehead up against a tree bark. Leaving enough of a mark to support the story he would spin.

Returning his focus to the task at hand, Alaric started his rehearsed speech. He had always been good at public speaking; he put it down to his mother's insistence on a scholarly education, and frequent hours in church learning how not to keep people's attention. He stood tall as he began, "Men, you know me. I'm one of you. I bleed with you, I train with you, and it's an honour to serve Nottingham with you."

A round of applause echoed around the room and Alaric felt the encouragement to continue. "We are living in precarious times. What I am about to share with you is the truth that would see my own father, the Sheriff, order my death. But I trust you men to take the righteous course of action." The room was deadly silent as they hung on his every word.

"The Sheriff is plotting to overthrow the King of England. He is forcing you, honourable men, to enforce unjust taxation on our people of Nottingham, to pay the barons to turn a blind eye and support his claim to the throne, when the King has been murdered. I cannot be a part of this blasphemy. The Sheriff is my own father, but I cannot witness this act against God's chosen King on earth, or his faithful people of Nottingham. Men, I ask you now, will you stand with me against tyranny?"

Alaric made a point of making eye contact with every man he could and the sound of support from the men was deafening. He soaked in the cheer and the glory of delivering the first successful pitch. When the room was quiet again, Alaric added, "Speak this truth to no one. Wait for my signal and we will be victorious!" Applause sounded again and then Alaric ordered the men to get to their duties.

He repeated his speech to the night shift workers and received the same unanimous support. After, he visited his elite guards who had private barracks. Their support he had never questioned, but he toyed with whether to tell them the truth about Aengus. After much deliberation, he decided against it. Instead, he manipulated the truth slightly to ensure Scarlett didn't become a target for vengeance. When his men were gathered, he started his speech.

"I have some grave news to share with you. Aengus is dead." Alaric allowed his grief to show. He held his hand over his heart as he continued, "You all know I loved Aengus like a brother, but my own father, the Sheriff, tasked Aengus with murdering me because I learned the truth. A truth I will share with you today.

You have to believe me when I say that if there was any other way, any way Aengus could have been beside me now, I would have ensured it." His men hung on his every word as he shared the truth about the Sheriff's ambitions. The men rallied behind him, but at least to Alaric, the anguish of Aengus's death lingered in the air.

It was mid-morning and Alaric knew his father would be breaking his fast anytime now in the banquet hall. He swung by the armoury to pick up as many weapons as he could conceal on his person and then sauntered to the hall. His father didn't even look up when he entered. Alaric started whistling a merry tune as he grabbed an apple from the centrepiece. He perched on the edge of the table, waiting for the Sheriff to notice. He kept his eyes trained on him and he eventually looked up as Alaric took a big bite from a juiciest red apple.

His father instantly recoiled seeing Alaric before him. It had been a full day since he had seen Alaric or Aengus. He'd assumed Alaric had killed Aengus when he realised he was following him. When he had heard nothing by yesterday evening, he had ordered a guard to check if Billy was still chained up. The guard had returned, sheepishly confirming that every detainee claimed to be Billy. The Sheriff had rolled his eyes and then had to personally check the prisoners before he established that Billy was missing.

If Alaric had realised who had sent Aengus to follow him, it was brazen of him to saunter about the castle like nothing had changed. The Sheriff gave a sideways glance to the guards charged with watching over him to make sure they were alert.

The Sheriff decided to focus on the physical bruising that he could see to establish what game Alaric was playing. "What have you done to your forehead, boy?" He shouted down the length of the table.

"That's a long story, but it warms my heart that you are concerned for me."

Gruffly the Sheriff replied, "Concern has nothing to do with it. Whilst you share my name, you are a reflection of me."

"How true that is, Father. Our wagons are truly melded together through life."

"Don't speak in riddles," the Sheriff demanded.

"You will be pleased to know I have foiled an attack against your life."

Intrigued, the Sheriff sat up and put his fork down. "How so?" He inquired.

"I regret to inform you that one of my most trusted men, Aengus, was plotting against us. He tried to escape with one of the prisoners and assassinate you. I managed to foil his plan and eliminate him, but unfortunately, the prisoner managed to escape. He banged me up pretty good, hence the head wound."

"And you are sure it was Aengus?"

Alaric swallowed hard, promising to send a prayer for forgiveness up to Aengus in heaven when he was alone. "Positive. He had us all fooled. Me more than most. He bragged about how he had won your confidence and tricked you into thinking it was me who was working with Robin, not him."

The Sheriff was distrustful by nature, but deep inside he wanted to believe that was the truth. He rose from his chair and greeted Alaric warmly. Alaric held his ground, fighting against the temptation to end his father's life here and now.

He looked at the guards around the room. He knew them well. Alfred had been his trainer. He might be older now, but he was still an excellent fighter. Alaric knew he would be dead before he had time to explain if he attacked now.

Through gritted teeth, he accepted his father's greeting and made a mental note to pull Alfred for a chat as soon as he could. He was a loyal man, who had been in service long before Alaric was even born. He would be the toughest man to convince to betray the Sheriff; Alaric only hoped his loyalty to the crown and his friendship would sway him.

The Sheriff left the hall straight after and ordered Alfred and his personal guards to remain within ten feet of him at all times. He told them threats had been made on his life, and no one was to be trusted. He even demanded a guard be stationed outside his bed chamber door. He wasn't convinced by Alaric's account and ordered that guards trail Alaric as well. Outwardly, this was on the premise of it being for his own safety, but the Sheriff wanted to know all of Alaric's movements and this was a secure way to know if Alaric was a traitor or not. What the Sheriff had miscalculated, was that the loyalty Alaric had from his men was beyond what he could buy.

Scarlett woke after a blissful sleep. It wasn't until she opened her eyes that she remembered, and her world came crashing down around her once again. She rolled over, hoping that a glimpse of Alaric might fuel her rage and stop her melancholy, but she was shocked when he wasn't there. She scrambled to her feet and looked around the makeshift camp. "Where's Alaric?" She screamed.

Everyone in camp shifted their eyes to the ground, including Beth. As her blood began to boil, she marched over to Beth, demanding, "Where's Billy?"

Beth cautiously looked up and begrudgingly admitted, "By the lake, giving Susanna a bath." Scarlett marched off in the direction of the lake to confront him. Billy had been vocal in his support of Alaric and Scarlett knew he would be the only one who would go against her and release him.

She saw him on the bank swaddling Susanna and she had to curtail her anger because of the baby. She shouted at him, "Did you let Alaric go?"

Calmly, he responded, "I did."

Exasperated Scarlett yelled, "Why did you do that?"

"You know why," he responded as he continued to cuddle Susanna, knowing she was a shield against Scarlett's rage. "I don't believe he was involved and he can help us as a turncoat on the inside."

"The man is a pathological liar. His father murdered our father and now Robin is dead."

"And those things have nothing to do with Alaric. You can't judge a man for the sins of another. He said he was going to make things right and I believe him."

"Then you're a fool!" Scarlett cried.

"Maybe I am," Billy admitted, "But I would rather believe in people than live a jaded and scared life alone. You push everyone away without seeing the good in anyone. You have feelings for him, don't deny it, but you would rather blame him and push him away, than take a chance at being happy."

"You don't know what you're talking about," Scarlett snapped back in response. "I'm not scared, and I will not sit around while more of our men die. It's time to make a stand."

Billy nodded, then confidently stated. "I'll stand by you, and when we get to the gates of Nottingham castle, you'll see Alaric standing with you as well."

Scarlett was confused by the feelings welling inside of her. She stared into the face of her twin brother, the only family she had left and she wanted to believe him. He was so adamant and she realised she longed for his words to be true. Hope wasn't a tangible feeling, but that didn't make it any less of a driving force pushing her onward.

Back at camp, she rallied the men and they hurried to the closest village. Now was the time to incite a riot. It was time to get vengeance for her father and for Robin.

CHAPTER 23

Scarlett climbed into the back of an empty ale wagon and took a deep breath. Billy had rallied the villagers. She took another deep breath and looked into the crowd. There was a mix of faces, some she knew well and others she didn't. Men and Women. Old and young. There was a mixture of disgruntled expressions and inquisitive ones.

She centred herself, ready to deliver the most important speech of her life. It would be no easy feat to convince hardworking, ordinary people to fight alongside her. She knew she had to give them a cause worth fighting for. A reason beyond the ones personal to her. She needed to inspire them and she knew that passion was the key.

Night after night, she had sat with Robin by the fire and listened to his war stories from the Crusade. Robin had instilled in her that men who were willing to die for what they believed in, were more powerful than thrice the number of hired guards. Greed was only a motivator for so long, but passion won wars.

Billy caught Scarlett's eye and she nodded. Billy shouted into the crowd, asking them to keep quiet. Once he had finished and the noise of the crowd had lowered significantly, Scarlett started her speech.

"Many of you know me. I'm one of you, a citizen of Nottingham. Yet, the Sheriff labels me an outlaw, because I live my life free from his dictatorship.

I don't lie, or steal like he does, hiding behind the laws he invents. The Sheriff charges taxes. Why? So he can pay high-ranking men to look the other way, whilst he plans to murder the King of England. The Sheriff's own son and commander of the guards confirmed this to be true. If the Sheriff gets his way, a war is looming. Do you intend to fight and die for a man like the Sheriff? A man who sends mercenary's to kill you while you sleep.

Last night the Sheriff took my brother from me. How long before he takes yours?

Will you fight against injustice?

Will you fight for freedom from tyranny?

He keeps us divided, because he knows that united together, we are an unstoppable force that legends are made of. Stand with us, in memory of everyone he has ever taken from you. I stand with you in the memory of Robin of the Hood.

Join us now. Fight for freedom."

The crowd erupted into cheers around her. She looked each person in the eyes and knew she had won them over. Her eyes met Billy's and his smile widened with what she thought was pride. Happiness began to surface in her chest, until she remembered all that they had lost to get to this point. She would need to ensure their success to make their sacrifices worth it. She buried the feeling down into the pit of her stomach and allowed the numbness to spread like ice.

They determined they would need two days, to rally enough of the villagers to take on the castle guards. The blacksmiths went into overdrive and even the children were helping to pluck chickens to make arrows.

Scarlett noticed a messenger on horseback approaching the village and suddenly she had an idea. She marched across to greet him, as he stopped to allow his horse to drink. The horse had clearly been travelling at speed as the steam from his coat was visible. The messenger washed his own face and neck with water to cool down. When he noticed Scarlett, he sneered at her before remarking, "Begone with you beggar, you won't get any coin from me."

Scarlett ignored him; his rudeness only fuelled her

determination. "Will you take a message to anyone?" She asked, pushing her chest out and placing her hands on her hips.

The messenger eyed her suspiciously before responding. "For the right price, but I'm currently on an important job," he replied.

"Well, what if I pay double your normal fee, will you delay the job you're currently on and deliver my missive first?"

"I've got my orders love and they're from an important person."

"Well, my missive needs to be delivered to the King, so I think my letter trumps your other patron. Do you know where to find the King?" Scarlett added, hoping her goading would be taken to encourage him rather than anger him.

The messenger puffed out his chest and proclaimed, "I'm the best at what I do. I can find anyone."

Scarlett spoke in her most upper-class-sounding voice, accentuating each word and pronouncing every consonant. "The missive I need to send is to be delivered to the King. It is of grave importance. From his own cousin, the Lady of Nottingham." The white lie escaped her lips before she realised how stupid she would look, when the messenger tried to deliver a letter from a distant relative that the King knew was dead.

Nevertheless, Scarlett could see the cogs whirling around in the messengers brain. She wasn't going to accept 'No' as an answer, so she followed up with, "You drive a hard bargain, sir, I will pay you thrice your usual rate, but I want you to personally put it into the hand of the King."

Scarlett knew she had hooked him when she said thrice, his greedy eyes lit up. He held his hand out for the letter and payment.

"Ah, I have not yet written my missive. Do you have parchment and a quill?"

The messenger stared at her blankly, before mockingly commenting, "Do I look like I can read and write? It's one of the job requirements. You need to be a fast rider and illiterate. No high-born men want me reading their private letters."

"Oh, that poses a problem. Stay here a minute whilst I ask around."

Scarlett cast her gaze upon the village and she quickly came to the realisation she wasn't going to find what she needed here. Turning back to the messenger she said, "Take me to the monastery due east of here. It's not far. I'm sure they will have what I need."

The messenger was already seated in his saddle and he rolled his eyes but held out his arm. Scarlett ignored it and pulled herself up using the saddle. She sat astride with both legs pinned to the horse's side behind the messenger. Unfortunately, there was no way around it, she had to wrap her arms around his waist to hold on as his horse set off at full speed due east.

Scarlett had only visited the monastery once, on a visit to Nottingham as a child one Christmas. She knew the monks weren't allowed to talk to women, but that didn't mean they couldn't listen. She let herself in through the unlocked front door. The room was laid out like a small chapel. She made her way up to the pulpit and found a quill with ink and parchment. There was no one around so she wrote her missive to the King, warning him of the plot against him and urging him to visit quickly to support the people of Nottingham rallying against the Sheriff.

She was out of practise and her handwriting was shaky. She would have received a wrapped knuckle from Edith if she had seen her penmanship, but it was at least legible. She went to sign it by her name, as she did her missives as a child between friends, but luckily caught herself. She signed it with her official title Lady Loxley, followed by her family motto. She just hoped the King would understand her deception to the messenger. There was no wax around, unless she lit a white candle from the alter, so she didn't bother to seal it.

Just as she was about to leave, a monk entered the room from the far side. He took one look at her and bowed his head low. Scarlett had done what she had set out to do, so she turned towards the door to leave. The monk froze as she approached and Scarlett felt like she had to explain. "I left a donation in the box when I entered. I needed to borrow some parchment and ink to write a missive for the King. I hope that's ok, there was no one to ask." Scarlett stared at the monk looking for any sign of an answer.

The monk nodded and Scarlett breathed a sigh of relief and headed for the exit. Outside she entrusted the missive and the money to the messenger, with strict instructions to put it directly in the hand of the King. He offered her a lift back to camp but she waved him on. The quicker he delivered her message the safer the people of Nottingham were. She ran to the next village where she had arranged to meet Billy and the others.

The group ventured from one village to the next, delivering the same speech and receiving the same resounding success.

In the village closest to the main road into Nottingham, a handful of guards on foot were milling around. Scarlett's men held their weapons ready as she started to deliver her speech. Much to everyone's surprise, the guards did nothing but listen. By the time the people were cheering and raising whatever weapons they had in the air, the guards had disappeared. It gave Scarlett hope that their numbers alone would be enough to scare the guards. Her hope of this working relied on a large portion of the guards deserting the Sheriff, a whole heap of luck, and the hope that God was on their side.

Alaric was in his father's office, helping him to plan the execution of the outlaws, when a guard he knew well knocked on the door and asked to speak to him privately. Alaric was pleased with the distraction. His father was intent on making this a spectacle, but the bookkeeping scribe kept interjecting at the cost of making such a show about the event.

The whittling was giving Alaric a headache. He knew

that soon, his father would just insist the scribe be part of the condemned, if he continued to restrain his ambitions. Alaric was convinced the only thing stopping his father from ordering Alaric to kill him on the spot, was the fact that educated scribes were hard to come by.

The guard insisted they walk some distance from the Sheriff before he divulged his information. Alaric led him through into his mother's gardens. He faked interest in a bush and the guard double-checked that they were alone before he delivered his news.

"A group of outlaws, led by Robin Hood are stirring up the villagers and inciting war. You said you wanted to be kept informed of any unrest and for us not to act. Do we need to plan a counterattack now, before their numbers get too strong?"

"Have no fear man, I have a plan." Robin patted the man on the back, "You did a good thing coming to speak to me privately."

As the guard turned to leave, Alaric asked, "Was a redhead with this group?"

Perplexed, the guard turned back around. "Aye, she was the one doing all the fancy talking and inciting everyone to the cause."

Alaric couldn't hide his smile and his reaction puzzled the guard even further. He smiled out of politeness, believing he had done a good job in reporting what he saw and left the garden.

Alaric was bursting with pride that Scarlett was leading the revolution. She might be using her brother's name, but she was leading them and now he needed to be ready for when her army arrived. He marched inside, back to his father's office.

"I hope I didn't miss too much?" Alaric cheerfully inquired, as he slipped back into the room.

The Sheriff threw a book at the scribe as he entered. Turning to Alaric, he replied, "Nothing just this bumbling idiot telling me we can't afford any of my ideas."

Alaric held the door open mercifully and demanded, "Scribe leave us." The scribe scurried through the door holding his nose as blood poured from it.

"Father I don't know why you entertain him. We can make this hanging a celebration of your triumph. Just give me three days to levy the taxes on all brothels and taverns and you will have your funds."

The Sheriff stared into his son's eyes and mistook the joy in his demeanour, believing it came from the thought of persecuting the taxpayers, along with the joy of slaughtering bandits. He patted Alaric on the shoulder and said, "Come my son. Let's drink and discuss my plans."

CHAPTER 24

The day had finally come and Scarlett could feel a mix of anticipation and trepidation from the gathering of men and women that surrounded her. The numbers were fewer than she had hoped for. Clearly, in the few days it had taken to convince the villagers and gather weapons, the fear of failure had crept in. Still, Scarlett was optimistic that the numbers would be enough. They would outnumber the guards three to one. She looked at the faces of those surrounding her and it instilled in her a determination to succeed. She would not be leading these innocent, hardworking people to die. Together, they would liberate themselves from tyranny.

She had used the last of the money they had repurposed from the Sheriff to pay a farmer handsomely for two horses. Billy and Scarlett rode them proudly, becoming a focal point for hope and yet at the same time a target for the enemy. The majority of the villagers were on foot, so they made their way slowly to the gates of Nottingham to ensure that no one was too tired to fight when they arrived.

Scarlett was armed with her father's dagger, her quiver filled with arrows and her bow. From the elevated position on the horse, she would have an advantage with her aim. Many of the villagers were only armed with pitchforks and clubs. Not a true weapon in sight. Even if they had found time to secure some, without the right training, it wouldn't have made much difference. She told herself that with a strength of heart and a cause worth fighting for, even a pitchfork could be deadly against a hired guard only fighting to line his pocket.

As they marched closer to the gates, the castle came into view. They were still too far out to see any movement, but there was no chance that they could creep up on the castle without the alarm being raised. The castle had been built for such attacks and had the advantage. Doubts started to creep into Scarlett's thoughts and she looked over at Billy for reassurance.

His steely expression comforted her. He felt her staring at him and turned. He flashed her a smile that was identical to Robin's. Her heart grew in size and she thought about how proud her father and her brother would be that they were standing up for what was right. It wouldn't be easy to win this battle, but it would be worth it. She smiled in return and then proceeded onwards.

The closer they got, the more of the castle's defence they could see being put into action. Guards were piling into the courtyard. The turrets were manned with archers. It was hard to see physical features yet, but Scarlett could make guards on horseback. One of them must be the Sheriff, unless he was that much of a coward that he would stow himself up in the castle, away from the fighting.

When they were a mile out, Scarlett rode out to the front of the group, causing them to halt. She rode back and forth, looking each and every member in the face, whilst delivering words of inspiration.

"We fight today for what is right. For justice. For our King. God is on our side. We will be victorious. Now is the time for our loyalty and faith to be tested. Are you with me?" The rabble cheered as Scarlett raised her dagger into the air.

Shouting at the top of her voice, she cried, "For Robin, and for every family member the Sheriff has taken from you. Let's deliver him to God, to pay for his crimes."

The cheers went up a level and Scarlett felt an overwhelming sense of pride. She turned her horse around and rode ahead, leading the rabble into battle.

The group ran towards the castle but the guards lining the

walls did nothing. No one approached them and Scarlett was suddenly suspicious. What trap had she walked into?

She was in clear line of sight of the castle archers now, but they didn't react. She stopped her horse and held her hand to stop the group from travelling any closer.

She could see the faces of those on horseback now at the back of two lines of guards. The Sheriff was on a huge horse, hiding at the rear. He looked furious and was shouting obscenities. He was surrounded by guards in full armour on horseback. He appeared to be struggling to keep his horse under control. The horse clearly didn't like being pinned in, or ridden; Scarlett couldn't tell which one. His face was bright red and he seemed to be particularly angry at a guard in full armour to his left.

Scarlett stared at the strange scene, trying to work out what advantage the enemy was trying to play. She studied the ground to make sure there was nothing that could ignite. Then she glanced to the sides to make sure that no gunpowder was stationed in barrels. Lastly, she looked at Billy, knowing the fear would be visible on her face, but she saw his expression change from confusion to a gleeful smile.

Scarlett followed his line of sight to see the guard whom the Sheriff had been shouting at remove his helmet. It was Alaric. Behind him, the Sheriff was being shielded by the other guards on horseback. Bile rose in her throat at the cowardness of the Sheriff and the brazenness of Alaric, to consider them so little a threat that he would remove his helmet. He rode out to the front of the line of defence.

Scarlett glared at him with all the hatred she could muster. After everything, how could he stand in defence of such a man? She reached into her quiver for an arrow and nocked it onto her bow. She used the strength in her thighs to signal to her horse to remain still. Scarlett took aim as a tear fell down her cheek. Her usually unshakeable arms trembled. Could she really kill the man her heart had been tricked into loving?

Alaric raised his arm into the air, his fist clenched tightly.

He was clearly giving a signal to the guards who stood to attention. The sound of their feet stomping in unison was impressive. His eyes fixed on hers and locked her into an unbreakable trance. His steely expression was indecipherable.

Her arrow rattled from the shakiness of her arm and she relaxed the tension and lowered her bow. With the amount she was shaking, there was no point in firing, it wouldn't hit her target.

Alaric moved his arm out to the side and unclenched his fist at the same time he shouted, "Now!"

Scarlett's heart sank. She had failed. She had led these innocent people into a trap. She wasn't even strong enough to shoot one of the enemy dead. Scarlett gave her own order and cried out, "Attack!"

The rabble around her ran forward, waving the weapons they had and she kicked her heels to encourage her horse forward, but the opposition did nothing. As the crowd of villagers got within reach, the guards turned to the side, creating gaps for the villagers to pass through. Not one guard armed themselves. No guards fought back. The villagers passed through the blockade unharmed. Scarlett found all eyes on her as she approached Alaric. The men on the castle walls had put down their weapons.

Alaric was smiling and nodded to Billy as he approached. Billy held out his hand and Alaric shook it. Both men turned to Scarlett, but her attention was drawn to the Sheriff, who was being pulled from his horse by his own guards.

Scarlett dismounted her horse and marched over. Alaric followed. The guards who were restraining him looked to Alaric for further instructions. One asked, "Commander, what should we do with him?"

The Sheriff spat back, "You will all hang for this! Traitors the lot of you! And you," he glared at Alaric and spat in his direction. "You are no son of mine. You will never be a prince. I strip you of your title as my heir."

Standing in front of his father, Alaric mocked, "And you

will never be King." Turning to Scarlett, Alaric asked, "What punishment do you see fit?"

Scarlett averted her gaze from the man she hated the most in all the world and stared into the eyes of the man she loved. How someone so good could be raised by someone so evil was a matter she couldn't comprehend. Alaric had saved countless lives today. He had done the right thing for the right reasons, no matter the cost to him personally. His strength of character astounded her. She pulled her gaze away from him as the Sheriff called her a 'whore' that had bewitched his son.

She snarled at him and raised her dagger to his throat. Did she have the strength to murder him in cold blood? Her hand wasn't shaking any longer and the Sheriff's goading wasn't helping his case. She pressed the blade closer to his jugular, a bead of blood trickled down his throat.

Then a deafening sound of trumpets rang through the courtyard. Scarlett turned around to see the men part and allow a procession of guards bearing the King's livery enter the courtyard. Men carrying the King's banners surrounded them. Scarlett looked into the distance to see several knights on horseback, with the best armour money could buy trot towards them.

One man stood out from the rest with the King's emblem welded into his breastplate. Two young squires helped him down from his horse. The man lifted his helmet off his head and passed it to a squire, who bowed his head on receipt. A royal crier stepped forward and announced, "All bow for his royal highness, King John."

Everyone in the courtyard took a knee, except for the men restraining the Sheriff. Scarlett was dumbstruck. Alaric had knelt to the side of her. She felt his fingers tickling hers and he gently pulled her down. His touch distracted her and she bent into a low courtesy. It had been years since she had acted like a Lady and the action felt unnatural.

Addressing the couple, the King gestured for them to rise. "Lady Loxley, I assume, and you?"

"Alaric, Commander of the guards of Nottingham, Your Majesty."

The King nodded, "Of course. When I received two letters by the same messenger warning me of a plot against my life, I decided to take action. Especially, when one was from my dead cousin and the other her son. However, it appears I had no need to worry. The loyal people of Nottingham are capable of standing against injustice in my name."

Scarlett blushed, but then realised that Alaric had also sent a message to the King. If she hadn't led a riot he would have still overthrown the Sheriff by alerting the King. He had chosen his side. She squeezed his hand in acknowledgement of the sacrifice he had made. He smiled in response and her heart felt like it would burst out of her chest.

The King peered between the couple to see the Sheriff being detained behind them. Scarlett went to release his hand to part for the King to pass, but Alaric held her tighter and tugged her towards him.

Now with a clear line of sight, the King addressed the Sheriff. A clear look of disdain on his face. "I wasn't keen on you when your betrothal to my cousins dear cousin was announced, but when she died in childbirth, I felt sorry for you. It was because of her that my father bestowed on you this castle and all its finery. From the hand of your own son, I have proof of your treacherous ambition. Here you stand before me as a dastardly knave. Do you have anything to say in your defence?"

With a murderous look in his eye, the Sheriff spat at the King's feet. Several guards raced forward, but the King detained them with the same gesture Alaric had used. A common military signal, it appeared. The King's expression never altered; he showed no fear.

The King turned his attention back to Scarlett. His features softened as he gazed upon her. "I know you were about to hand out your sentence, but if I may, I would like to be the one to enact justice, as you have taken away my ability to save the day."

Scarlett bowed her head in respect, "Of course, Your Majesty."

Turning to the crowd of onlookers, the King projected his voice to a level Scarlett would never have been able to reach. "I extend my gratitude to all the people of Nottingham. Today, you have shown the Lord our God your allegiance to his representation on earth, by supporting those who plot against the crown. Death is too easy a sentence for a traitor. The dungeons of my castle have been bare for too long under my righteous reign. I sentence this heathen to spend the rest of his life in my dungeon. This is a warning to every evil traitor. You can die every day for your sins, and when you leave this world, you will pay further in hell when the devil becomes your master."

The King was clearly an accomplished public speaker and the crowd erupted into applause. The sound was deafening and the King turned back around to face the leaders of the rebellion. He placed his hand on Alaric's shoulder and pointed to the castle. Scarlett could barely make out what he said but she got the gist. The King wanted to go inside.

A procession of guards surrounded the three of them as they made their way through the hallways to the banquet hall. The King spotted a serving wench and ordered meats and ale to be brought to him. The young girl cowered in front of him, but Alaric took her to the side and calmed her. She scurried away to fulfil his order and the King entered the great hall. Scarlett looked adoringly at Alaric and he winked. His smile sent a tingle down her body to her core. She bit her lip and flashbacks from their time together in the forest replayed in her mind. They left the darkened hallways and entered the large room behind the King's entourage.

The King had already taken a seat at the head of the table, in the Sheriff's usual seat, and his guards were stationed around him. Alaric pulled the chair to his majesty's right out from under the table and nodded his head for Scarlett to take the seat. Scarlett wasn't used to the gesture and floundered before composing herself. She sat up tall and straight like nursemaid Edith had taught her as a girl and ensured her elbows were not on the table. She felt awkward and stiff, but then she was in the presence of a King. There was no better time than the present to act like the Lady she had been brought up to be.

Her eyes followed Alaric around the room as he sat on the other side of the table. It was only when she heard the scraping of the chair beside her, that she realised Billy had followed them into the castle. When the three were seated, the King addressed the group, looking specifically at the right side of the table.

"I have only recently become aware of your family's plight. For that, I am truly sorry. My brother, King Richard, God rest his soul, placed too much trust in his noblemen in the north of England, a mistake I will now rectify." Pointing at Billy, the King asked, "You sir, are William of Loxley?"

Billy nodded and sheepishly replied, "Aye." Scarlett kicked him under the table and he jolted forward and frowned. Scarlett turned and mouthed, "Your Majesty," which promptly jolted Billy to follow up with, "Your Majesty."

The King smirked and Scarlett relaxed her shoulders. It seemed he was amused by the lack of propriety, rather than angry.

The King continued, "My scribe tells me you have an elder brother. Where is he?"

Billy hung his head, as did Scarlett; both siblings were avoiding the King's gaze and line of questioning. Sensing the tension, Alaric interjected. "Your Majesty, Robin was killed a few days ago by the Sheriff."

"I see," replied the King, "Then the title and lands are yours, Sir William. They were unlawfully stripped from your family and my scribe will ensure everyone in the land is aware of my decree, you will now and forever be known as the Earl of Loxley."

Scarlett and Billy's heads flew up. Both had the same shocked expression. Scarlett reached for Billy's hand and squeezed it. Shock faded away with merriment and both siblings were grinning. Billy stuttered out his thanks in gratitude.

The King turned his attention to Alaric, who only had eyes for Scarlett. The King followed his gaze and smiled. He turned his attention to Scarlett and held out his hand, palm side up. Scarlett reached forward and placed her hand in his. The King kissed her slender fingers in response.

"Lady Loxley, I will be forever in your debt. Ask me for anything and it shall be yours."

Scarlett blushed at the compliment. "I want for nothing that you can bestow upon me. Seeing my brother claim back our family lands and title is more than generous."

"Come now, surely there is something I can grant you," the King insisted.

Scarlett shook her head, "There is nothing I desire, Your Majesty."

The King eyed up Alaric and Scarlett individually again, then turned his focus to Alaric. "You look like him, but you have your mother's skin tone and there's something about your eyes that reminds me of her." Alaric nodded in agreement. "I owe you a debt as well, and to repay that debt, I bestow on you a title you have earned rather than have been given. You will be the new Sheriff of Nottingham. I trust under your watch, taxation will be fair and my laws will be enacted."

Alaric tried to contain his smile as Scarlett stared at him adoringly. She could see how happy he was to have earned that office for himself.

The King clicked his fingers. A feeble man dressed in brown robes with a quill and parchment in his hands moved forward. Without glancing behind, the King stated, "Scribe, make sure you write this down and proclaim it across the whole of England. Furthermore, for the bravery and loyalty shown to me today by both of you," The King cast his gaze from Alaric to Scarlett, "I bestow on you, Alaric a second title, Baron of Nottingham. As a Lord, you can marry a high-born Lady, if one so chooses to accept your proposal."

Alaric's face lit up and his attention immediately diverted

to Scarlett. Her face reddened by the heat in his gaze and the astuteness of the King. Just then, the food arrived and the King reached forward to help himself. Alaric's trance was broken as a ham hock was placed in front of the King and he remembered his manners. He thanked the King for the honour.

Billy excused himself to tell his wife the good news. Alaric and Scarlett entertained the King whilst he ate. Alaric offered the King a bed for the night, but he declined stating he had business north with the Baron of Loidis. He said his farewells and Scarlett could have sworn she saw the King smirk at Alaric, as he privately whispered in his ear.

CHAPTER 25

The majority of the villagers had long since returned home, and with the departure of the King's entourage, the Castle courtyard seemed quiet. Alaric's fingers intertwined with Scarlett's as they waved goodbye to the royal procession. The door to the tavern opened and a drunk man stumbled out. The sound of the merriment within billowed into the cool night air.

Alaric led Scarlett to the side entrance of the main building, the one that led to the private gardens. Alaric turned his full attention to Scarlett and she saw desire burning in the depths of his eyes.

His hand caressed her cheek as his thumb traced her bottom lip. His eyes dropped to her mouth and he dipped his head. He paused above her just out of reach. His breath was hot on her lips and her need for him grew stronger, until she couldn't take it any longer. She leaned up on her tiptoes, but he anticipated her move and rose an equal distance higher.

A teasing smile burst across his face as he retorted, "You once said you wouldn't kiss me if I were the last man on earth."

Scarlett smiled as a giggle escaped her lips, a flashback to an earlier memory danced across her mind. She knew as soon as he gave her the authority to pass judgment on the Sheriff, that she would end up in his bed tonight and every other night, but she couldn't resist toying with him. Their banter had been what sparked the attraction between them. It was obvious for all to see that Alaric felt the same as she did.

"I seem to remember it was you who first turned me down

when you were a damsel in distress and I a knight who had just saved you."

Alaric laughed out loud, his smile broadening. "Well, neither of us are a damsel in distress and I think we've saved each other. So how about that kiss?"

His eyes were smouldering as he gazed into hers. The look of pure desire had her insides melting. She grabbed the front of his shirt and pulled him toward her, closing the gap between them. That was all the confirmation that Alaric needed. He dipped his head and his lips locked onto hers. His hand moved to cup the back of her head to support his passionate embrace. His other hand grasped her rear and his groan escaped into her mouth.

A door creaked open as a kitchen servant entered the garden. It brought Alaric to his senses. Regretfully, he pulled away from their kiss and rested his forehead on hers as he caught his breath. In a voice far more gravelly than his usual tone, he stated, "We shouldn't behave like this in public."

Although he didn't say the words, his question hung in the air with anticipation. Scarlett bit down on her bottom lip as she thought of what pleasures were to come when she gave in and said yes like the wanton woman she was.

His hand covered her cheek and his thumb traced the line of her bottom lip. His gaze was intense and she stole a kiss that elicited a moan from his lips. His hand shifted to his breeches and Scarlett's eyes followed the movement.

In the same dark tone, Alaric admitted, "You do things to me I can't control."

Knowing that Alaric was too much of a gentleman to ask, Scarlett leaned up to his ear and whispered, "Take me to your bed chamber, Alaric." She met his eyes as she stepped back and the desire within them was front and centre. Alaric took her hand in his and hurried inside the castle.

As soon as he locked the door his need for her took over.

He spun her around so her back was pushed flush against the door and his lips were on her. She moaned in pleasure as he caressed her breasts. He pressed against her and she revelled in the feeling of his hard length. Her body instinctively reacted like it knew what to do. Her undergarments were soaked from her need for him. Their clothes were quickly shed, discarded within seconds on the floor.

The two stood breathlessly staring at each other. The moonlight that shone through the window cast an ethereal glow, enhancing their naked forms. They both took a moment to visually explore each other's bodies, until the tension was so palpable neither could hold back any longer. They met in the centre and kissed passionately as their hands roamed eagerly.

Scarlett playfully pushed him back onto the bed taking control. Alaric was mesmerised as Scarlett asserted herself as the dominant lead.

She confidently took his hard shaft in hand and teased the tip with her tongue. Alaric moaned in pleasure and it gave her the green light to continue. She trailed her tongue down the side of his length and then took one ball at a time into her mouth, giving each a gentle tug. Then she took him fully in her mouth, using her hand to pump his shaft until she tasted pre-cum on her tongue.

Alaric pulled gently on her hair to gain her attention and she crawled up the bed before straddling him. He pushed himself up to a seated position as he explored her breasts. Scarlett writhed, grinding and arching her back, allowing him greater access. He took a nipple into his mouth and sucked, as his other hand squeezed tight. A shudder rushed through her body and the ache between her legs grew unbearable. She moaned as her head snapped back.

She felt him teasing her entrance. One finger slipped inside easily and the sensation was delicious in a tantalising way. He nibbled at her neck as he muttered, "So wet for me already."

Scarlett rocked against his hand and she begged, "Alaric, I

need more."

Alaric slipped a second finger inside of her and her moans grew as he swirled his fingers inside of her, one particular spot made her writhe with pleasure.

Again she begged, "I need more."

Alaric withdrew his hand and lifted her up by the waist. When he knew she could hold her own body weight, he positioned himself at her entrance and slowly guided her down onto him. He could feel her stretching to accommodate him and he nearly lost control at the feel of being inside her.

Instinctively, she started rocking and Alaric lay back down on the bed. He watched as Scarlett got off on riding his cock. He felt her start to tighten around him as her breathing hitched and he felt her walls flutter as she came undone. She was breathtaking to watch.

He stared unashamedly as she rode the wave of ecstasy and then in one swift move, he switched their positions. Scarlett now had her back on the bed and he was above her, but most importantly, still inside her. He started slowly, but with each moan she elicited, he began to thrust more vigorously. Her leg rose next to him and he took the opportunity to trail kisses from her ankle down to her inner thigh.

In an attempt to prolong the ecstasy, he leaned down for a passionate kiss, before trailing kisses down her pale skin. His mouth found the bud of her nipple and he took his time caressing it.

When he resumed thrusting his pace was quicker. He brought his thumb to his mouth and sucked it. It made an audible pop when he removed it. Knowing Scarlett's eyes were transfixed on him, he winked. His smile turned devilish as he placed his thumb onto her swollen nub. His thumb made circular motions as he continued to thrust.

Scarlett felt her body react to every movement. Her mind was lost in the sensations she was feeling. She felt overwhelming love for the man looking down at her. He was right, he had never been her enemy. She realised it now.

A moan escaped her lips as the tension that had been rising in her body was ready to explode. She felt an intense sensation in her core as he stretched her further. Alaric cried out as he climaxed and the sensation tipped her over the edge into sweet oblivion. Waves of pleasure crashed across her body as she felt the most intense orgasm of her life.

When she opened her eyes, Alaric was gazing down at her with awe. He whispered, "You're breathtaking."

They settled into a comfortable position entwined with each other. Scarlett landed a soft kiss on his lips, before tracing her fingertips over his facial scar.

"I'm sorry for this." Her heart was full of regret for disfiguring him.

Alaric quickly responded, "Don't be."

Trying to justify her actions, Scarlett babbled, "I was scared. If I'd known your motives, I wouldn't have done it. I'm so sorry." Scarlett looked away, not wanting him to see her tears.

Alaric turned her back to face him. He used his thumbs to gently brush away the tears on her cheeks. His voice was soft and earnest as he replied, "Don't regret it, don't regret anything, without it we wouldn't be here, and right here is where I choose to be."

Scarlett knew in that moment there wouldn't ever be another man for her. Alaric was a man who accepted her for who she truly was. His quick wit challenged her mind and his kind heart fed her soul. Not forgetting his talents in the bedroom would keep her satisfied and warm at night.

As she started to drift off to sleep, wrapped in his arms, one question plagued her. She rolled over to face him, knowing that even if the King of England had asked him to keep it a secret, he would tell her if she asked.

"What did the King whisper to you?"

Alaric chuckled. "He told me not to let you slip through my fingers. So I'm holding on tight." He held up their joined hands, "See, holding on tight."

Scarlett let out a soft giggle, her eyelids started to grow

heavy as the enormity of the day suddenly hit her.

Alaric moved a stray strand of hair from her face. He took a deep breath and leaned in close. He brushed his nose against hers and stole a gentle kiss. Propped up on one arm, gazing down at her, Scarlett looked up and their eyes locked. He let out a long sigh and then asked, "Will you marry me and help me make Nottingham great again?"

Scarlett beamed up at him, full of so much love she could burst.

EPILOGUE

Scarlett took a deep breath and stared at her reflection in the looking glass. She barely recognised the woman staring back at her. Her long auburn hair had been tightly plaited when it had been wet. Now that the plaits were removed, she had waves that cascaded down her back.

The majority of her hair was free-flowing to her waist, as was the fashion in highborn society. Although she was still getting used to having her hair tickle her face, so she couldn't resist creating a crown out of two plaits that melded into one down her back.

Her gown was made out of the most exquisite fabric. It felt incredibly soft to the touch and appeared to change colour when you rubbed it. She had picked emerald green. It was her favourite colour and reminded her of Sherwood Forest.

It had surprised her how quickly she had readjusted to highborn life. These last few weeks, she had spent her days listening to the needs of the people of Nottingham and helping Alaric establish new laws. At night, he snuck into her bed chamber and worshipped her like a goddess. He included her in all the decision making and welcomed her advice. Together they made a formidable team.

Alaric would have been happy to marry immediately after she said yes, but Scarlett had wanted to uphold some formality. Mostly, she wanted to celebrate with everyone they cared about. Billy had only just settled into Loxley Castle and hired staff.

The rest of the outlaws had joined him. They had all promised to make the journey back to Nottingham for the big day and Scarlett was looking forward to seeing them again.

A knock at the door jarred her from her thoughts. "Come in," she shouted. The door opened and Billy stood in the doorway, looking handsome in a new tunic. He smiled when he saw her and she curtseyed. "Do you think I will pass for a lady?"

His face beamed as he replied, "You look like a princess. What was it Robin called you, Princess of thieves?"

A tear of happiness prickled in her eye and she attempted to blink it away. "I believe it was."

In light-hearted jest Billy extended his arm as he asked, "Well, Scarlett, Princess of thieves, are you ready to transform into the Lady of Nottingham?"

Scarlett nodded and took his arm, "I am."

As soon as she walked into the church on Billy's arm, she looked to the front for Alaric. He was staring right back at her with a look of awe on his face and desire in his eyes. Scarlett bit her lip in anticipation, knowing what that smouldering look did to her and how much she would enjoy tonight. As per tradition, they had spent the prior night apart and Scarlett had missed him terribly.

A baby's cry broke her trance and Scarlett remembered her guests. She smiled at them in the filled pews as she finished the walk up the aisle. Billy ceremoniously handed her over to Alaric and kissed her on the cheek before taking his seat in the front row.

As the newly appointed Lord of Nottingham, Alaric's social standing had risen considerably, and the Archbishop of York had insisted on presiding over the wedding. The church fell silent as the Archbishop began.

"We are gathered here today in the house of God to unite and bless this union. Repeat after me, I, Alaric, Sheriff and Lord of Nottingham, take thee, Lady Jorja of Loxley, to be my wife."

Alaric's smile morphed into a devilish smirk at the sound of her official name and title. She felt her centre grow damp and ache for his touch. They finished the vows and the Archbishop declared them husband and wife.

The guests erupted into a deafening roar of support as Alaric closed the gap between them. One hand slid perfectly round her waist and the other grazed her cheek as he took her mouth with his own. She lost herself in his touch and for a few seconds, she completely forgot where they were. As he pulled back from the kiss, his lips touched her earlobe as he whispered, "I'd forgotten your Christian name was Jorja. You will always be Scarlett to me."

And that was the story of Scarlett, the Princess of thieves. Now you may wonder why history forgot her name. Well, as you've just read, she never used her own name when she was an outlaw. In time, the name Lady Jorja of Nottingham stood for altruism and virtue. The name Robin Hood lives on as the renowned figure who robbed the rich and gave to the poor. The legend, who defeated the tyrannical Sheriff of Nottingham. Just as she intended.

BOOKS BY THIS AUTHOR

The Undercover Agent And The Lycan

If you enjoy urban fantasy why not try The Undercover Agent and The Lycan.

Morgan Hudson is a formidable female agent. Her next undercover assignment will shake the very foundation of the world she thinks she lives in, when she's suddenly thrust into a world of Vampires, Witches and Lycans.

Does she allow her mark to get too close and risk derailing her investigation? Something about him awakens her sexual desires and her magical powers.

Will she trust her heart or her training?

When the world is depending on her, is she powerful enough to make a difference?

AFTERWORD

Thank you for reading this story.

I hope you enjoyed reading it, as much as I enjoyed writing it.

If you enjoyed the story please leave a review on Amazon, to help others to enjoy it.

You can now follow the author on Instagram and be one of the first to hear about the launch of the upcoming sequel

@author_hannahhitchcock

Printed in Dunstable, United Kingdom

63865728R00150